SOME ENCHANTED EVENING

Men of KWESTT, Book 1

By Clari Dees

ISBN-10:1-944203-07-9
ISBN-13:978-1-944203-07-8

DEDICATION

To my sisters.
The JoyAnnes in my life.
I love you!.

(1)

"*W*ould you sign *me*, Kellan?" Heavily lined eyes flirted with him as the woman flipped a hank of hair darker than her eyeliner off her nearly bare shoulder.

Kellan's smile didn't falter. His facial muscles were too well-trained to drop their upward curve, and normally, he didn't mind the mild flirtation of the more daring female fans. "Sure. Turn around." He resolutely kept his eyes above the ends of the woman's ridiculously long earrings that brushed the skin bared by her spaghetti-strap top. Not that he could see much with spots dancing across his vision from the smartphone camera flashes that kept firing his direction.

She dropped her chin and flashed him a coy look through eyelashes that would make Snuffleupagus jealous. "But I want you to sign here." She drew a finger above the left edge of her low-cut top.

"Sorry." He wasn't. "I'll sign the back of your shoulder." He ignored the pout that was probably intended to be seductive and hastily inked his name along the top of the shoulder blade she reluctantly turned to him. Doing it without letting his hand rest against her skin was a skill he'd perfected on his first tour. He might play the role of bad-boy-slash-ladies'-man while singing and hamming it up on stage with his tour mates in their family friendly, theatrical-style music show, but he wasn't about to put his hands all over some female he'd never seen before and whose face would blur into the crowd two minutes later.

Kellan turned to the next eager fan and continued to slash his signature across CD inserts, T-shirts, ball caps, and various other items the merchandise tables offered at exorbitant prices. All because they had the names and faces of six guys who could sing. And dance a little—also known as following the highly-choreographed stage plan that Sandy, their music director, had drilled into them.

He surreptitiously checked his watch while signing a promo poster. Five more minutes before he could head backstage. The other guys were already there, chilling after the earlier meet-and-greet with the artist-circle ticket holders, but it was his turn to be the face at the merchandise table, and the clock couldn't tick fast enough. He loved singing and performing, and fans made that possible. But back-to-back tours this last year had worn him out and rubbed his tolerance thin. The latest tour had kept them on the road over four long months—so long he'd lost track of the cities they'd played.

He must be getting old. And cynical. He'd turned thirty-seven last month and the rest of the guys had taken to calling him "The Old Man." He was beginning to think they were right.

An arm snaked around his waist and he automatically lifted his head to smile into the nearest camera. As he forced away the fatigue threatening to flatten his smile, a flash of bright red drew his eyes over the crowd pressing in around him. The stiff wind that had roared around the back of the theater while he and the guys played a cutthroat game of basketball earlier was obviously still blowing. It accompanied the brightly dressed woman through the center doors in the gilded entrance of the massive lobby, ushering in the scent of rain. And freedom.

Tomorrow. He'd be free to disappear for two whole months after tonight. No solo appearances. No interviews. No back-to-back shows. He might even turn off his phone and forget to turn it back on.

The corners of his smile quivered in sudden amusement as the woman batted down the skirt of her dress while trying to hand her ticket to the greeter. The same wind that had threatened to steal his St. Louis Cardinals' cap earlier—they were on the famous redbirds' home turf, after all—had nearly recreated the famous Marilyn Monroe scene with the dark-haired lady.

Accepting her ticket stub, the woman strode gracefully into the lobby toward the busy merch table.

Kellan lowered his gaze to scrawl another signature across the bill of a KWESTT-logoed ball cap, but found his eyes lifting to catch another glimpse of the classy lady.

She had paused in the center of the lobby and was looking up at the ornate rotunda, slowly twirling as if taking in the impressive architecture for the first time and making the full skirt of her cardinal-colored dress swirl around her knees. The younger females that attended their shows wore everything from jeans and T-shirts sporting his group's logo to ostentatious dresses that showed plenty of skin. But this woman appeared to have stepped from a more polite, more gracious era. The era when acts like Frank Sinatra or Bing Crosby played this magnificent old theater. He half expected a Cary Grant lookalike to appear and offer the woman his arm.

And he'd clearly been watching too many old movies to pass the time on the bus lately and not getting enough fresh air.

Two more-soberly clad women flocked the pretty cardinal, surrounding her with smiles and plenty of chatter—by the way their mouths were moving. After a flurry of hugs, they tugged her toward the staircase that led to the mezzanine level of seats.

Kellan's eyes trailed them until the shapely calves and black high heels below the hem of a certain red dress disappeared from view as he unseeingly autographed another ball cap.

He accepted another program to sign, but a tap on the shoulder and quiet word in his ear reminded him of the time.

Finally! "See you all in a few minutes." He flashed a bright smile to the groaning latecomers who hadn't gotten their items—or persons—signed before slipping between the gap in the curtains behind the merchandise table.

The woman in the red dress had been a brief, sharp stillness in the middle of the frantic blur of the merchandise table meet-and-greet, but now it was time to earn his bread and butter by entertaining this crowd.

He quickened his steps and headed backstage to slug a bottle of water before hurrying into the first outfit of the show. Five hours until vacation officially started. And counting.

(2)

She'd made it with a few minutes to spare. JoyAnne slid into the plush seat and exhaled noiselessly before grinning at the elaborate stage. It had been months since she'd ventured further afield than the small county seat where she bought groceries and supplies, went to church, and visited the public library. So while she hadn't enjoyed the big-city, four-lane rush, the excitement of the upcoming show, the beautiful theater, and spending the evening with her friends was enough to make up for the long drive that left her with too much time to think about past road trips. With her parents. With Micah. And how abruptly and finally those days had ended.

"We thought you were going to miss the opening. What happened? Your phone kept cutting out so we

couldn't understand anything except that you'd be late."
Alyce plopped down on JoyAnne's left and tucked her
purse beneath her seat.

"Sorry 'bout that. It's on the fritz." JoyAnne
shoved away the lingering wisps of sad memories to
concentrate on the present.

"Again? What'd you do to it this time?" Jordyn's
eyes sparkled with sympathetic humor.

"Phones don't like to go swimming. Who knew?"
JoyAnne shook her head and grinned. "I forgot it was in
my pocket when I had to rescue a camper's spoiled
Pekinese that discovered it couldn't swim *after* jumping
off the boat dock last week—you should've seen the
fat, bedraggled thing when I carried it out." She
grinned. "Funniest sight of the week. I dried my phone
out in a bag of rice afterwards, but now *it* decides when
I can call or text. Not me."

Alyce rolled her eyes. "You go through more
phones than anyone I know."

"Which is why I buy *cheap* ones." She pointed the
remark at Jordyn who'd accused her of being allergic to
technology with her refusal to purchase a so-called
smart phone. "Anyway, there was an accident of some
sort that blocked the highway for a while. Sorry I
messed up dinner plans." JoyAnne's stomach twinged
at the thought of the missed food.

"No problem. The restaurant we want to take you
to stays open late even on Sunday nights, so we'll eat
after the show. We're just glad you're okay," Jordyn
gave JoyAnne's shoulder a friendly nudge with her
own, "and hope you like your birthday gift even if you
did have to brave weekend city traffic to get here."

JoyAnne laughed at her friend's gentle, teasing

verbal jab. "I know. I've become spoiled about not having to fight traffic. But who cares? I can't believe I'm finally seeing KWESTT in person!" She lowered her voice to keep from squealing like a teenage girl, but the last couple of words still jumped an octave.

She'd been speechless when the sisters had handed her a birthday card containing the ticket two weeks ago when home to visit their parents—JoyAnne's employers. The only thing that would have made this birthday better was if she'd been able to enjoy their company on the drive south, but Alyce and Jordyn lived in the St. Louis area with their husbands. They'd invited JoyAnne to come down a couple of days early for some serious "girl-time and pampering," but May was the beginning of Wad-a-Wa Campground's busiest time, and multiple days off—especially around the weekend—weren't a good idea if Joy wanted to stay on top of the controlled chaos that was camping season.

The houselights dimmed, and a voice crackled through the speakers, requesting the audience to silence all cell phones and reminding them that taking pictures or video of the show was strictly forbidden. After a few more housekeeping announcements and a final entreaty to enjoy the show, the faceless voice went silent, and shadowy band members slipped into their places to quietly tune their instruments accompanied by a light smattering of applause.

JoyAnne grinned at her friends, not bothering to hide her growing excitement. Left to her own devices, she would've ignored her birthday and spent the afternoon following Sunday church service tackling the never-ending list of things to do around a campground until it got too dark to see. But her friends' generous gift and the chance to really dress up, feel pretty and feminine, and spend the evening seeing her favorite performers in concert had overcome her reluctance to leave her comfort zone. Besides, she was only going two-and-a-half hours away from home for the evening, not moving to another country.

The instruments fell silent, the band members stilled, and an expectant hush fell over the ornate concert hall.

JoyAnne pressed the toes of her high heels against the narrow strip of concrete between her and the row of seats in front of her to keep from tapping her feet in delicious anticipation.

Smoke rolled over the stage. A faint, throbbing drumbeat broke the silence, growing in volume as the stringed instruments added their low-pitched, pulsing rhythm. Other musicians joined in, instrument by instrument, building the anticipation of the audience.

JoyAnne had sung along to the recorded version of the poignant ballad a hundred times or more, but the sudden appearance of the vocalists through the white smoke caught her off guard. Their powerful voices joined the melody, and her breath hitched. They were so much more impressive in person. Not even the sound quality of Victor's Bose speakers had done them justice.

The show was everything she'd dreamed it would be and more. Not even gnawing hunger pangs distracted her from absorbing every note of music, every expression of the performers. She perched on the edge of her seat and couldn't help singing along, but she did manage to keep it under her breath so as not to disturb those around her who'd paid to hear the professionals.

Talent poured out of the six members of the male group backed by a full band. Re-imagined versions of a range of musical styles from American and Celtic folk songs, pop ballads, and Broadway tunes, to contemporary favorites and classical crossovers showcased each singer's powerful voice and the group's unique sound and style of harmonies as a whole. It was no wonder their audience consisted of fans of all ages. From a curly headed toddler bouncing and clapping her chubby hands between her mommy and daddy, to gray-haired couples holding hands and nodding in time to the music.

The men at the front of the stage also demonstrated their mastery of several different instruments—piano, guitars, violins—and effortlessly performed coordinated movements and footwork while singing. They appeared as if they were having an absolute blast, even though they must have sung the songs thousands of times.

JoyAnne's eyes lingered on each performer in turn. She'd never been able to pick a favorite among the handsome guys, although she thought Sawyer might be the most attractive with his flashy dark looks. She loved the distinctive qualities of each singer's voice, but Kellan's rich, smooth baritone occasionally rang from her speakers a little more frequently than the other singers' solos. She didn't care for the shoulder-length, slightly wavy brown hair that fell around his face and his short beard, though. It went with his bad-boy persona—if it was a persona—when he took the part of the scamp or scoundrel in the story ballads the group sang and acted out, but she'd never liked the look. His voice, however, almost made her forget the dislike. Especially when she only saw his face on a CD cover or caught the tail end of a KWESTT TV special after she'd dragged in from a long day of work.

The guys ran from the stage as the last notes of a rousing show tune faded away and the houselights came up accompanied by the announcement of a fifteenminute intermission.

"How can the first half be over already?" JoyAnne collapsed against the back of the seat, using it for the first time since the music started.

Alyce laughed and stood to stretch. "I wish you liked your birthday gift just a little more, JoyAnne. I hate to see you so disappointed."

JoyAnne grinned and sighed. "They sound so *good*! And their *band* is so good! I *love* their music!"

"Because it's so *good*!" Jordyn mimicked JoyAnne's emphasis with a smirk and pulled her to her feet. "Come on. Let's visit the ladies' room while we don't have to climb over people to get out of our seats."

They joined the flow of traffic toward the restrooms. The long line moved quickly, and upon exiting the ladies' room, JoyAnne decided to do something about her noisy belly.

"I'm getting a snack and something to drink before intermission ends. You two want anything?"

"No. I got something while we waited on you earlier so I'm heading back to my seat." Jordyn replied.

"And I don't want to do all those stairs again in these heels." Alyce pointed to her pointy-toed stilettos. "I kind of regret giving into vanity and not choosing a more practical pair of shoes for the evening."

"But the way they finish off your outfit is worth the

cramped toes, right?"

"Right!" Alyce laughed and nodded. "You know me well."

JoyAnne grinned and headed toward the stairs that led to the concession area. "Yep. Meet you back at our seats."

The smell of warm, salted pretzel dough made JoyAnne's stomach rumble in appreciation, and she silently urged the line at the counter to move faster. She didn't want to miss a single second of the show.

As she placed her order, the overhead lights flicked off and on in a two-minute warning. She slapped down her money before grabbing the warm treat and icy water bottle and rushing toward the stairs. Their seats were nice ones. Center stage and three rows from the edge of the mezzanine, but there were three flights of curving stairs between them and the lobby concessions.

Slipping the neck of the sweating water bottle between the fingers that held the salty pretzel, she snatched off her heels with her free hand and took the stairs two at a time, arriving at the mezzanine level in half the time it had taken to go down them earlier. Her knee-length, poufy skirt might have tried to turn traitor on her in the whirlwind that sucked through the front doors as she entered, but its fullness came in handy for sprinting up a long stair case.

The houselights lowered, and colored spotlights swept the audience from floor to ceiling, emphasizing the opening notes of the swelling music as she hurried to her section. When she reached it, she paused and grimaced. She should have ignored her stomach and foregone the snack. Now everyone on the end of her row would have to stand up so she could traverse the narrow strip of floor between the seats.

Ooh! Maybe not. She hesitated before taking the two steps down to their row. Only one row of seats lay between her spot and the walkway that separated the mezzanine section from the rest of the balcony. The occupants of the three seats directly behind hers and Alyce's and Jordyn's seats hadn't returned from the break yet, either.

Not waiting to talk herself out of the notion, she headed toward the empty seats, glancing around. The ushers would not like what she was about to do.

Jordyn glanced over her shoulder and gave a relieved smile upon spotting JoyAnne. In one smooth move, JoyAnne stepped over the low railing and onto the flip-down cushion.

Eyes wide with a mix of surprise and laughter, Jordan hastily tilted down JoyAnne's own seat in preparation for her unorthodox arrival.

JoyAnne grinned and lifted her foot to step over and down again, but a white strobe light passed over her face, temporarily blinding her. Her bare toe stubbed the top edge of the seat back and she stumbled, barely recovering in time to keep from tumbling head over heels onto the unsuspecting heads in the lower two mezzanine rows.

Her landing was ungraceful and closer to a slide into home plate than a ladylike return to her fancy, high-priced theater seat, but she made it without dropping her shoes, her water, or her pretzel. And, more importantly, without flipping her full fifties-style chiffon skirt over her head.

Alyce clapped a hand over her mouth to smother a laugh, and Jordyn shook her head, a smile spoiling the quelling look she'd perfected on her two- and four-year-old girls.

"You can take the girl out of the country and put her in a dress, but I guess you can't take the tomboy out of her." JoyAnne whispered with a grin before setting her shoes and water bottle on the floor. She liked dressing up, but she would always be a tomboy and that stunt proved it. At least KWESTT was so spectacular nobody but her friends seemed to have noticed the comical balcony scene.

JoyAnne took a bite of her hard-won pretzel. The salty treat had nearly made her miss the opening of the second half, but maybe her stomach would quiet down so she could hear the rest of the show over it.

"In the tradition of all KWESTT shows, we invite anyone who's celebrating a birthday today to stand." Kellan Campbell, the long-haired singer, spoke into his mic when the song ended and shaded his eyes from the spotlights.

JoyAnne took another bite of her pretzel and craned her neck to look at the audience seated in the floor sections as the houselights brightened.

"Only four? Wow. That's a first for us. Anyone else willing to admit they're getting older? How about the balcony? Any May third birthdays up there?" Enoch Johnson, the group's rich bass singer, pointed toward the mezzanine.

JoyAnne nearly choked on her pretzel when Alyce and Jordyn shot to their feet and pulled her upright, pointing to her and simultaneously waving wildly to get the group's attention.

"Ah! We do have a couple more." Kellan grinned. "And one of them appears to be having her birthday treat already. Did you bring enough to share with us?"

Half the audience twisted to look at her as her friends plopped into their seats, giggling. JoyAnne shoved her partially eaten pretzel behind her back and swallowed to empty her blazing chipmunk-cheeks.

"Guess not. But we'll sing to her anyway. Ready, boys?" Kellan chuckled then led the group in the birthday song.

JoyAnne stood frozen in place as Jordyn plucked the napkin-wrapped snack from her hand. She'd read about this concert tradition somewhere on the internet, but since she'd never actually seen it happen, she'd forgotten about it. And out of several thousand people in attendance, how were there only a handful of people admitting to celebrating a birthday today?

JoyAnne darted a look at Alyce who grinned broadly. She would suspect a setup except not even Alyce and Jordyn could manipulate an entire theater full of people.

She returned her eyes to the stage and found six handsome, incredibly gifted singers focused on her for a full five beats of music before splitting their attention between her and the other birthday celebrants. Their beautiful, intricate harmonies floated around her and a huge smile grew as her embarrassment faded. This was the best version of happy birthday she had ever heard.

The song ended and Kellan, Westin, Enoch, Sawyer, Trevor, and Tyrone bowed low.

When they straightened to the applause of the audience, they looked up at her one last time. JoyAnne's grin nearly split her face as she mouthed a thank you and sank into as low a curtsy as was possible in the narrow row. If she were still alive, Mother would be proud her daughter retained a hint of old fashioned etiquette in her tomboy soul.

The intro for the next number began and JoyAnne smoothed the back of her skirt to lower herself back in the plush seat. She'd been sung to by KWESTT. Life was good. She grinned at her favorite group, eyes landing on Kellan whose attention remained on the mezzanine level. Her knees gave way, dumping her the last few inches to her seat with a soft thump.

She couldn't possibly have seen what she thought she'd seen. But it really looked like Kellan Campbell, performer with world-renowned, chart-topping KWESTT had winked. At her.

And the appeal that had made female fans cluster around him at the lobby merchant table suddenly made sense.

(3)

*K*ellan's smile had come easier since intermission. Or to be more accurate, since he'd looked up in time to see the lady in the red dress reemerge in a blaze of light from the shadowy blur of the audience and nearly tumble out of the balcony. He'd caught his breath in surprise and alarm, dropping out of a crescendoed note and earning a sideways glance from Sawyer. Thankfully, no one else had seemed to notice.

When the overhead lights brightened for the traditional acknowledgement of birthdays in the audience, he'd had to swallow a chuckle at the satisfied grin on the woman's face as she bit into her pretzel. She dressed like Grace Kelly and acted like Doris Day. An interesting combination that gave him something to focus on besides his fatigue and increasingly scratchy throat.

Kellan ran across the front of the stage, hit his next mark in the ever-changing positions of the choreographed up-tempo folksong and lifted his gaze to the upper level of the packed house. It was harder to pick her out through the glare of the spotlights, but he knew her location now and could spot her and the friends that had forced her to stand for the birthday number.

Grin widening, he sang with more energy than he'd had all night. Watching her expressive face morph from shock, to chagrin, to a full-fledged smile as they'd sung the birthday song had been the most fun he'd had for more shows than he cared to count. So much so he'd been unable to keep from tossing her a wink in appreciation of her unselfconscious, sheer enjoyment. The kind of enjoyment that held no trace of flirtatious behavior.

Unlike the females that had responded to the wink with ear-splitting shrieks.

Should have thought twice about that impulsive gesture. The younger members of the group still enjoyed that kind of shallow adulation, but it had stopped stroking Kellan's ego a long time ago.

The last few numbers flew past, and the rousing finale brought the entire audience to their feet, clapping and singing along. Thunderous applause and whistles begged for an encore and they obliged with another chorus. Taking their final bow, the loudest whistle Kellan had ever heard pierced the thunder of applause. He followed the sound, not completely surprised to see Doris Day's lips pursed around the shrill sound, and her friends' hands clapped over their ears as they winced, grinning.

"Thank you!" Kellan grinned and saluted the young woman who'd been as bright a spot in his evening as a cardinal in winter time. "And good night." His voice cracked on the last word, and he turned and jogged off the stage ahead of the rest of the group.

He grabbed a towel and water from one of the stage hands as he exited and wiped his face before slugging half the bottle to lubricate his throat. It wasn't normal to finish a show with a strained voice. Either he'd pushed too hard on the last half or his body was signaling its need for long overdue rest. Probably both.

Enoch smacked him between the shoulder blades. "You sure had the crowd in the palm of your hand tonight. What's with the winking? You haven't done that in... forever."

Kellan shrugged, adrenalin draining from his muscles, the familiar fatigue that had dogged his steps for months flooding into the void it left behind. "Old habit, I guess." He stepped into the dressing room and snatched up his duffel bag. "I'm gonna hit the showers."

Enoch eyed him but didn't press further. "We still on for supper or did you decide to head out tonight?"

They still had the busses and trailers to load, but Kellan needed the reviving effects of stinging-hot water first. "I'll be there."

The late supper was a noisy affair as the gang celebrated the wrap-up of another successful tour. When the hands on his watch neared one a.m., Kellan stood and stretched. "See you guys later."

"When you headed out?" Westin's keen, watchful green eyes belied his habitually calm, quiet voice.

"Whenever I wake up." The shower had helped, but a definite rasp had taken up residence in Kellan's throat.

Sawyer punched him in the shoulder. "Where you off to this time?"

"Think I'm going to check out this state for a while."

"Why?" Trevor pulled a face. "Last I heard, Missouri doesn't offer any kind of skiing or mountain climbing or white-water rafting. And they definitely don't have good surfing." He smirked.

"Sounds dull." Tyrone, the quieter twin but no less an adrenaline junky, shuddered.

Kellan grinned at the brothers' disgust. "Hey. I'm the old man, remember? Dull sounds good. The only plan is to see how lazy I can be. And maybe drown a few worms."

"Better you than us." Trevor shook his head. "Ty and I are taking off for Colorado and the Arkansas River. We're gonna raft The Numbers." The twenty-seven-year-old twins performed an elaborate fist-bump ritual, clearly pumped about their upcoming whitewater adventure.

"The rest of you should come. It'll be a good 'team-building' experience." Tyrone's smirk matched his brother's earlier one exactly as he mimicked one of their tour director's favorite phrases.

"I'm in. Ain't got nothin' else more exciting to do." Sawyer tapped Trev's outstretched knuckles with his own.

"No, thanks." Westin replied blandly. "Going down a Class V river with you three showoffs makes as much sense as a kamikaze pilot wearing a helmet. I prefer to walk away from my vacations. Not be carried away."

The twins scoffed at the rest of their tour mates' lack of courage, and after a few more good-natured, back-and-forth verbal jabs, Kellan took his leave. He would miss these guys.

Eventually.

Enoch caught up with him outside the restaurant and matched Kellan's long strides. "It's been a good tour."

"Yeah."

"But it'll sure be good to go home. Video chats don't cut it. I miss being able to hold my girls." Enoch had a cute pair of curly haired girls, ages two and four, and one very beautiful, devoted wife.

"I bet you do." After a couple of failed attempts at relationships, Kellan had concentrated on his music and singing career to the exclusion of all else. But lately, the longing for a wife and kids of his own was burrowing deeper and nudging him more frequently.

"Why don't you go home, Kel?"

"Don't have one." He was too tired to gloss it over.

Enoch frowned at him as they approached the multi-story hotel. "What about your place in California?"

"That's not a home. It's a condo." An empty building with no one waiting his return. Not even a dust bunny thanks to an efficient cleaning service.

Enoch dropped a dark-skinned, beefy arm around Kellan's shoulders. Though only about an inch taller than Kellan, the man's frame matched his resonant voice. Both were big. And deep. "Come home with me. You know my babies love having their Uncle Kel around to spoil them."

Kellan grinned at the thought of the two little girls who could wheedle just about anything out of him, but he shook his head. "I'm not intruding on your time with your girls. We'll be back on the road before we're ready for it."

"You gettin' tired of the ramblin' life?"

Kellan stopped and looked up at the hotel. Its architecture—or lack thereof—could be in any number of cities he'd visited. Nothing about it was remarkable, and for half a second he couldn't remember which city it stood in. "I don't know, Enoch. I'm too worn out to think logically about it."

"You need roots, Kel. To keep you grounded."

Kellan snorted. "And how exactly does one grow roots when you spend half your life on a bus, Enoch?"

"You need a family."

The word hurt. The grief of losing his parents then his grandparents had mellowed, but the loss of anyone to belong to, of anyone that belonged to him, that feeling grew a little more each day. "Enoch—"

"Don't bite my head off, Kel. You could get married and start your own family."

Anger burned through the road fatigue. "And who exactly am I supposed to marry? One of the rabid fans that follow us from town to town but don't know anything beyond the persona they see in our stage productions or on the internet? I'm not into one-night stands! Or maybe you think I should hop on one of those matchmaking sites? I'm sure plenty of women would jump at the chance to be Kellan Campbell's 'match.' Until they discover that Kellan C. *Davis* is not quite the person in real life as he is on stage."

His agent hadn't thought his last name had enough "star power" when he'd signed with her years earlier, so they'd used his first and middle as his professional name. She'd also changed his home state to California and convinced him to let his thick, wavy hair grow to shoulder length and adopt the scruffy-face look to project a kind of bad-boy image that—she claimed—women liked. The woman's instincts had proven correct, and she'd cleared many obstacles out of his path so he could now claim a successful music career, but sometimes he wondered where plain-old-farm-boy Kel Davis had disappeared to.

"*Man*, I forgot how cranky you get at the end of a tour." Enoch's dark eyes twinkled in spite of his scowl. "I don't think any of those things, and if you'd crawl out of your bad mood, you'd know that. I *think* you should use your vacation to find someone normal. It's time you fell in love and started growing those roots, creating a home to return to. Those things ground a man."

"Normal? Huh! What *normal* woman wants a man whose profession keeps him on the road for months at a time?" Kellan yanked his keycard out of his pocket and jammed it in the horizontal slot beside the hotel's side entrance.

Enoch followed him through the door and continued his siege. "A woman who loved you. Although, come to think of it, if she fell in love with *you*, *she* wouldn't be normal."

"Ha ha. Don't give up your day job, Enoch. You'll never make it as a comedian."

"Maybe you should think about giving up *your* day job if you're that tired of it all."

Kellan slapped the stairwell door open and jogged to the third floor squinting under a growing headache. He reached his room, Enoch still hard on his heels. He unlocked it and slapped on the overhead light before wearily turning to face his friend. "And what would I do with the rest of my life?"

"Whatever God wants you to. Raise a family maybe."

"I really didn't have much of an example on how to do that." When his mother died after Kellan's eighth birthday, he'd gone to live with his grandparents. Seven years later, his father—an international, jet-setting businessman who was gone more often than he was home—died in a plane crash, leaving Kellan with plenty of cash in the bank and few memories of a father. Kellan's grandparents had given him love and stability, and life on their farm had taught him the value of hard work and love of the outdoors. But during his senior year of high school, they'd died within three months of each other, leaving the void of family emptier than ever. A void that even his close friendship with the other KWESTT members hadn't filled.

Enoch's eyes hardened. "You have a Heavenly Father who will teach you whatever you need to know."

Though three years younger than Kellan, Enoch should be the one called "Old Man." He had more wisdom than the rest of the group put together. It had been Enoch who'd led Kellan to Christ four years ago—something Kel's grandparents had prayed about for years. That surrender had filled a huge hole in Kellan's life, and he'd experienced a contentment he couldn't remember feeling since before his mother died. Lately however, that contentment had disappeared into thin air.

"You taking your Bible with you?"

Kellan frowned. Lack of contentment didn't make him a heathen, did it? "Of course."

"Then spend some time reading it while you're sitting on a river bank. Jesus liked to fish, too, you know." He yanked Kellan into a rough hug and slapped him on the back before releasing him. "Call or text me some time to let me know you haven't drowned, and I'll see you in a couple months."

"Tell Evie and your girls Uncle Kel says 'Hi.'"

"Will do." Enoch flashed a bright smile at the mention of his girls. "Night, man."

"Night." Kellan closed the door and walked to the king size bed and flopped onto his back in the middle of it.

He stared at the ceiling while thinking over his friend's advice. "Find a wife. Right. Because Enoch found one worth her weight in gold, he thinks it's as easy as buying a new shirt." Rolling over, he yanked one of the pillows free of the bedspread and stuffed it under his cheek. He'd undress and crawl under the sheets in a minute. Right now it felt good to close his eyes and enjoy the silence.

If he could find someone in real life who caught his attention like that Doris Day, Grace Kelly woman had, he'd consider taking Enoch's advice. But she was probably too good to be true. Kind of like KWESTT's full stage productions with all the costumes, smoke, and colored lights that made everything more dramatic and eye-catching than it really was.

Or as fake as the bad-boy, lady's-man stage image his agent and the show's producers had created out of

Kellan Campbell Davis. In reality, just an Arkansas chicken farmer who happened to be pretty good with a guitar and could sing a little.

(4)

"*H*ey, Girl! How was your show? I'm almost jealous—even though it *wasn't* a country music concert." The college-age female standing behind the registration desk hooked a strand of royal blue hair behind her ear and pushed out her bottom lip.

"Hi, Tayleigh." JoyAnne grinned. "It was pretty incredible. I think you would've enjoyed it, too, in spite of having the poor taste to not be a KWESTT fan." She kicked the door shut to prevent more of the campstore's conditioned air from escaping and dropped her armload onto the counter with a thud, smacking a hand on top of the stack of mail that threatened to slide off the two boxes of travel brochures from the state's tourism division. "Blue, huh?" She pointed to the girl's unnaturally streaked blonde hair.

A junior in college who juggled classes with her work schedule, Tayleigh had carried a solid 4.0 GPA every year. She was intelligent, dependable, and a hard worker, but you wouldn't know it if you judged the girl by her fashion style. Especially her hair. Which changed colors nearly as often as the weather.

"It's Ryan's baseball team's jerseys' color and embarrasses my little brother to death when I show up at his high school games." Tayleigh smirked, deftly wielding the box cutter to get to the new brochures for various Missouri attractions. "But enough about me. How was the concert? Spill, Girl! Are you ready to run away to the big city so you can enjoy the nightlife on a regular basis?"

"Absolutely not." JoyAnne laughed and described the theater, some of the musical numbers, and the stage production. "I loved the show, but I'm glad to be back where it's quieter and traffic is limited to two-lane highways." And where life stayed safe and predictable.

Tayleigh's blue-gray eyes studied the computer screen in front of her. "Not so quiet. We're almost at capacity, and that family reunion group is keeping everybody hopping, getting them all settled in today."

"Tell me about it." JoyAnne pulled a chilled water bottle from the insulated tub of ice in front of the counter and took a long swallow after breaking the seal. "A couple of guests drove their RVs like they were the size of a compact car—oh, make a note that we need to repair the one-way sign at the Y in section three." Joy shook her head remembering the embarrassed driver who'd swung too wide and clipped the edge of the metal placard, "I've helped set up three brand new, out-of-the-box tents today. This weekend is shaping up to be interesting, and it's only Thursday afternoon." Some days she wondered if her title shouldn't be baby-sitter instead of campground manager.

"Speaking of interesting…" Tayleigh let the sentence trail as she wiggled her eyebrows before sliding some of the new brochures into empty slots on the tourism information rack.

JoyAnne swigged another long drink and stepped around the desk to view the dry-erase map of the camping sites. The season was starting off with a bang. If it kept up all camping season, they'd have a banner year.

Tayleigh tapped the toe of a bright purple Converse that somehow didn't clash with her yellow shorts and blue Wad-A-Wa Campground shirt. The mishmash of colors fit the girl's personality. If Joy'd tried that combination, she'd only look like an explosion at a paint factory.

Tayleigh's purple-clad toe tapped harder.

"All right, all right. *What* is so interesting?"

The girl's grin flashed. "I thought you'd never ask. You *have* to check out 197 on your next go-round."

"Why? What's wrong with it?"

"Oh, it's not what's wrong, it's what's *right* with it. Or rather… *who*."

JoyAnne ran her finger along the map until she reached 197. The most secluded tent site they had—and that was saying something since they were all positioned to give each site a feeling of privacy. Rented out for… three weeks? It wasn't unprecedented, but it was unusual for a basic tent site. "What do you mean?"

Tayleigh waved her blue manicured nails in front of her wide-eyed, grinning, lightly freckled face. "I'm just sayin' if all the rugged outdoor types looked that hot, campgrounds would be the newest trend in matchmaking sites."

JoyAnne rolled her eyes. "You are terrible. Did this camper really rent the spot for three weeks or were you flirting so hard you messed up the dates?"

"Ha, ha." Tayleigh narrowed her eyes. "I don't mess up numbers. I wrote down exactly what he asked for. You should probably talk to him to confirm, though." Tayleigh's eyebrows performed jumping jacks again. "He's two years older than you—I know 'cause I checked his driver's license—and I didn't see a wedding ring. You aren't getting any younger you know."

The friendly barb stung, but JoyAnne's skin had thickened out of sheer necessity, and before she could stop it, her tongue shot between her lips in a gesture that belied the birthdate on her own driver's license. "Thank you, Miss Matchmaker, I don't do summer flings." She snatched the keys to the all-terrain utility vehicle from the pegboard below the counter. "If anybody needs me I have a walkie with me. Ladybug and I are going to check the beach and make sure everyone's playing by the rules." She grabbed another water bottle on her way out the door.

"You never know when a summer fling might turn into something longer." Tayleigh hollered before the door slapped shut.

JoyAnne aimed the utility vehicle for the barn, her foot pressing the accelerator a little harder than necessary. She knew exactly how old she was, thank you very much. But she hadn't always been single—which might be why it stung more these days. Tayleigh was a sweet girl and a hard worker but sometimes... "As if a romance with a paying guest would be feasible even if he is staying three whole weeks—which I doubt. There's summer fling and then there's complete insanity." She braked hard outside the barn and threw it into park.

Entering the large, old-fashioned but well-maintained structure that sat about three hundred yards behind the camp store, she grabbed a halter and brush and strode out the wide rear doors to the large pasture bordering the east side of the campground. A sharp whistle brought the heads of five horses up, and a mare the color of a new penny cantered toward JoyAnne.

"Hello, pretty girl. Wanna go exploring this afternoon?" JoyAnne slipped the green rope halter over the horse's nose and fastened it before palming a cookie.

The mare nickered low in her throat and lipped the treat off JoyAnne's hand. Wad-A-Wa Campground boasted two-hundred-and-fifty campsites and had the prerequisite golf carts and a couple of larger utility vehicles to carry staff, campers, and supplies around the sprawling property, but horses had less impact on the acreage surrounding the primitive campsites and on the walking trails. Not to mention, they were a lot more fun.

In ten minutes, JoyAnne had the horse brushed and saddled. She stuffed the water bottle into the saddlebags that held extra radio batteries, a first aid kit, and a few other tools that came in handy for her Jill-of-all-trades job. "Let's go, Ladybug."

She swung into the saddle and guided the chestnut toward the wide finger of Dogwood Lake that the campground butted up against. Unlike other crowded recreational lakes created by hydroelectric dams in the state, miles of national forest surrounded much of this one giving it a secluded, wild feel. And although plenty of boat traffic invaded the main body of the lake on weekends and holidays, this portion of it tended to be quieter. Perfect for those wanting the slower, peaceful pace of camping.

Perfect for people who needed a break from the so-called real world. Or people who wanted to avoid it all together. Like herself.

Which is why she loved her job. Her life now.

JoyAnne and Ladybug reached the stretch of sandy, private beach and rode along the edge of the water. Although the swim area was cordoned off from the rest of the lake, it was a swim-at-your-own-risk beach since there was no lifeguard posted.

The patch on her polo shirt proclaimed her position as campground manager, and she greeted everyone with a smile. When needed, she quietly restated a few beach rules to those pushing the boundaries then handed out horse cookies to a few curious youngsters to feed to Ladybug.

An hour later and without making a conscious decision, she emerged from a trail and directed Ladybug down the narrow strip of blacktop that wound through the primitive camp sites. The regulars in this section tended to be pretty self-sufficient, but they were always friendly and she received many smiling waves and was frequently stopped to chat for a few minutes.

Until she reached campsite 197.

JoyAnne lifted an eyebrow at the emblem on the rear of the shiny black car parked on the campsite. With the availability of compact, lightweight camping gear now days, cars were as common a sight as trucks and SUVs around the tent sites. But a brand new Mercedes? Not so much.

She whistled under her breath. Thanks to Micah and Victor, she recognized an expensive automobile when she saw it, and this one reeked of money.

A man walked around a tent so new JoyAnne could smell it. He'd gotten it upright and straight—points for him on that one—and now grabbed a tent stake to secure the fabric structure to the ground.

"Hi. Are you getting settled in okay?"

He glanced her direction without the smile she normally received from happy guests, jerked his chin up in a semblance of a nod, then picked up a camping hammer and squatted to pound the first stake into the hard-packed soil.

Or tried to. Dressed in a gray t-shirt and faded jeans, the man looked fit enough for the job, but he missed every other blow and nudged up the brim of his navy-colored ball cap to wipe his forehead like he was pounding railroad spikes rather than a tiny tent stake.

One corner of JoyAnne's mouth slanted down and she shook her head slightly as she dismounted Ladybug. Flipping the reins over the horse's head to trail the ground, JoyAnne left her to nibble the short grass. If the man's choice of transportation was any indication, the city slicker had probably never camped a day in his life.

"Can I help you finish up there?"

The camper straightened and shot her a frown. His body language emphasized his croaked denial before returning to his painstakingly slow task.

Tayleigh was right. The man was hot. Running a fever hot if his voice and reddened cheeks were any indication. He was handsome, too, though, under that unnatural flush. Sunglasses hid his eyes, but not his strong jawline, and a firm mouth. The way his arms and torso filled out the material of his long sleeved t-shirt, he could grace the cover of any outdoor magazine. Until they saw his hammering skills.

"Why don't you sit down and let me do that for you?"

The man pushed to his feet. "Why?"

She didn't take the growl personally. "Because you don't look like you feel well."

"Doesn't mean I can't put up a measly tent."

"No. But the way you're going about it, it'll take the rest of the afternoon."

He turned his back on her, leaned over, and poked the pointy end of a second stake in the ground. At least he knew which end of the stake went where.

He swung the hammer, and missed.

JoyAnne was grateful for the hoarseness that kept her from understanding the word he uttered. "You hammer like lightning."

He straightened again and rubbed his forehead before tugging on his ball cap and crossing his arms across his muscled chest, camping hammer gripped in his right hand like he wanted to hit something besides tent stakes. "What are you talking about?"

JoyAnne grinned. "You never strike the same place twice."

When he continued to stare at her without moving, she swiped the hammer from his hand and proceeded to make short work of setting the last of the stakes to secure the tent. She laid the hammer on the lid of a small ice chest when she finished. The man hadn't moved, and his arms remained tightly folded.

She returned his scrutiny. "Are you out here all by yourself?"

"I was."

Ah. The grumpy, loner type who resented intruders. "Are you sure you're well enough to be camping alone? We're a long way from a hospital if you became really ill."

"I'm fine." His stance softened a little. "Just dizzy from the decongestion medicine."

"Leaning over with full sinuses will do that, too." Poor guy. Trying to escape the pressures of city life and finding you were allergic to the wilderness would make anyone grumpy. "Do you have a cell phone with you?"

He silently fished a slim black device from his pocket and showed it to her, his mouth gaining a wry twist.

She grinned again. "Okay. Dumb question. Our office number is on the registration card that goes in your vehicle window. There is someone on call for emergencies twenty-four hours a day during camping season. Don't hesitate to use it if you have any trouble."

He acknowledged the invitation with another silent chin lift.

"And I'll ride around in the morning to check on you." She picked up Ladybug's reins and swung into the saddle. The man was a grown adult. If he wanted to camp out while sick there was nothing she could do to stop him. She'd just have to keep an eye on him.

"Don't bother."

She gave the grump a grim smile. "It's not a

bother. It's my job." *Wad-A-Wa Campground manager and chief babysitter at your service.*

(5)

A fish broke the surface with a splash, ignoring Kellan's baited hook for the tastier bug that had made the mistake of landing on that spot on the lake to take a sip.

Kellan leaned against the trunk of a big oak and took in the beauty of the wide expanse of water edged with a mix of cedars, oaks, hickory, and other deciduous trees occasionally broken by rocky outcroppings. Enoch had advised him to use time like this for prayer and devotions, but he'd forgotten his Bible at his campsite in his groggy haste to gather fishing supplies and get to the water early. He'd remember to bring it next time. He'd also remember to fix himself some decent coffee-to-go, too. The small cup of instant he'd managed to fumble together had not done the job.

The peaceful view was worth dragging himself out of the tent before sunup, though, if he did have the mother of all colds. Rest, fresh air, and sunshine would do more to heal him than that vertigo-inducing decongestant he'd made the mistake of picking up at a gas station after the first brand he'd purchased hadn't lessened his symptoms. When his head cleared, he'd make a mental note to never buy either brand again. It had made him look like a complete idiot in front of that cute campground employee. Not the blue-haired one at the camp store, but the one who'd looked capable of pitching her own tent, catching her own supper, and cooking it over the fire she'd started with two sticks.

Kellan grinned. It had taken his foggy medicine head a full ten minutes after she'd ridden away to catch up with her "hammer like lightning" comment. He'd watched too many old movies in hotel rooms over the last few years. The woman sort of reminded him of classic-movie actress Debbie Reynolds. A spunky, capable, outdoorsy girl-next-door with a quick sense of humor.

If he had any intention of following Enoch's advice, she'd be worth a second look. But since he'd already fouled up the other part of Enoch's uninvited wisdom, he should concentrate on laying low and kicking the bugs out of his system.

He rubbed the prickly morning-stubble on his jaw. The laying low part should be easy enough. His new super-short haircut and clean face had kept him incognito while he'd rented a vehicle and crisscrossed the metropolitan city to fill it with ultra-lite camping and fishing gear. And cold medicine. Throw in a ball cap and a different style of sunglasses than he normally wore, and no one in this rural area had recognized him yet. Especially with plugged sinuses and a roaring case of laryngitis.

The sense of rootlessness that had plagued him for months jabbed him again. He didn't even have an automobile to his own name. When the old pickup truck he'd gotten in high school had finally died, he'd never replaced it because it made more sense to rent or get a short-term lease whenever he needed a car rather than let one sit in a long-term parking lot somewhere or gather dust in a parking garage at one end of the country or the other. But every rental agreement was becoming a stark reminder that he still had no place to really call home. No one to leave an automobile with when it was time to board a plane or bus for the next round of travel. No one to drive it to meet him when he landed in an airport or stepped off the bus at the end of a long tour.

His stomach rumbled, and he reeled in his line and caught up the empty hook with a frown. "At least somebody got breakfast this morning." He grumbled, picking up his tackle box and squinting toward the sparkling water. "Don't get used to the free meal. It won't happen again. I've got my mouth set for some fresh bass."

A splash mocked him as he hit the trail back to his secluded corner of Wad-A-Whatever-its-name-was campground——must be some kind of old Indian word. Good thing he'd never intended to subsist on what he caught and had other food items in his ice chest to pick from. After breakfast, he'd go find the showers, clean up, and explore some of the trails he'd seen signs for as he'd driven in. If his full head didn't insist on a nap first. This virus was wearing him out, and he was suddenly thankful he'd opted for a nice, groomed-campground version of roughing it instead of backpacking all his gear into the wilds of a mountainous national park.

Kellan exited the wooded trail onto his campsite and stopped short at the sight of a female peering into the tent window he'd left unzipped. "Can I help you?"

She jerked upright and spun to face him. Kellan didn't have to read the logo on her red shirt to recognize her. The tent-stake-pounding woman.

"Oh. *There* you are. I see you survived the night." She didn't look the least bit guilty about invading his privacy but tilted her head and studied him with a clear gaze.

What had he left lying on his air mattress beneath that screened opening? It would be impossible to remain anonymous if the woman found something identifying him as a member of KWESTT. Five of their albums had landed on music charts not only in the U. S. but around the world, and the last two had peaked at the number one spot for world music album sales. All it would take was one person recognizing him and posting it to some social media site and his new clean-cut disguise would be blown. Then he'd have to find a new retreat. Not just to keep fans from hounding him but also to keep his agent from tracking him down to give him another earful about going dark when he should be "capitalizing on your success and current popularity." Patricia wanted him trending in news feeds, not disappearing for two solid months. But he desperately needed a break, and besides, he had a promise to a wily bass to keep.

He dropped the tackle box on the picnic table and propped his rod next to it. "Did you need something?"

She gave a start. "Yes. I almost forgot." She spun on her heel and jogged to the green utility vehicle parked behind his car. When she turned to head back toward him, she had a Styrofoam takeout box in one hand and an insulated cup in the other. "Do you like coffee? I don't but most people do so I took a chance you would, too."

His stuffy nose sucked in the wonderful aroma of liquid caffeine. "Yes." Who didn't like coffee?

"Good! I brought you some breakfast, too, since I see you failed to catch anything. George said the fish weren't biting well this morning even for the experienced anglers."

That stung. They *had* been biting, just not on what he had to offer. "I can take care of myself. I'll have you know I come from a long line of hunters." On his mother's side, anyway. His father's side had given him a love for luxury cars. Which is why he hadn't been able to resist a short-term lease on a new Mercedes-Benz S-Class Coupe for his vacation rather than a more practical SUV. But life on the road had also taught him to appreciate a comfortable, quiet, powerful ride—even if it was impractical for a camping trip. And in spite of his achy head, it had been fun to drive on the hilly, curvy roads leading to this remote lake.

Her eyebrow lifted at his surly tone. "A long line of hunters, huh? I think you come from a long line of sourpusses. But maybe this will sweeten your disposition." She handed him the insulated cup and opened the white container. "There's sugar and creamer in the corner here if you like that in your stump water, but the—"

"Stump water?"

"Yes. It looks like rainwater that's been standing in a rotten stump for months and smells about the same." She wrinkled her nose. "But as I was saying. The pièce de résistance…" The sudden authentic-sounding French accent made him blink as she turned the takeout container toward him with a wide grin. "Eggs, bacon, buttered biscuits, and homemade applesauce." The accent disappeared as if it had never been.

His stomach growled appreciatively as he took the box. He wasn't going to lower his guard with this nosy female, however. No matter how intriguing she might be. "First you call me a sourpuss, then you try to feed me. What'd you do, poison it?"

A twinkle brightened her hazel eyes until they looked more gold than green. "No. And don't you believe the rumors, either."

The quirky woman was quickly breaching the protective surliness that had reared its head upon seeing her snooping around his things. He should keep his mouth shut. "What rumors?"

She glanced around as if there might be someone eavesdropping on the secluded, tree-surrounded tent site and lowered her voice. "About the previous camper at this spot."

The woman not only pounded tent stakes better than him, she fished better, too.

He rose to the bait. "What happened?"

Wide-eyed innocence replaced her conspiratorial expression. "He is no longer with us."

Kellan lifted the foam cup to hide his chagrin at

walking into the gag. This energetic, bright-eyed woman was making him feel old and slow. Of course the previous camper was gone. It's what campers did. They left. Checked out. Went home. Moved on.

"But I had nothing whatsoever to do with his demise." A quiver at the corner of her mouth and the twinkle in her eyes ruined the pious, innocent expression.

Kellan choked on the hot coffee and coughed to clear his throat. "Very funny." It *was* actually, but he wasn't about to encourage her. Not with his scratchy throat protesting that scalding liquid.

An engaging grin showcased neat, white teeth. "*I* thought so. Enjoy your breakfast before it gets any colder." She turned away. Stopped. Spun back toward him, digging in her back pocket. "Almost forgot." She pulled out a set of napkin-wrapped plastic-ware. "Here."

When he took them, she headed for the mechanical steed that had replaced the horse of the previous afternoon. "I'll see you around."

The vehicle sped away as Kellan stared at the curly ponytail bouncing and swaying with the same cheerful liveliness that exuded from its owner. "I can't wait," he muttered under his breath before taking another sip of really good coffee. To be honest, he *did* want to see her again.

A bad idea since her energy made him feel every one of his thirty-seven years.

(6)

*W*hat in the world had gotten into her? She'd teased and bullied that poor befuddled man as if he were Uncle George or Victor. No doubt he thought her looney tunes, but she hadn't been able to stop herself. He'd looked so uptight she'd instantly wanted to help him lighten up.

If Tayleigh could've witnessed any of that, she'd probably label JoyAnne's behavior as flirting. And no doubt approve. But she hadn't been flirting. Not exactly. Sure the guy was nice looking, but he didn't set her pulse racing or her stomach flopping like a freshly-caught bass. Not like Micah had.

JoyAnne's hands tightened on the steering wheel of the utility vehicle, and she breathed past the dull stab of pain the memory prompted. A steady pulse and calm stomach were good things. The reverse led to tremendous pain when they ended.

She was thankful the guy at camp site 197 didn't cause those things. She only felt sorry for him. He was obviously worn down and ill, but there was also a lost look in his light-brown eyes that she recognized. She used to see it in her mirror before George and Dorothy had given her a purpose and a place. So she would keep an eye on him and make sure he survived his attempt to camp out, and maybe she could gently bully him into a better mood. Wad-A-Wa Campground didn't need a grumpy bear prowling the grounds, scaring the other guests.

The mental picture brought another grin. He sure growled like a bear, but maybe that hearty breakfast would calm the savage beast and make him friendlier. If it didn't, well, they could always ask him to be the campground's mascot.

"Uh oh. I've seen that look before. What are you plotting now?"

JoyAnne braked beside the tall man standing along the blacktop drive. "Morning, George. Hop in." She kissed his sun-tanned cheek when he joined her on the bench seat. "Finish your morning walk already?"

"Yes, and none too soon, either. It's warm for this early in May." He wiped his forehead on the sleeve of his sunny yellow t-shirt that advertised their campground. "But don't change the subject. What are you up to?"

She darted a sideways glance at the man who was closer to a father than an employer. "Five-five last time I measured and I think I'm done growing."

For a man who didn't have an ounce of spare flesh

on him, George had the best belly laugh she'd ever heard. It was one of the things she loved about him, and it was nearly impossible to be sad around it. There'd been a couple of years when it didn't ring out, but it had returned. Richer and sweeter for the grief that had buried it for a while.

"You're wired for sound this morning, aren't you?"

"Just living up to our reputation." She gestured toward the slogan on the front of his shirt.

"It says we're the *happiest* campground in Missouri. Not the *pun*-iest." George scrunched his grin into a frown.

"Ooh! Someone ate their *witty-s* this morning." JoyAnne shot back.

He lifted his hands in surrender, eyes twinkling. "You win, Smarty Pants." George shook his head. "I get no respect around here. None at all. Give the woman a clipboard and a title and the power goes straight to her head."

"You can have the clipboard back anytime. Just say the word." JoyAnne pulled it out of the rack below the dash and offered it to him.

"Uh uh." He pushed it away with a grimace of distaste. "Been there, done that. I'm enjoying being the lazy, useless figurehead, thank you very much."

JoyAnne returned the clipboard holding the daily schedule, list of repairs, and various other reminders to its compartment. "Useless, my foot. Must have been a figment of my imagination that you spent all yesterday on the mower."

"Must have."

JoyAnne laughed at his innocent smile and drove around the back of the pool house. She had a water filter to check on. "So what have you and Dorothy got planned today?"

"Don't know. I'm afraid to ask what's on her agenda. I think I'll hide out with you a while longer. Besides, I'm curious."

"'Bout what?"

"What you were plotting earlier."

JoyAnne parked the vehicle and grabbed her clipboard, ducking her head to hide the instantaneous grin. "Not a thing."

George yanked the clipboard out of her hands and studied her with suspicion.

"Thought you didn't want that." She tried distraction.

"I haven't seen that particular smile in a long time, JoyAnne." His expression softened. "I've missed it."

Her mouth flattened. "It's a plain old smile, George. Nothing special. You wanna help me replace the filter? It's still not working right, and I'm tired of fiddling with it."

He studied her, disappointment replacing the twinkle as he returned the clipboard. "No. I think I'll go on to the house."

JoyAnne studied the toes of her khaki-colored boots. No matter how vigilantly she avoided the minefield of painful memories, invariably someone else stepped on a trigger and they exploded in her face. It wouldn't be so bad if they only hurt her. But the fallout hitting those closest to her was unacceptable.

She should have spent a few more minutes in Micah's Bible this morning. Concentrating on verses that talked about controlling the tongue.

"I'm sorry, George. I..." She clasped the clipboard

to her chest, unable to explain.

He gave her a quick hug and a soft smile reappeared. "Don't worry about it. I'll grill you later. After I've had another cup of coffee."

"Great." She dragged the word out but gave him a crooked grin.

"Don't work the rest of my employees out of a job today, JoyAnne." George issued the oft-repeated warning.

"I haven't yet."

"Not for a lack of trying, though." His smile faded but his brown eyes were gentle, entreating. "As much as I want this place to live up to our slogan and give people a relaxing, enjoyable vacation experience, there's more to life than this campground, JoyAnne."

"I know that." The words sounded defensive and she tried to soften her tone. "I thoroughly enjoyed taking a break to spend time with Alyce and Jordyn Sunday evening and sleeping in on Monday."

George's disapproval didn't diminish. "One day does not constitute a break, JoyAnne. You can't hide behind work and this place for the rest of your life. I'm praying you figure that out soon, Kiddo."

He turned and walked away before she could respond so she marched to the small structure that sheltered the large in-ground swimming pool's filtering equipment and took her emotions out on the recalcitrant filter.

There *had* been more to her life once. She'd traveled, explored the world, spread her wings. And when they'd been scorched, she'd plowed into the dirt and wallowed in her own pain until George, Dorothy, and Victor had dragged her to a place of safety. She would always miss her parents and Micah. The Barretts would never replace them, but they had filled some of the aching hole those losses had left behind. And she was happy here with them. Happier than she'd once expected to ever be again. And here she planned to stay. She loved her job. Loved seeing people relax. Loved that she got to help families enjoy themselves and make lifelong memories.

A faint smile returned as she wiped her hands and eyed her repair job. There was definitely someone on the premises this week who looked like he needed help figuring out how to chill out.

(7)

"*H*i. Nice day for a hike."

Kellan nodded and stepped off the well-worn trail to allow the young couple wearing hiking boots and loose-fitting, long sleeve button downs over t-shirts and cargo shorts to pass. With their hydration backpacks and trekking poles, they looked ready to tackle a small mountain. Not this groomed, level, tree-lined park path.

The young man paused as they came abreast of Kellan and leaned on his pole. "Are you hiking the green loop or the blue?"

"Haven't decided." According to the sign at the trail head, the two hiking loops accessible from it diverged about a quarter mile in, giving him the choice of a two-mile trek through the woods or a mile trek along a bluff overlooking the lake.

"You don't sound good." The woman eyed him with a sympathetic frown.

"Laryngitis." Kellan edged around them. He wanted to be hiking. Not socializing.

The man finished a long pull on the flexible straw that draped over his shoulder then tucked it away. "Well, if you decide to take the green loop, you'll need to watch closely for the trail markers. I think some of them have been stolen or something. We nearly got lost a time or two. When we get back, we're going to report it to the camp office."

As if a trail smooth enough to resemble a sidewalk wasn't enough of a marker. He stepped back onto the path. "Thanks."

"Sure. See you around."

Kellan tossed a wave over his shoulder and quickened his pace. Enoch was right. He was grumpy. Grumpier than he'd ever been after a long tour. Fans were his bread and butter, but if he had to deal with them in his current funk, he risked offending them at best, alienating them and their social media followers at worst. So he'd chosen to camp in the woods rather than stay in hotels, but maybe he should have rethought picking a campground that proudly proclaimed itself the friendliest or happiest or whatever that Indian name meant.

Yesterday's breakfast had been a pretty nice way to start his stay here, though.

Pretty nice?

All right, it had been downright delicious. But the more people he had to be around, talk to, or deal with, the greater chance he would be recognized. He wasn't normally so antisocial, but back-to-back tours, hours in the recording studio when he wasn't on the road, and tussles between himself and his agent and record label upper management had drained him. Burnt him out. Left him craving privacy. He needed this time to be a nobody. And for the first time in years not to think, eat, drink, and sleep music, showmanship, and persona.

Would you like some cheese, too?

Kellan took the right fork of the trail, following the blue markers at a jog along a gradual rise. Okay. So he was whining. He had a good life. A life people envied. And he'd been careful with his inheritance and earnings and had a fat bank account to show for it. He'd traveled the world and could spend his vacation anywhere he wanted, doing anything he wanted. Almost. But he could no longer ignore the creeping emptiness, the sense of drifting without an anchor.

Besides the love of making music, what was he doing all this for? Who was he doing it for? What difference did he make in the world? Fame and fortune were no longer adequate reasons to keep doing what he did, nor did he have any motivation to pursue a different course.

Enoch had nailed the fact that Kellan had no roots. Acknowledging that fact did nothing to remedy the lack, though. It would be nice to have a wife and kids, but he'd been burnt twice before and the thought of wading through the dating game again in search of someone whose attraction wasn't based solely on his or his group's fame made him shudder.

His schedule didn't leave much time for meeting the right woman. He supposed he could sign up for one of those websites that were advertised everywhere now days, but there again, he ran into the problem of his identity.

The glint of sunlight on water flickered through the thinning tree line, and Kellan slowed to a stop when he reached the clearing at the top of the bluff. The trail hadn't been steep but taking it at a jog had worked up a light sweat and the view was worth stopping for.

"This is more like it." With no other hikers in sight and no boats on the water below him, he could imagine himself alone in the wilderness.

Kellan leaned against the waist-high stone wall that provided a barrier along the top of the bluff. He stared out over the water, and took a deep breath through marginally clearer sinuses.

Fresh air, space, and silence. Wonderful silence. No one trying to get his attention. No one pushing him to make decisions. No one pulling him in directions he wasn't sure he wanted to go.

He half sat on top of the wide rock wall, bending his knee and planting one foot on it while keeping the other foot on the ground. Closing his eyes, he absorbed the silence until he heard the sounds of life that throbbed around him. The soft rhythm of water lapping against the rocky bluff below him. The melody of the light breeze playing through spring-green leaves. The sweet harmony of bird song.

The natural music worked its soft notes into the knots that had taken up permanent residence in his neck and shoulders. This was what he'd been needing. Peace. Solitude. Not something as intangible and indefinite as roots.

He lost track of time thinking about absolutely nothing until new sounds pierced his awareness and made him look up. He turned his head to listen, easily identifying the sounds of people coming his way.

His eyebrows lowered. So much for solitude. He stood and dusted off his backside as three children of various heights rushed into the clearing, shouting and laughing.

A man and woman appeared behind the three youngsters. "Slow down and don't climb on the rocks." The short-haired woman caught sight of Kellan. "Hello. Sorry to interrupt the quiet."

Kellan shook his head. "No problem. I'm leaving." Sooner than he'd planned, but he wouldn't grudge the eager boys and their sister the enjoyment of the pretty overlook. He'd just have to find a place farther away from people. Even if that meant folding his tent and striking out for wilder, less populated country.

(8)

"*I*'m going to grab my lunch break while it's quiet. You okay here for a bit?"

JoyAnne glanced toward Tayleigh who stood in the doorway of the storage room and nodded. "Take your time."

"Thanks, Boss." Tayleigh saluted and disappeared from view.

JoyAnne returned to clearing the head-high shelf that ran above the tubs and bins of gift shop inventory. It had wiggled ominously when she'd pulled down a box of children's hoodies earlier. Upon closer examination, she'd discovered one of the support brackets starting to pull away from the wall. If ignored, it could dump its load of boxes on an unsuspecting head. And wouldn't that do wonders for their insurance

55

premiums.

She pulled off a neat stack of tees and placed them on the table behind her. When she finished, she'd better take a look at the floor-to-ceiling shelves on the other wall and make sure they were solid. Just what she needed at the start of a busy camping season. To be repairing shelves. Why hadn't she noticed it over the winter while doing inventory?

She banged her knee against a waist-high barrel, sending the extra inventory of wooden hiking staffs clattering to the other side of the container as she reached for another box. She ignored the racket and carefully lifted an unwieldy box off the unstable shelf. Clothing should be lighter than this. Especially when her shoulders ached from running the weed eater for three hours yesterday afternoon.

"Excuse me?"

JoyAnne jerked toward the unexpected voice, lost her grip on the box, and dropped it against the edge of the shelf. The flimsy tape across its cardboard bottom split open, dumping a rainbow of thick cotton on her head. The weakened bracket pulled free of its moorings and one end of the shelf smacked her shoulder.

"Ow!" She stumbled backwards, batting away her colorful blindfold.

Firm hands gripped her arms above the elbows, halting her frantic movements before lifting the pile of hoodies off her head.

She blinked at the man standing in front of her.

"You okay?" Forehead creasing beneath the brim of his cap, the man from campsite 197 ran his eyes over her.

"I... I think so." She scooted backwards, rubbing

her smarting shoulder. "I didn't hear you come in."

His hands fell to his sides. "Sorry. Didn't mean to startle you. I came in as the girl with the… the blue hair was leaving. She said I'd find you back here if I needed help."

"Tayleigh." It had been three full days since she'd seen the taciturn camper, and his voice had lost much of its strained hoarseness.

But it hadn't gone far. She'd just found it.

"What?"

She cleared the rasp from her throat. "The girl who left. Her name's Tayleigh."

"Oh." He frowned and fiddled with the aviator sunglasses tucked over the neckline of his cocoa-powder-brown t-shirt. "Are you sure that board didn't hit your head?"

"No. And it was loose already—the board, not my head." She grinned. "I was clearing it off to fix it. So wouldn't you know it would crash *after* I lightened its load? That's gratitude for you. But at least I know gravity still works."

His frown faded but before she could see if an answering smile took its place, he bent and began to pick up sweatshirts from the floor. "Where do you want these?"

"You don't have to do that. I can take care of it." What had happened to the grumpy camper who'd seemed anxious to be rid of her the first two times she'd talked to him?

He ignored her offer and draped two more sweatshirts over the ones already hanging over his arm.

"Well, if you insist. Lay them on the table, and I'll refold them after I fix the shelf." At least she wouldn't have to launder the hoodies since Tayleigh had mopped the storeroom floor yesterday. She scooped up the last three. "Was there something you needed?"

"Do you have a drill?"

JoyAnne dumped the crumpled sweatshirts on the table beside his neat pile, her eyebrows scrunching together. "What in the world do you need a drill for?"

"To put that shelf back up." Arms crossed, he studied the damaged drywall.

"Umm, that's okay. I can handle it from here." What would a luxury-car-owning city boy know about repairing a shelf?

His head turned slowly, eyes narrowed. "You don't think I can do it, do you?"

Apparently she hadn't scrubbed the skepticism from her voice. "Not at all, but you're a guest. You're here to relax, not work."

"You want to repair the drywall first?"

JoyAnne cocked her head. "You do know how to relax, right?" She could see this man being some high-powered attorney. Driven, focused, used to getting his own way. Put him in a suit instead of a t-shirt and jeans, and he could be the star of a prime-time lawyer drama.

K. C. Davis. The name on his campground registration form even sounded like some pricey lawyer.

"Or do you want to just get the shelf right back up?"

She crossed her arms and studied the stubborn man who waited for her reply.

Or maybe not. The glint in his eyes might be impatience rather than stubbornness. Or was it irritation? Her skepticism must have stung his ego into proving her wrong.

Uncrossing her arms, she lifted her palms in a small shrug and circled the table to the tool bucket she'd brought in earlier and pulled out the rechargeable drill, a container of long screws, a measuring tape, and a level. Dumping them on the corner of the scarred work table, she waved her hand over them. "Knock yourself out." She wasn't looking forward to holding that drill above shoulder height anyway. "But not literally, please."

"Thank you." A tiny smirk lifted one side of his mouth and satisfaction brightened his eyes. The man looked positively pleased with himself as he picked up the drill and tested the trigger.

Yep. Driven and unwilling to lose. "I hope you handle that better than your camp hammer." She couldn't resist the dig.

He didn't so much as blink. "Watch me." He turned and set to work unfastening the other end of the tilted shelf and its twisted bracket. "Do you have another set of brackets I can use?"

"Oh. Yes." JoyAnne rummaged through a corner cabinet and found two extra brackets. She laid them beside the other tools.

The bell over the camp store entrance jangled and the chattering voices of several children reached her ears. "Tayleigh's not back yet, so I need to go see if they need any help." She gestured toward the store. "I'll return quick as I can."

"Go ahead. I've got this." Holding the end of the shelf with one hand, he backed out the last screw and lowered the whole thing to the floor.

JoyAnne edged toward the door. "All right. Holler

if you need any help." She should radio George and see if he could come finish the job.

"Don't worry. It'll be level when I finish." He tossed her a glance over his shoulder.

JoyAnne stared at him. That dimple had *not* been in his cheek before. Was he laughing at her?

A little dazed, she hurried to check on her customers. Who would have thought the grumpy camper was capable of teasing? There might be hope for him to relax and enjoy his vacation after all.

Why do you care one way or another?

The silent question drew her up short, but she shook off the sensation. It was her job to care about their guests. Especially ones who looked like a vacation was ten years overdue. Wad-A-Wa Campground was a place to relax and refortify oneself to face the world again.

Like you're *facing the world?*

One of the small boys needed help with a purchase, allowing her to shove away the mental inquisition as she assisted the young cousins from the family reunion figure out how many pieces of penny candy their pocketful of change would purchase. When they headed out the door, an older couple came in to register for an RV site. By the time the store emptied again, the annoying inner voice had grown quiet.

The sound of the drill drew her back to the storage room in time to see Mr. Davis tighten the last screw, lay down the drill, and set the level on the edge of the shelf. How had the man accomplished the task that quickly and by himself? Not only was the shelf level, it had been adjusted so he wasn't putting new screws in old, stripped-out holes.

"Okay. I'm officially impressed."

He turned and his eyes smiled although it didn't quite make it to his mouth. "Better than my tent peg skills?"

"Definitely."

The smile finally arrived and put the dimple in his left cheek on full display. "Good."

JoyAnne's breath caught and her heart kicked in her chest. Oh goodness. That smile should be illegal. Or at least come with advance warning. It could turn a girl's head before she knew what was happening.

Guilt instantly assailed her. She hadn't been attracted to anyone since Micah. And she wasn't ready to risk that heartache again. She might never be ready.

(9)

*W*hat had he said? Kellan scrambled to recall what he might have done to cause the flicker of pain that washed the smile from the woman's expression. He'd spoken barely ten words since she'd returned so it couldn't have been something he'd said. Could it? Maybe the shelf had injured her more than she let on.

He laid the drill on the table, dusted off his hands, and walked toward her. "Are you sure that shelf didn't do any damage when it hit you?"

She blinked, and the darkness in the depths of her eyes disappeared. The teasing sparkle that had been present in all their past encounters failed to return, however, and he missed it.

"I'm fine. I really appreciate your help, though. Now I can get back to my other chores." Her smile rose no higher than her cheekbones.

"It was the least I could after that breakfast delivery the other morning."

"You don't owe me for that." She shook her head before walking out of the storage room.

Kellan followed her. "But I do. I think it cured my cold."

She scurried behind the desk and wiggled the mouse to a computer. "I thought you sounded better today. I think it's due to all the fresh air out here, though."

Kellan leaned against the high counter that comprised the front of the registration desk. He'd successfully avoided all but a couple people for three days and had planned to continue doing the same today until he'd realized how low on firewood he was. Then as soon as he'd seen *her* again his plan to duck in and out of the camp store had fallen to pieces along with that supply shelf. His grandfather would've rolled over in his grave if Kellan had left her to deal with that mess alone. Not to mention, he flat hadn't wanted to pull himself away from the cute woman's upbeat, sunny personality so soon.

What *was* her name, anyway? "By the way—"

"What did you—"

They spoke simultaneously.

Kellan motioned for her to continue.

"I'm sorry." The woman smiled slightly. "What did you need?"

Kellan rested his arms on the countertop and studied her a second. For a woman who had gone out of her way to check on him, she now acted impatient for him to state his business and be on his way. Something had definitely happened to change her lighthearted mood, and it piqued his curiosity enough to delay his return to solitude.

"I don't know your name."

Her eyes widened. "That's what you came in here for?"

He shook his head. "No, I came for a couple more bundles of wood, but then I realized it would be nice to know your name." His grin felt genuine for the first time in months. "After all, I did repair your shelf."

She ducked her head and quietly cleared her throat before straightening and stretching her arm over the counter with a slight smile. "I'm JoyAnne."

He grasped the short-nailed hand in his own, not surprised at the strength in her grasp. She was trim, but could probably work circles around most people. He'd noticed the muscle definition in her arms and legs. "Nice to meet you, JoyAnne. I'm K.C."

"I know." Her smile grew.

Kellan stiffened. "You do?"

"Of course." She rapidly typed something into the computer, clicked on the mouse, then turned the monitor toward him and pointed. "See? K. C. Davis, site 197. Are you really planning to stay until the end of the month or did Tayleigh put the wrong dates down?"

Relief freed the breath trapped in his chest. The name on his old credit card. The one he used to stay low profile on vacation. "Yes. Those are the dates I gave Tayleigh." Whether he planned to stay until then depended entirely on how well people left him alone. With the exception of JoyAnne, maybe. "Is there a problem?"

"Oh, no. Just confirming. Now. About that wood.

How many bundles did you want?" A business-like tone accompanied her exit from the small cubicle.

"Two." He pulled out his wallet. "How much?"

She shook her head, heading for the entrance. "This one's on me."

He followed her onto the campstore porch. "That's not necessary."

JoyAnne grabbed the handles of two plastic-wrapped bundles of split wood from a metal rack and handed them to him with a firm smile. "And I say it's on the house."

Kellan crossed his arms. "I'll take them on one condition." For a man who'd craved solitude like a drowning man craves oxygen, he'd suddenly developed an irrational desire to hang around JoyAnne until the sparkle in her eyes and her quirky sense of humor reappeared.

"What condition?" She asked slowly, setting bundles on the decking between their feet.

"I caught a fat bass this morning that I'm going to fry up for my supper. I'll take that wood on the condition you stop by about... say 6:30... to share it with me." And since he was on vacation, he wasn't going to waste a single moment weighing his motives for asking her in the first place.

She shook her head again. "You already paid me back for breakfast."

"No. If I hadn't startled you, you wouldn't have dropped the box which brought down the shelf and made a mess, so it's only right I helped repair it. That means I still owe you for breakfast."

She huffed a small laugh and some of the sparkle returned to her eyes. "You just made a mud hole out of clear water. That is the most convoluted reasoning I've ever heard."

"Did it convince you?"

Her forehead scrunched up. "Can you cook? Fish?"

"Even better than I repair shelves."

She sucked in a deep breath then let it go. "All right. I'll make you prove that boast. But you better have hushpuppies or it's an automatic fail."

"Done." He stuck out his hand.

JoyAnne took it automatically, but she yanked away quicker than he would've liked.

Kellan slid on his shades, snagged the bundles, and straightened. "If the fish doesn't taste good I can always blame it on the quality of the wood in the fire and how the smoke flavors the meat. Right?"

"Huh uh." Her pony tail swung back and forth as she shook her head. "That's cheating."

He stepped off the wide porch that ran the length of the camp store and held several inviting rocking chairs and pots of red and white geraniums. "The challenge is on then. See you at 6:30?"

Her nod was slow in coming and not very encouraging but he'd take it. "Sure."

Kellan headed toward his car in the blacktopped parking lot fighting the sudden urge to whistle. As he dropped the bundles of wood into the trunk, the slogan on the brightly painted sign set in a well-tended flower bed caught his eye. *The happiest campground in Missouri.* It didn't seem like such a corny motto, now.

Maybe he'd picked the right place to vacation after all.

(10)

*T*his was a bad idea.

One she'd regretted five seconds after Mr. Davis had disappeared from view. Her ill-thought-out plan to help the uptight camper start enjoying himself and relax had backfired in her face. But she couldn't blame him for that. It was her fault for becoming aware of how really good looking he was. A completely unexpected reaction that had caught her off guard.

Fortunately, she'd been so busy through the afternoon, she'd only had time to wash her hands and face and tighten her ponytail before hopping on the utility vehicle at 6:25. If she'd had even ten more minutes, she'd have been tempted to shower and change clothes. A worse idea since this *wasn't* a date. The man had simply asked her to share his supper because she'd been kind to him when he felt bad and maybe to brag on his fishing skills. Nothing more, nothing less.

Her hands loosened their grip on the steering wheel and her jaw relaxed. Besides, who could resist the lure of fresh fish? Not her. Though a lake comprised much of their backyard, the campground kept them all so busy that fishing often took a backseat during the summer months, and she didn't get to indulge her taste buds as often as she wanted. And she intended to enjoy this meal to the fullest.

Unless K. C. Davis had highly overrated his cooking skills. In which case, she'd find a way for him to make it up to her.

JoyAnne chuckled. They could always use an extra pair of hands to help with the children's outdoor arts-and-crafts session tomorrow afternoon.

She parked beside the black Mercedes.

Mr. Davis straightened with a smile from the skillet positioned over a thick bed of glowing coals in the fire ring. "Good timing. The fillets are almost done." He took off his sunglasses and perched them above the brim of his hat.

JoyAnne hesitated just slightly before hopping to the ground and walking toward him.

Okay. His flashing dimple might make her pulse jump, but she could enjoy his nice smile without falling victim to it. If his choice of vehicles was any indication, he probably had any number of svelte, sophisticated women tripping over themselves to catch his attention. He didn't need a stocky, sunburnt campground manager fawning over him. "I hope that tastes as good as it smells."

"Me, too." He pointed a fork toward two folding canvas chairs beside the fire ring. "You want to sit by the fire or at the picnic table?"

"Table. It'll be easier." And less cozy.

"Table it is." Davis carried over a paper-towel-lined plate holding several pieces of golden fish. "Drinks are in the cooler under the end. Grab what you want and a bottle of tea for me."

JoyAnne spotted the blue cooler and opened the lid to find an assortment of bottled water, tea, and a few different kinds of soda on ice. She pulled out two sweet teas and set them by the plates. He'd thought of everything. Small containers of ketchup and tartar sauce, plenty of napkins, and even a carton of coleslaw.

She picked up the clear plastic package. "Where'd this come from?"

Mr. Davis glanced at it before continuing his task of placing two pieces of fish and multiple golden-brown hushpuppies on both plates. "Oh that's a little something I whipped up in my spare time."

JoyAnne narrowed her eyes. "Uh huh. I believe that like I believe the moon is made of green cheese."

"You mean it isn't?" He set one of the plates on her side of the table. "Have a seat."

She stepped over the plank bench and sat, grabbing a paper napkin and spreading it across her lap. "I can't believe you said that with a straight face."

He sat down across from her and lifted one shoulder. "So… maybe I ran into town to pick up a few ingredients and happened to make a stop in the deli."

"You didn't cheat on the fish, too, did you?" She eyed the battered and fried meat.

"I give you my word this is the bass I caught this

morning. I cleaned him, filleted him, dipped him in my grandmother's batter recipe, and fried him up with my own hands."

"Okay. I believe you." Good thing her heart had developed a thick barrier of scar tissue or those twinkly brown eyes surrounded by thick lashes might have made it do something silly. Like go all soft and gooey.

"Do you mind if I pray before we eat?"

Pleased surprise relaxed her shoulders. "I would prefer it, actually."

His dimple flashed again before he bowed his head. *Oh, dear.*

She didn't hear a word of his short blessing and barely managed to duck her head and send a flare-prayer skyward for her sanity before he finished. Keeping her gaze down, she picked up her fork, twisted off a piece of fish then plopped it in her mouth, chewing quietly.

Her head flew up and she stared at Davis who hadn't started eating but sat watching as if waiting for a verdict. She swallowed. "This is *good!* I mean really good!"

The dimple flashed. "Thank you." He stuck a hunk of steaming meat in his mouth.

JoyAnne bit into another piece. "It's so good I don't think I even want to put ketchup on it And half the reason I love fried food is because it gives me a reason to eat ketchup."

"I'll take that as a compliment."

He watched her take another bite but his scrutiny didn't bother her. She'd regained her emotional footing and now felt nothing more than a comfortable sense of camaraderie. It had been a hectic, tiring week and between that and George dredging through old memories, her mood had gone a little whacky. That's all it was.

JoyAnne grabbed the ketchup bottle, squirted a glob onto her plate, and coated a hushpuppy before biting it in half.

"Uh oh. What's wrong with the hush puppies? Give it to me straight."

JoyAnne shook her head. "Nothing." She quickly swallowed the bite. "They're fantastic."

Davis tapped the small bottle of red sauce. "Then why the ketchup?"

She grinned, the light conversation restoring her emotional balance. "It doesn't have a thing to do with your cooking skills. A girl's just got to have ketchup with this kind of meal. It's the rule."

He dipped a bite of fish in tartar sauce. "The rule, huh?"

JoyAnne took a swig of her bottled tea then checked the label. Not a brand they carried in the camp store. Maybe she'd order a couple of cases and see how it sold in the store. It was good tea for store-bought. "Don't tell me you've never heard it."

"Nope. Can't say that I have."

She rested her hands beside her plate and eyed him with stern curiosity. "Where did you grow up that your education is so sadly lacking?"

His attention returned to his plate. "Arkansas."

"What?" She infused her voice with mock dismay. A shadow had crossed his face and she wanted to erase whatever caused it. "Don't tell me people in Arkansas don't eat ketchup with their fish and hushpuppies?"

"Don't blame the whole state. We simply preferred

tartar sauce at my grandparents' house." He squirted another dollop of the white stuff on his plate.

"Well…" she dragged the word out. "I suppose I can overlook your poor taste in sauces since your grandmother has the best fish-batter recipe I've ever eaten."

He bowed his head. "Thank you. I can breathe easier now."

She grinned at his mock gratitude. "So what do people call you? K. C. or Kasey," she blurred the initials together, "or something else entirely?"

He swirled a flaky piece of meat in the white sauce. "Hmm… I think I prefer K. C. 'Something else entirely' is too much of a mouthful." He popped the bite between his teeth then grinned. The shadow had faded.

Joy laughed before concentrating her remaining energy on enjoying the meal. When she'd cleaned her plate along with a few more of the hushpuppies, she twisted on the bench and stretched her legs along it to face the trees at the back of the tent site. "That tasted wonderful. I was starving."

"I think you might have overlooked a hushpuppy." He offered the lone ball of fried dough to her.

"Are you calling me a glutton?" She had eaten a lot, but she hadn't had time for lunch today. Add into the equation one of her favorite meals and there was no way she was going to pick at it like some skinny chick worried about fitting into size four jeans.

"Not at all. I take your appetite as a compliment to my efforts. But since I've had all I want, if you don't eat this last one it'll go to waste."

"When you put it that way…" She popped the

hushpuppy in her mouth.

His laugh made her grin as she chewed. He sounded so much better than that first day. His voice was rich and warm and very easy to listen to. "By the way…" She watched a squirrel jump from one tree to another. It felt good to sit after trying to outwork memories from her old life all afternoon.

"Yes?"

"If you're from Arkansas, where's your accent? Although, come to think of it, you do have a hint of an accent, but it's not a southern twang. It's more of a… an international flavor, I guess." She should know. Her own speech patterns held traces of many of the places she'd lived.

Silence greeted her question and she glanced over to find him frowning at his plate. "I left Arkansas a long time ago."

"And done a lot of traveling since, if I had to make a guess."

K. C. stood and started gathering the condiments. "Yeah."

JoyAnne climbed to her feet to help him clean up but he waved her away.

"And if I had to guess, I'd say you've been on your feet all day." He smiled, but it had a stiffness to it. The same stiffness she'd noticed on their first meeting.

She wanted to apologize for unwittingly touching on a subject he preferred not to discuss, but she wouldn't. She knew from personal experience an apology didn't help when someone inadvertently trod over a sore spot. "I don't mind helping you clean up."

"No. I've got it. I appreciate you sharing it with me, though." The sun had dropped below the tree line, but he took his reflective sunglasses off his hat and slid them over his eyes.

"I'm the one who should be thanking you. It was fantastic."

"You're welcome." His smile softened but a thicker barrier than his polarized shades had gone up and he stood waiting as if for her departure.

The old "here's your hat, what's your hurry" routine? She'd really hit a sensitive spot. Maybe the reason he was hiding in the woods instead of vacationing in a five-star luxury hotel by some beach had to do with whatever job afforded him a Mercedes and plenty of travel. Had he lost that job? Left town to lick his wounds? Camping in Missouri was definitely cheaper than a tropical vacation. "Then I think I'll head toward home and a hot shower."

"You don't have too far to go, do you?"

She couldn't tell whether he really wanted to know or was just making polite conversation. "No. I live on the grounds. I'll be home in less than five minutes."

"I'm glad I didn't cause you to have a late night at work, then."

JoyAnne swallowed a laugh. Late night? It wasn't even 7:30 yet. There were days she didn't stumble across her threshold until after midnight. And not because she was on a hot date.

"Thanks again for supper." She rubbed her stomach. "It made me as happy as a jaybird in a cherry tree."

His return smile seemed to come easier. "I'm glad. Good night, JoyAnne."

"Night, K. C." She turned and jogged to the utility vehicle and waved as she pulled away. At least she'd left him smiling.

(11)

*T*he sleek black phone buzzed again and again, happy at having its power turned on and full of news of missed calls, voice mails, texts, and emails. Kellan ignored all of them but Enoch's. He smiled as his friend's message appeared on the screen.

Hope the fishing's good. Stay out of trouble. Praying for you. E.

Kellan typed in a brief reply. *Fishing's great. Prayer appreciated. Hug the girls 4 me. K.*

He needed the prayers to help him figure out the appeal of a certain campground manager. Then again, Enoch's prayers might be the reason behind this sudden fascination with the woman.

Kellan shrugged the notion aside and touched the weather app. He hadn't bothered checking the forecast or radar since he'd arrived because the days had dawned clear and bright, but this morning's sky held heavy, brooding clouds that threatened rain if not something more severe.

The app took longer than normal to open and finally an error message appeared in the middle of the black screen. He checked the phone's signal bars. Nothing. No service.

Strange. It had had service for a second, but no matter where he held it now, the signal bars remained blank.

Kellan powered the device off and tossed it into the console with a shrug. The lack of cell service didn't bother him since it gave him a valid excuse to ignore the rest of his messages. All of which were no doubt from his agent and manager whom he thought he'd convinced to leave him alone for at least a month before hounding him for further career decisions. But the woman's unshakable persistence would put an over-the-phone salesman to shame. Patricia Banks had Kellan's career's best interests at heart, though, and had kept him from stagnating in the backwaters of county fairs and small-town venues.

After hearing him sing at a benefit concert, she'd pursued him like a heat-seeking missile. Her appreciation for his talent and her flattery had turned his naive head and he'd thought she was as interested in him personally as he'd been in her. When he'd signed the contract to make her his agent, he'd hoped the business relationship would turn into something more personal. It had taken longer than it should have to realize she only wanted him for one thing—a ride to the top of the entertainment industry. And he was the ticket for her fledgling talent agency. As his star had risen with the growing popularity of KWESTT, so had hers.

In the end, his pride had suffered more than his heart and their business relationship had survived—due mainly to Patricia's single-minded ambition. But a wall of cynicism had sprung up around his heart, growing thicker with every passing year.

Kellan shoved away the unproductive memories and his eyes landed on a hard-sided case lying on the back seat. He hadn't touched the instrument inside it since the last night of the tour and he had no desire to. That scared him worse than the possibility of never meeting a woman who could see past his alleged fame to the real man beneath. Scared him worse than not having written a lick of lyrics for four months. He'd had a guitar in his hands on a daily basis since his fifth birthday when his mother had given him a tiny child's version and taught him his first chords. The love of music she'd nurtured within him had been a tangible piece of his mother he'd been able to hang onto even after she died.

Had that piece finally died, too?

He slammed the passenger door with more force than necessary and clicked the lock button on the combination key and remote. Shoving it into a pocket in his running shorts, he pulled his Cardinals cap low over his sunglasses and started off at a slow jog down the narrow blacktop lane curving through the secluded tent sites.

The cool wind blowing off the lake made the temperature perfect for running and he did. He lapped the quiet tent site section several times before venturing through the RV and cabin sections. With no idea what the distances of the neat, paved lanes were, he just ran. Ran till there was nothing but the wind in his face, the swish of his clothing, the rhythm of his breathing, and the beat of his feet.

The abrupt spatter of moisture against his face yanked him out of the zone and he stumbled to a stop, gripping his knees and panting heavily. He checked the sky. The clouds had lowered till they nearly scraped the treetops.

The sprinkles escalated to full-fledged rain, and a bright flash followed by a rolling boom forced Kellan's protesting legs back into action. Getting soaked didn't bother him, he was already dripping with sweat, but he'd prefer not to be fried.

"Hop in!" JoyAnne appeared alongside him in a partially enclosed UTV, her approach covered by the noise of the storm. "It's not the best ride for these conditions, but it's better than nothing."

Kellan lunged onto the bench seat as the storm intensified, dumping rain in blowing sheets. He pulled off his wet sunglasses and swiped a hand over his face. "Thanks. Where did all this come from?"

"They've been predicting it for two days." She shouted to be heard over the downpour. "I stopped by to warn all the tenters about it yesterday afternoon, but you weren't there so I taped a note to the front of your tent."

"Must've blown away. I never saw it." No wonder the rustic campsites had been so empty. He'd wondered about that since they were headed into the weekend but had appreciated having it almost all to himself yesterday evening.

"I'm sorry. I knew I should've come back and

warned you in person." JoyAnne zipped around a corner at a speed that made him grab for handholds. The nearly simultaneous flash of blinding light and deafening thunder indicated the storm stood directly above them.

Rain lashed at the open sides of the utility buggy. If the wind kicked up any stronger, his tent would be flattened. Good thing he'd left his valuables in the trunk of his automobile.

"Not your fault. I could've turned on a radio to check the weather myself."

A large barn loomed out of the solid curtain of rain, and JoyAnne aimed toward the center of it without reducing her speed. Just as he was about to duck, they whipped through a tall, narrow opening and into the dry. JoyAnne braked and the vehicle skidded to a stop.

"Whoo! That was fun." Her wide eyes and comical grimace said otherwise.

The building muffled the storm enough to speak without shouting, and they exited the small vehicle and turned to watch the rain sluice past the partially open double doors.

"Thanks for the ride. I saw the storm clouds but didn't expect the rain to start this quick, otherwise I would have delayed my run till afterwards."

She threw him a strange look. "It didn't start quick. I first saw you running over an hour ago like something was chasing you. What are you? Some kind of marathon runner?"

Kellan shook raindrops off the face of his waterproof watch and checked the time. No wonder his muscles quivered. It had been months since he'd had that much time to spend outdoors beating the pavement with his shoes. He'd been limited to indoor treadmills much of his last tour. "No. Lost track of time is all."

Disbelief arched her eyebrows. "Lost track of time? There is no way I would lose track of time while running. I'd be counting the minutes until I could stop. How many laps did you do around this place?"

He shrugged. "I didn't count. I regret that now. I'd kinda like to know how far I ran so I could estimate my speed."

"Well if you ever feel that crazy again, the loops through the campsites are right at three miles total. If you add the driveway out to the main road and back, that adds another mile."

"I know I did the loop through the tent section more than once, but I lost track when I headed this way."

JoyAnne's eyes widened, her wet, spiky lashes emphasizing them. "Good grief you must have run nearly five miles. How are you still standing?"

At the pace he'd set, he'd undoubtedly run farther. But he'd needed the workout. It had cleared away a few mental cobwebs and left him tired but invigorated. "You were watching?"

The woman blinked at him and her cheeks suddenly rivaled the red shirt that peeked past the neck of her raincoat. "I couldn't help but see the idiot running into the teeth of a storm while I was bringing the horses in." She pulled off the yellow rain slicker and went to rub the nose of the horse poking its head out over a stall door.

Her irritation tattled on her. She *had* been watching him. He'd developed a sort of immunity to being watched, but he didn't mind that she'd been doing it. In fact, he kind of liked the idea. But since she wasn't watching him now, he'd take his turn.

The red shirt she wore clung to her sides, emphasizing the curve of her waist before tucking into a worn pair of jeans. The clothes showed signs of being broken in, but they sure flattered her athletic figure. And the color looked good against the dark hair cascading in damp waves from a low ponytail. She was trim but not so skinny she looked like a stiff breeze would blow her away. No. This woman looked like she could tackle anything she set her mind to and not shudder at the thought of a little dirt under her short nails. She looked... normal.

A normal woman. The kind with roots who would probably have trouble appreciating or understanding his nomadic lifestyle even if she could see past his professional persona. Even if her job had her dealing with travelers every day.

He ran his eyes over her again. A little slower this time, and lingering on her red shirt. The color reminded him of someone... Ah! The woman at the theater. Like he'd known it would, the lady's face had faded into the abstract blur of all their audiences. But her unique flair had caught his attention then, just like this woman's kindness and humor had caught it now.

JoyAnne glanced over and caught him studying her. Her brows dipped. "What?"

He grinned. "Did you come out into the storm looking for me?"

The slight blush gave her away again. "I was already out double checking things, and it would be bad for business if one of our guests was struck by lightning."

"Nah. You'd say I was 'no longer with you but that you had nothing to do with my demise.'" He tossed her earlier words back at her and swiped at a drop of water rolling down the side of his face.

She rewarded him with a quick grin and crossed the barn aisle to a closed door. "You'd better believe it." Unlatching the door, she stepped inside. "We should have some clean towels in here somewhere…"

(12)

*T*he thunderstorm vented its fury on the barn, but the solid old structure had been built to withstand nature's temperamental blasts and protected those who sought shelter within its sturdy walls. It reminded her of the way George and Dorothy had taken her in when Victor had dragged her home and given her a place to hide and recover from the storms that had left her broken and drifting.

JoyAnne glanced overhead at the thick trusses as she exited the tack room with a couple of the old towels they kept on hand for emergencies. The barn shielded her from a physical storm today, but it couldn't do anything about the unsettling disturbance that brewed inside her. One she couldn't figure out how to avoid or even if she wanted to. The one that caused her to stick a note on K. C. Davis's tent and not return to see if he'd gotten it. Maybe if she'd not been such a coward, she wouldn't be stuck in the barn with him now.

She handed one of the worn cloths to the dripping man whose eyes seemed to follow her everywhere. "Sorry I didn't think of this sooner. If I had some dry clothes to offer you, I would."

"No problem. These will dry soon enough." He shucked off his red ball cap and tossed it on the seat of the gator then scrubbed the thin towel over his face, head, and neck. Draping the first one over his shoulders, he accepted a second one to wipe his arms.

JoyAnne turned back to Ladybug as he bent to wring out the edges of his running shorts and rub the towel down his legs. Time had enabled her to appreciate a man's physique again without feeling unfaithful, but it still made her uncomfortable to notice *this* man's well-defined calf muscles and thick, toned forearms. And affected her breathing more than she wanted to admit.

She needed a distraction. "So, I'm curious. What does the K. C. stand for?"

He straightened, a slight frown creasing his forehead. "What?"

"Your initials. Around here when we say K. C. we mean Kansas City."

His frown disappeared. "No. They don't stand for that."

"Are you laughing at me?" Joy cocked her head and studied his twinkling eyes.

"Nope. Just thankful my mom didn't decide to call me Kansas City. Sounds like some cowboy from an old western." His smile lit up the dim barn alley.

When he didn't elaborate, Joy crossed her arms. If he wouldn't tell her, she'd have to guess. What names would be awful enough that a man preferred his initials? "Then what about Kinney Clifford?"

K. C. blinked at her. "What? No. Thankfully."

"Okay... How 'bout... Keats Cassidy?"

He grimaced and shook his head. "Uh uh."

"Keith Cavanaugh?"

A laugh rumbled out of him. "That one's better, but you're still colder than ice."

And he didn't appear to have any intention of giving her a hint either. How many male names started with K anyway? She tried to concentrate on that instead of his close proximity and the cozy, secluded feeling of the storm-soaked barn.

The hand-held radio squawked from the front of the gator. "JoyAnne? Where are you? Tell me you aren't still out in this mess."

She rushed to pick it up—thankful for the interruption—and depressed the talk button, perching on the edge of the seat. "Okay, I am not still out in this mess."

"Ha, ha, JoyAnne. Be serious." The radio static did nothing to disguise the irritation in the voice.

"I am serious, Vic. When did you get back?"

K. C. Davis plopped down on an overturned bucket against the wall directly in front of her, not bothering to hide the fact he was eavesdropping.

"Right after you took out on the gator according to Dad. Where are you?" Victor barked the question over the radio. "This lightning is nothing to mess around with."

"Chill out, Bam Bam. I'm in the barn and fine as

frog hair."

K. C. choked.

JoyAnne grinned and waited.

After a short silence, the walkie-talkie crackled again. "You're not alone, are you, Squirt?" Victor drew the question out in a way that promised reprisal for using the annoying nickname.

JoyAnne laughed into the radio. "Nope. Rescued a camper from the storm and we're waiting out the rain."

"When it dies down, get over here to the house. I want to see you."

"Only if there are no ice cubes within a hundred feet of you."

A devious laugh rolled out of the small speaker. "I promise nothing, Squirt. Over and out."

JoyAnne tossed the radio on the seat behind her. "Spending the afternoon cleaning the barn suddenly sounds very appealing."

K. C. smiled quizzically. "What was that all about?"

"Bam Bam is an old nickname Victor's cousin started calling him for some unknown reason when they were kids. And although it fits perfectly with his profession, Vic's only okay with it as long as we don't use it in public. It doesn't suit His Honor's dignity." And only recently had she been able to use it again, which meant they were both doing better. Another indicator of how far they'd all come.

"He's a judge?"

JoyAnne nodded. "He's also the son of George and Dorothy Barrett, the owners of Wad-A-Wa Campground." She smiled at the memory associated with the funny name but continued with her explanation. "And as close as a brother to me."

"Ah." He nodded understanding, but she could tell he didn't.

Further explanation was too complicated for a virtual stranger, though.

She shoved upright and walked toward the end of the barn to check the sky. The rain had begun to lighten. If the forecast was correct, the worst of the storm would be over soon with only a fifty percent chance of brief periods of light rain the rest of the day.

"So were you in the military?" K. C. joined her at the door.

The question broadsided her. "What?"

"The combat boots? They look like the real thing."

"They are." She lifted the toe of her khaki-colored footwear and eyed the red laces crisscrossing her instep. "Today's Friday."

Brow puckered, he lifted his gaze and studied her. "I'm missing something, aren't I?"

"Have you ever heard of R.E.D. Fridays?"

"Guess not."

"R.E.D. stands for Remember Everyone Deployed. And wearing the color red on Fridays helps remind us and others of our soldiers and their service and sacrifice. These combat boots are from a great group who sell the real things to civilians so we can—in a very tiny way—walk a mile in our service men and women's boots. And the proceeds from the boots go to help veterans and their families. It's one way to honor and support the ones who fight for our freedoms."

"You sound really passionate about the subject."

She was. But she hadn't meant to get quite so carried away. "Just call me a flag-waving American."

She forced a chuckle through a tight throat.

"Is someone in your family deployed or in the military?"

"No. Not anymore." JoyAnne stared at her boots, remembering another worn pair that used to walk through her door. A pair that now resided permanently in the corner of her closet with a pair of dog tags.

She jerked her head up and focused on the weather. *Think about something else!* Anything *else!* "The rain's letting up enough we can take the utility vehicle out without getting drenched. How about we check and make sure your tent is still standing?"

His answer was a bit slow in coming. "Sure."

"Okay. Hop in." JoyAnne yanked on her raincoat, climbed in the vehicle, and cranked the engine. "If your stuff has gotten wet, you can use the laundry room dryers and bunk in one of our cabins until your tent dries out. We have an empty one that hasn't been booked for the weekend." She kept her voice businesslike and without a quiver as she backed out of the barn and into the light spatter of rain.

Showing her support for military men and women and their families was something near and dear to her heart, but talking about it sometimes poked at tender scars. And with an anniversary she didn't want to remember creeping up on her and a set of intense brown eyes seeming to absorb every nuance of her tone, today had been one of those days.

(13)

*O*nce again Kellan found himself grabbing for a handhold as the woman beside him whipped the steering wheel of the utility vehicle to the right while reversing. A light tap on the brakes, and she shifted the machine into drive and gunned it to the left, spitting gravel.

The woman had missed her calling. She should be driving for NASCAR. Or a cab company in New York City.

"Uh oh…" JoyAnne stomped the brakes.

Kellan braced himself against the dash. "What's wrong?"

"That." She nodded toward a massive pickup truck rolling down the middle of the unpaved drive toward the barn.

JoyAnne shifted into reverse and gunned their smaller ride backwards into the dry barn alley.

The truck's powerful engine growled as it followed them inside, the stainless steel flames of the grille looming above the shorter vehicle with a menacing presence.

The UTV jerked to a stop.

Kellan gritted his teeth until the larger machine halted its advance. For a second there, he'd wondered if it planned to. He'd never seen a souped-up truck from this angle before. It made him feel like a bug. On its grille.

A quiet huff yanked his attention away from the impressive automobile. JoyAnne glared at the driver behind the truck's rain-spotted windshield, her arms crossed.

"Who is that?" The distorted figure sitting behind the tempered glass looked nearly as big as the truck he drove, but Kellan wasn't a shrimp, and if this was some upset camper or abusive ex, he'd have to come through Kellan first.

He jumped out circled the back of the UTV, calmly but quickly placing himself between JoyAnne and the man in the silver truck. "Who is this guy?" He asked her under his breath.

"It's Victor."

Kellan blinked at her grumbled response as the pickup's big engine cut off and the driver's door swung opened.

This was the guy Joy Ann had talked to over the walkie-talkie? The judge? The man she'd called Bam Bam?

The tall, blonde giant who squeezed between the

bumpers of the double-cab truck and the utility vehicle looked as much like a judge—or even a Saturday morning cartoon character—as the vehicle he'd arrived in looked like an environmentalist's dream automobile. He planted himself in front of Kellan with crossed arms and narrowed eyes.

Kellan returned the scrutiny. He lifted weights and worked out on a regular basis himself, but the man in front of him had the physique of a body builder. Or a linebacker. Put him in black robes and he'd be enough to scare a juvenile delinquent straight into a choirboy.

"Welll?" JoyAnne impatiently interrupted the silent standoff.

"Well, what, JoyAnne?" Victor's gaze never flickered from Kellan.

"Are you going to move that monster so I can drive our guest back to his campsite or do I have to run over it on my way out?"

Kellan had to bite the inside of his cheek to hold in a startled laugh at the thought of the golf-cart-on-steroids climbing over the custom tank in front of it.

Victor only lifted one tawny eyebrow. "I'd like to see you try, Squirt, but in case you hadn't noticed, it's still raining outside."

"A little rain never hurt anybody, so if you don't mind scratches on your big baby..." JoyAnne powered up the vehicle and revved its small engine.

Kellan couldn't help himself. A chuckle escaped as he reached over the steering wheel to disengage the key. "As a neutral country, I'm declaring a truce."

"Hey!" JoyAnne snatched for the key and missed.

Kellan stepped forward and stuck out his hand. "Hi. I'm K. C. Davis. JoyAnne took pity on me and gave me a place to wait out the storm." And nearly gave him a heart attack when she'd started trying to guess his name.

"Victor Barrett. So you're camping here with us, are you?" The judge stood a couple of inches taller than Kellan, and his calloused grip tightened uncomfortably before letting go.

"Yes. It's a nice place." Kellan resisted the urge to shake out his hand.

There was more between JoyAnne and Victor than employee and boss's son. And his bone-crushing grip and steely gaze said Judge Barrett took the relationship very, very seriously.

"You're not from around here, are you?"

"Nope."

The judge—if that's what he was. JoyAnne might be pulling his leg—didn't like the one word reply. But Kellan didn't feel like giving him more information.

"May I have my key back, now?" JoyAnne stuck her hand under Kellan's nose.

Kellan held it out to her, but Victor snatched it.

"Vic give that back. You're being a pain."

Victor stuffed it into his right front jeans pocket. "You won't need it. I'll give Mr. Davis a ride back to his site and then take you home." He held up his hand to forestall JoyAnne's protest. "Come on. It's still raining. The truck will be a lot dryer."

JoyAnne squinted at the big man. "Only if I get to drive."

"No." The response was immediate and definite.

"Then no deal. Give me my key."

Kellan's eyes flicked between the dueling parties, trying to figure out their relationship.

Victor made no move to do as JoyAnne demanded. "I'll let you pick the radio station."

"Pinky swear?" With a doubtful expression, she stuck her little finger into the air.

The blond giant scowled. "I do *not* 'pinky swear,' Squirt. And for that matter, since when do you?"

A grin lit her face. "Okay. We'll ride with you. But I get to pick the music." She covered the few feet separating her and Victor and threw her arms around his waist. "It's good to have you home again even if you are too bossy and drive like a menace."

"You're one to talk, Squirt, but it's good to *be* home." The big man hugged the woman in his arms, picking her feet off the floor.

A darker emotion replaced the hitch in Kellan's breathing that had developed with JoyAnne's infectious smile. He'd been in the woman's company less than a handful of times so he really shouldn't have a problem with another man hugging her.

The giant set JoyAnne down. "Climb in, you two. Let's go."

Kellan stepped forward and opened the front passenger door for her.

She shook her head and scooted around him. "I'll ride in the rear seat. I don't mind."

"You can't run the radio from there." He reminded her. "And I don't mind the rear seat, either."

A twinkle danced to life in her hazel eyes. "You don't have to ask me twice... Kildaire Claude?" She paused expectantly. Kellan shook his head, repressing a grin with difficulty, and she shrugged. "Oh well. I'll keep trying. But it's not often Vic lets me switch his precious radio from its boring presets. The opportunity is *not* to be missed."

Victor twisted the key in the ignition and the powerful engine roared to life. "I have a feeling I'm going to regret this offer."

JoyAnne and Kellan climbed into the truck, and JoyAnne laughed, her hands already reaching for the radio knobs. "You just don't appreciate good music when you hear it, Mr. Tone-Deaf."

"When I hear any good music I'll let you know." The man behind the wheel twisted to look over his shoulder and backed out of the barn.

The radio came on, blaring a popular syndicated talk radio program.

"Sorry!" JoyAnne shouted and quickly lowered the volume and punched the search button. "See what I told you?" She threw a quick glance over her shoulder towards Kellan. "No taste."

"What site are you staying at, Mr. Davis?"

Kellan raised his eyes to see the judge watching him in the rearview mirror. What *was* between those two? "197."

Victor grimaced. "I hope you still have a tent. According to the weather radio, there were some forty to fifty mile-an-hour gusts in that storm."

"I don't think we had any that strong here, but we'd better check on all the occupied sites on this end before heading to K. C.'s." JoyAnne spoke over the music stations she scanned past.

Kellan didn't remember any gusts that strong either, but if they'd happened while he and JoyAnne were in the barn, he'd been too busy studying her to notice. And wondering what had made her suddenly shut down. "I can go get a motel room for the night if I need to."

"You won't need to—Oooh!" JoyAnne's squeal made Kellan jump and Victor wince. "This is a good one!" She stopped scanning stations and turned up the volume.

"Must you be so enthusiastic?" Victor wiggled a finger in his ear.

"Yes. This is my favorite group. Now hush so I can hear them!" She cranked the sound higher.

Kellan stopped breathing and yanked his gaze toward the passenger window, blanking any expression from his face. He'd recognized the music the instant she'd paused on the station. The original song had shot to the top of the charts when it had been released two months before KWESTT's most recent tour and had resulted in sold-out venues at every stop. And while he liked singing the song, he preferred not to *listen* to himself sing it. Thankfully he didn't carry the lead after the first verse and chorus, but handed it off to Westin to modulate it a key higher and pick up the tempo.

Kellan tugged his cap lower, thrust his sunglasses on, and tried counting the passing campsites to keep from sliding down in his seat. Any minute they were going to add K. C. Davis and Kellan Campbell together and come up with the sum of Kellan Campbell Davis. Sitting in the back of their pickup truck.

It would be fun packing up wet camping gear to hit the road. Not.

He wouldn't need gear if he decided to spend the rest of his vacation in a beach-front hotel in Cancun, however, so he could always sign the wet gear with a Sharpie and leave it for them to do whatever they wanted with it—probably sell it on E-Bay. Which is what had happened to his favorite leather jacket. The one he'd loaned to Meredith. His first and *last* attempt at a relationship with a KWESTT fan.

A sweet sound penetrated the sour memory and pulled his attention forward. His eyes snagged on JoyAnne's reflection in the large side mirror outside his rain-streaked window. She was singing along with the radio—harmonizing actually. In a beautiful soprano that tempted him to lean forward and lower the volume on the speakers in order to hear less of the guys and more of her.

He shifted in his seat as quietly as possible in order to view JoyAnne's profile without the blurring effect of rain. Peering through the rain-streaked window at each campsite they drove slowly past, she bobbed in time to the music, singing as if no one were around.

Movement caught his peripheral vision and he caught Victor's gaze in the rearview mirror.

This time, Kellan saw nothing but tolerant amusement in the big man's eyes and mouthed, "She's good."

Victor nodded, silently mouthing a reply. "And loud."

Kellan grinned and returned his attention to JoyAnne, watching her until the music crescendoed to an end in a crash of cymbals and a swirl of violins. The song had been written for KWESTT by their band leader, but it had never sounded better.

JoyAnne turned down the volume as another song began then leaned into the seat with a sigh and a huge smile. "I love that song."

"Really? We couldn't tell." Victor shouted as if the music still blared.

She wrinkled her nose at him. "You are such a wimp. What are Bose speakers for if not to turn up the volume?"

"Turning them up is one thing, Squirt. Deafening our passenger is another." He jabbed a thumb over his shoulder at Kellan.

JoyAnne clapped a hand over her mouth and jerked around in her seat to stare wide-eyed at Kellan.

He sucked in a deep breath. *Annnnd here we go.* It was show time.

She lowered her hand. "I am so sorry! I didn't even think about how loud it would be back there. You should have said something."

Relief trickled through the tension. "I'll be fine. In an hour or so." He mimicked Victor's earlier action and wiggled his finger in his ear.

JoyAnne's cheeks turned pink, and she scrunched up her face. "Sorry." She faced front and flopped against the seat. "I just *really* like that song. But it's even more incredible in person."

Kellan's teasing smile froze on his face.

She whipped back around. "Have you ever seen KWESTT in concert?"

"Uhh…"

"Not everyone is obsessed with that group like you are, Squirt. They can't even spell the word *quest* correctly."

"According to the music charts, people *are too* obsessed with them, Grumpy Pants. And their name is an acronym of the first initial of each of the guys in the group." JoyAnne stuck her tongue out at Victor. "Kellan, Westin, Enoch, Sawyer, Trevor, and Tyrone. But I am not obsessed. That requires stalking them on social media sites—which I don't do because I don't have time. I just like listening to them. But seeing them perform live was the best birthday present ever. I still can't believe I got to do that." She aimed a "gotcha" grin at the driver. "Thanks for dropping that idea into your sisters' heads, by the way. It was so much fun seeing it with Alyce and Jordyn."

Kellan stared at the brunette head in front of him. The Grace Kelly in the cardinal-red dress. The Doris Day who'd nearly tumbled out of the balcony.

JoyAnne!

Evidently he couldn't add two and two together, either. How in blue blazes had he not recognized her? Especially with her wearing a bright red shirt today? He couldn't blame the lack of recognition on the fact he'd seen her only from a distance or that her hair had been long and curly around her face that night and pulled back into a pony tail or braid every time he'd seen her since. He could only blame it on the cold medicine and the mental fog of exhaustion he'd been in.

But a sudden thunderstorm had scrubbed the air clean for the first time in months. And since neither Victor nor JoyAnne had added up the identity of the passenger in the rear seat, he would hang around a while longer and pretend to be a normal guy. Getting to know a normal—or maybe not-so-normal girl.

(14)

JoyAnne would normally sing along with the song that next floated softly from the truck's high-quality speakers, but she'd made a big enough idiot out of herself for one afternoon.

Warmth touched her cheeks and she looked out the side window, counting the seconds until they reached Mr. Davis's campsite. Vic drove slowly, dodging downed tree limbs on the road and watching for any signs of damage to the campground or its guests. She pretended to do the same, but she couldn't wait to escape the close confines of the pickup. What must their guest think of the crazy woman in the front seat?

She was so used to annoying Victor by cranking his fantastic stereo system on a great song ever since he'd purchased this truck that she hadn't thought twice about singing along with KWESTT's latest radio release. *Loudly* singing.

She'd discovered the group after Micah had died, so there were no painful memories associated with their eclectic range of music. In fact, it had been one of their humorous, upbeat ballads that had first attracted her to the group, and they'd helped pull her out of many a sad funk since.

But singing along at the top of her lungs like a hyper teenager instead of acting like a mature campground manager wasn't the best way to impress a paying guest.

The truck slowed and JoyAnne sucked in an audible breath. "Houston, we have a big problem."

Victor whistled as he pulled in beside the shiny black car on site 197. "At least it missed your vehicle, Davis. Nice ride. Is it one of the new S-Class Coupes?"

K. C. leaned between the front seats and peered out the rain-dotted windshield in between intermittent passes of the wipers. "Yep. But it's insured. Glad I decided to go for that run instead of hanging out here, though."

The three of them stared at the sight before them in silence before slowly exiting the truck to examine the damage closer.

The thunderstorm had been short but violent, and a bolt of lightning had hit one of the large, old trees at the edge of woods ringing the campsite and exploded it into a splintered, mangled mess. Part of the top had landed on K. C.'s tent, crushing it. If he'd been inside when it had happened…

Victor let out a long, low whistle. "Hope you weren't attached to that tent. It's a mess."

"It's replaceable."

"And we'll replace it." JoyAnne hastened to assure him.

K. C. took his gaze off the flattened tent and blinked against a spat of wind-driven rain drops. "Why should you?"

"Because it happened on our property." He didn't seem at all upset over how close he'd been to serious injury or worse. While she, on the other hand, was weak in the knees at the thought. And she barely knew the man.

"You don't control the weather."

"No. But our insurance will cover your replacement." And if it wouldn't, she'd take care of it out of her own pocket. Even if the thought of replacing that brand new tent made her wince a little. The sheer lightweight compactness of it put it in the pricey category of camping gear. But at least this was something she *could* control.

"That's not at all necessary."

"Why don't we discuss this in the dry?" Victor interrupted as the sprinkling rain started to intensify again. "We'll have to wait for it to quit raining before tackling that mess. Do you have any dry things in your automobile to tide you over until we can get the rest of your belongings unearthed?"

"Yeah. I only had bedding in my tent. I tossed my duffle bag and valuables into the trunk before going on my run."

"Good thinking. Why don't you follow us in your vehicle, and we'll set you up in a dry cabin?"

"Sounds good." K. C. unzipped a pocket on the side of his running shorts and dug out a high-tech-looking key.

"And then you're going to eat supper with us, and we can discuss replacing your tent." JoyAnne jumped back into the conversation. Victor lifted one eyebrow at her but didn't protest.

K. C. glanced at Victor then at her. "I don't want to intrude."

"You won't. Dorothy always fixes plenty, and I'll warn her I'm bringing company while you clean up." She ignored Victor and whatever opinion he might have and focused on K. C. and his slow smile. It didn't help steady her knees any.

"All right. I'll take you up on it."

"Good." She returned his grin and headed toward Vic's truck. "Follow us."

Victor didn't speak until he'd backed onto the road, straightened out the truck, and put it into drive. "What was that all about?"

"What do you mean?" JoyAnne watched K. C. follow them in the reflection of the side mirror.

"Inviting a stranger to dinner?"

"He's hardly a stranger. We've talked several times, and he even helped me repair a shelf in the storeroom after it fell on top of me." The instant the words left her mouth she wanted them back.

Victor's dark gold eyebrows lifted as he glanced her way. "Exactly how long has this guy been hanging around you, anyway?"

Wouldn't Vic like to know they'd already shared a meal, too? "He's not 'hanging around.' He's a guest who happened to be in the store when I needed a helping hand."

"Mmm hmm." Skepticism twisted his mouth.

"Vic," she warned, "quit making something out of nothing. I'm only doing what George would do. Mr. Davis's home-away-from-home has been destroyed. Offering him a meal is the kind thing to do and replacing his damaged gear is the right thing to do."

"I know that. Just make sure *you* aren't making something more out of it." Pain flashed through his eyes. "I don't want to see you hurt again."

JoyAnne stared out the windshield. "I know, Vic. And I love you for it. But nothing's going on."

Victor reached over and gave her hand a quick squeeze. A frown tightened his mouth.

She sighed. "What?"

Victor glanced in the rearview mirror. "Casey Davis. Something about that guy bugs me. The name isn't familiar, but I feel like I've seen him before."

JoyAnne rolled her eyes. "It's K. C." she emphasized the letters, "not Casey. And if you tell me he's appeared before your bench I think I'll smack you."

Victor didn't respond to her exasperated tease. "No. That's not it."

"Maybe he's an attorney or something." She shrugged. Being a judge sometimes made Victor overly suspicious of people. Couple that with his promise to protect her, and she was feeling a bit smothered.

He frowned over at her. "You don't know his occupation?"

"No. We've only talked a few times." And though the man had shut her out when she'd ventured past the topic of where he'd grown up and had yet to tell her his full name, she felt a disturbing protectiveness for him in the face of Victor's curiosity. "Now quit acting like a judge and start acting like the owner of a campground. One who *likes* people."

Victor's mouth relaxed. "In other words… get my nose out of your business?"

JoyAnne poked his arm. "As if that were an actual possibility. Micah used to say it was no wonder you became a judge given the way you like to order people around."

He smiled but she caught his hard swallow. "I miss him."

"I do, too, Vic. But maybe… maybe it's time to…"

"Move on?" He turned onto the lane that led to the cabins.

"I don't know. I guess so." She pointed to the small log building at the end of the row. "That one's empty."

He pulled to the side of the road and motioned K. C. to pull into the parking area. "About the time I think I've grown used to Micah being gone, I catch myself reaching for the phone to call him. And then remember." He shook his head slowly. "I don't know if I know how to move on. Especially not this time of year."

JoyAnne returned his solemn gaze. She was trying very hard to treat this month as any other on the calendar. "I don't either, but I think it's time to figure it out. Micah wouldn't want us to spend the rest of our lives living in the past." The words coming out her mouth surprised her. George's soft advice over the last few months must have taken root.

"No. He wouldn't. Just be careful that you don't rush it, Joy."

JoyAnne opened the door, pulling a master key from her pocket. "I won't, Vic. You wouldn't let me anyway." She gave him a faint smile and climbed out to unlock the cabin.

She wasn't ready to examine what had made her suddenly willing to open herself up to new possibilities, but the tendrils of new growth in a heart that had been frozen for nearly four years felt good.

(15)

Kellan rubbed his hand over his jaw and peered into the mirror above the sink in the small room. They'd given him a log cabin with bathroom facilities which meant he hadn't had to traipse through a persistent drizzle to the shower houses. He shook the water off his razor before dropping it into his toiletries bag and pulled out his toothbrush.

The cabin was small but contained a queen-sized bed, comfortable chair, built-in table, and a tiny bathroom. The rate on it had to be double, if not triple, what he paid a night for the tent site but after JoyAnne had unlocked the door for him and given him directions to supper, she'd told him he could spend the rest of his stay here if he wanted and not to worry about the difference. She hadn't given him time to argue but had hurried back to Victor's silver truck.

The upgrade in sleeping arrangements was to his liking but the extra cost would not be coming out of her pocket. As little as a day ago, Kellan might have taken the flattened tent as incentive to move on, but things had changed. He wanted to know more about JoyAnne. Find out what made her tick and what cloud occasionally obscured her upbeat, sunny disposition.

Find out what lay between her and the protective, possessive Victor Barrett.

Feeling competitive, are we?

Kellan rinsed his mouth and grinned into the mirror. "Could be." He set the toothbrush aside to dry and reached for the polo shirt hanging on the back of the door. After tucking it into his belted, dark-wash jeans, he ran a dollop of gel through his short hair to give it a spiky texture then checked his appearance one last time.

Although he was having supper with JoyAnne's employers, he felt a little like a teenager meeting a cute girl's parents for the first time, but he liked the new zest she'd brought to his weary soul. He'd come here looking for solitude and rest but he might have discovered something else. At all events, he'd definitely found a path worth exploring to see how the land lay.

After locking the cabin door with the key a young campground employee had delivered shortly after Victor and JoyAnne's departure, Kellan climbed into his Mercedes and followed the directions to the Barrett's house.

He turned at the metal maintenance barn onto the road marked *Private Drive* and wove through the woods about a half-mile before entering a wide clearing on a slight rise that held a modest log home with a covered, wrap-around porch. Three gable windows peeked past a green metal roof, and a stone chimney stood tall at one end.

The rain had finally stopped, and the sun put in a tardy appearance, making up for lost time by gilding the air with golden, late afternoon light and covering the lake that created a gorgeous backdrop for the house with millions of sparkling diamonds.

He slowed to admire the view as longing spiraled through him. His condo in California was more than nice by the pickiest standards, but it would never exude the sense of warmth and welcome this place did.

Of course, that might have something to do with the pretty brunette who stood on the front porch.

He pulled alongside Victor's silver truck on a parking pad that lay at right angles to the paved drive— leaving the approach to the detached double garage clear—and quickly exited his vehicle.

"You're wearing red." Joy had changed into jean shorts and a gray flag-emblazoned t-shirt. Her damp wavy hair was held off her face by a red headband.

"Someone told me it was appropriate to wear red on Friday."

"They were right." Her smile lit up her fresh, pretty face. "We're hanging out on the patio. Come with me, Kenneth Craig."

Kellan laughed as he joined her on the porch. "My friends call me Kel."

Joy's eyes sparkled. "Ooh! A hint. Kel. I like it. So what's it short for?"

"Greedy, aren't you?" Joy nodded at his tease. "Sorry. That's all you're getting." He wanted to get to know her better without Kellan Campbell getting in the way. He changed the subject. "This place is beautiful."

"It is, isn't it? Hard to believe it was so wild and stormy earlier."

"Yeah. You said you lived close the other night. Do you have a view of the lake, too?"

She grinned. "Every day."

"I don't mean while you're at work. I mean—"

"I know what you mean. But come on, I want you to meet George and Dorothy." She pivoted and strode along the porch around the side of the house.

He followed and dropped his voice. "Thanks for the invite, but I'm feeling a little odd crashing your employers' mealtime."

"You're not crashing anything." A hearty voice preceded a tall, older gentleman who appeared around the back corner of the house.

Kellan recognized the silver-haired man as the one he'd seen mowing around the campground earlier in the week.

"George, this is K. C. Davis. K. C., this is George Barrett, owner of Wad-A-Wa Campground. He also has supersonic hearing and can see around corners." JoyAnne teased.

"Welcome, K. C." George stuck out his hand and shook Kellan's with a hearty grip. "As I was saying, you're not crashing anything. JoyAnne is like one of my own daughters and we're thrilled she brought a new face over. It can get boring looking at the same people over the table every night so you're more than welcome."

"Thank you, Mr. Barrett. I appreciate your hospitality."

"Call me, George." The man led him and JoyAnne onto a deep deck that ran almost the entire length of the rear of the house. Furnished with a rectangular, six-seat outdoor dining set, thickly-padded lounge chairs, and surrounded by a variety of blooming, potted plants, it had an fantastic view of the lake with its private beach and dock.

"Pull up a chair and take a load off. Vic and JoyAnne have been telling me about what happened to your tent. I'm glad you're all right." The man sank into a chair that showed no signs of being doused in the storm earlier.

"I am, too." Kellan grinned, nodded a greeting to Victor, and chose a chair that faced his host.

"Food will be ready in about ten minutes. What would you like to drink?" JoyAnne gave him several choices.

"Tea sounds good, please."

"You like..." she caught herself and glanced at Victor, "Uh... it sweet?"

"I'm from Arkansas. Is there any other kind?" He grinned, remembering the bottled sweet tea they'd both drunk at his picnic table. Something she obviously didn't want Victor to know about.

She smiled weakly. "Good answer. I'll be right back."

"Arkansas, huh?" Victor asked when the sliding patio screen door closed behind JoyAnne. The question sounded like mere small talk, but the man's gray eyes held a hard glint. "Your vehicle has Missouri plates."

"I don't live in Arkansas anymore." Kellan looked at George. "You have a beautiful place here. I don't think I've ever seen this big of a recreational lake as pristine and uncommercialized as this one."

"It is definitely a hidden treasure and a tiny piece of heaven. It helps that most of the land is national forest and the rest is still privately owned by individuals rather than corporations. The state park provides another campground and boat access, and there are a couple of small motels in town. It can get crazy during the fishing tournaments and around holidays, but otherwise, since we're twenty miles to the closest town of any size, it stays much quieter than your typical recreational lake. And we like it that way."

"I can see why." Kellan accepted the tall glass of cold, amber liquid JoyAnne handed him. "Speaking of fishing, I caught a nice bass the other day."

"They're good eating if you know how to fix 'em right." George said.

JoyAnne's eyes twinkled before she dropped her gaze and walked over to the table with the pitcher of tea she'd brought out with her.

"I thought it tasted pretty good." Kellan swallowed a smirk along with a mouthful of tea.

"I assume you have a current Missouri fishing license then?"

"Yep."

"Victor!" JoyAnne's exclamation covered Kellan's calm answer.

"Just checking." Victor's answer wasn't apologetic in the least. "Guests don't always realize what the laws are."

"Which is why we post that information in the campground office and sell fishing licenses at the front desk." JoyAnne planted her fists on her hips and glared at the stony-faced judge.

Interesting. JoyAnne was sticking up for him. Kellan took another swallow of tea to hide his pleasure.

"Dinner's ready." A short, soft-spoken woman stepped onto the patio carrying a stack of plates, napkins, and utensils. "Vic and Joy, you may carry out the dishes while I meet our guest. George, set the table, please."

"Yes, Ma'am." The three adults sprang to follow her smiling orders.

Kellan stood to greet the woman, his hand tightening around his sweating tea glass when Victor placed his hand on JoyAnne's back and ushered her through the door. If the man wanted to stake a claim on JoyAnne, he'd better do it with a ring, because Kellan didn't intimidate that easy.

"I'm Dorothy Barrett. It's nice to have you with us. The meal's nothing fancy and we like to eat out here whenever the weather cooperates. Which it seems to be doing now."

Kellan smiled down at the lady who was short to her husband's tall and round to his spare leanness. Their son had inherited his father's inches and his mother's blond hair and gray eyes. But where Victor's were hard and watchful, hers twinkled with warm welcome.

"K. C. Davis, Ma'am. I appreciate your hospitality on such short notice. If the aromas drifting out that door are any indication, I'm in for a treat."

"Flattery like that will earn you an extra piece of pie, Mr. Davis." She claimed a seat at the end of the frosted-glass rectangular table.

"Call me Kel, Mrs. Barrett." He'd liked the woman even before she mentioned pie.

"And you can call me, Dorothy."

JoyAnne set a large bowl of potato salad on the table along with a small dish of assorted pickles.

"Kel." Victor cast him a speculative look as he set two platters, one containing fried chicken and the other corn on the cob glistening with melted butter, on the table. "Anyone ever call you Kelly?"

Kellan felt Joy's curious gaze on him at Victor's prying question. "A few have tried." Kellan's mouth watered as he held the chair cattycorner to Dorothy out for JoyAnne. "But I had nothing whatsoever to do with their demise."

Joy dropped into a chair with a laugh. "Touché, Mr. Davis."

Victor scowled.

George and Dorothy chuckled. "Sounds like you've heard JoyAnne's joke about the mysterious disappearance of former campground guests." George shook his head with a fond smile at Joy.

Kellan claimed the chair on Joy's other side, effectively blocking Victor from sitting beside her, and bit back a smirk. If Victor's narrow gaze was any indication, he fully recognized Kellan's outmaneuvering of him.

"I heard it from you first, George." She shot back.

Victor sat across from JoyAnne, leaving an empty chair between himself and George who sat at the opposite end of the table from his wife.

George leaned forward with an appreciative sniff. "My Dear, everything smells wonderful. Let's bless it so we can dig in. These boys are eyeing each other like that chicken might fly away if one of them so much as blinks."

(16)

*T*he meal flew by with plenty of conversation and laughs, but JoyAnne learned nothing new about K. C. Or Kel. Which if she were honest with herself was half the reason she'd extended the invitation. They talked about fishing, boats, weather, the history of the lake, and current sports. But even there she failed to discover if he had a favorite team that might give a hint as to where he'd gone to school or currently lived.

The blame for that failure could be because his arm had brushed hers as they'd reached for the platter of oven-fried chicken tenders at the same time and her brain had fritzed out for the rest of that particular topic.

It didn't help that Victor sat directly across from her and every time Kel adroitly parried one of his prying questions, Vic shot her an "I don't trust this guy" look.

Her own curiosity aside, she was enjoying the way her cousin-in-law continued to get stymied at every turn. It wasn't often the associate circuit court judge got so thoroughly stone-walled.

"Do you have room for apple pie, Kel?" Dorothy returned to the table with a tray of sugar-dusted, homemade turnovers.

Kel's eyes lit up when he saw the tray. "Yes, ma'am. I haven't had a pastry like that since my grandmother passed away."

JoyAnne's ears pricked at the first bit of personal information he'd let drop since their previous meal together. He'd mentioned his grandparents then, too, before shutting down. She glanced at Victor fully expecting him to jump on the subject with both feet, but he kept his attention on his own piece of dessert.

"Mmm." Kel swallowed and looked up at Dorothy. "It's as good as hers were. Thank you."

JoyAnne's heart tugged at the quiet, somber note that threaded through his voice. He'd known loss, too.

"Memories are hard things to live up to, so I take that as a great compliment, Kel." Dorothy patted him on the shoulder before sitting the pastry-filled platter in front of him and heading back to her chair. "Have as many as you want. I have another batch in the kitchen and will send some with you for your breakfast if you'd like."

"Yes, Ma'am, I'd like!" Kel's emphatic nod made Dorothy laugh.

"Hey. I thought those were for me." Victor complained around a mouthful of baked apples.

"Don't worry, Vic. There's plenty for the rest of

you to pig out on."

"Watch your language, wife. I never 'pig out.' I merely appreciate your culinary talents." George assumed an air of injured indignation, but his twinkling eyes betrayed him.

"Then after three pieces of chicken, two helpings of potato salad, and two ears of corn, you won't want another turnover." Dorothy calmly forked a piece off her turnover instead of holding it in her hands to eat as the rest of them were doing.

"Now I never said that, Dotty. It is impossible to fully appreciate your talent after only one turnover."

Laughter broke out around the table at George's meek, placating expression.

"That kind of flattery earns you the privilege of doing the dishes." Dorothy passed the plate of pies to Victor who eagerly snatched another one.

"I'll be happy to help Victor clean the kitchen." George gave her a big grin and bit the corner off his second pastry.

"Wait a minute. How'd I get roped into this squabble?" Victor protested.

"Because you're a judge, Son. Dealing with squabbles is your job." George grinned broadly at Victor who groaned.

"I'll help wash up." Kel offered, polishing off his second apple turnover.

"No. I have a rule. First-time guests do not do dishes. Next time you're here, you're no longer a guest and can take your turn at KP duty with JoyAnne. Until then, she can show you around the place."

JoyAnne licked the sugar off her fingers and grinned at Victor's glower. The poor guy had been outmaneuvered all evening but she had no pity for him since she rather liked Dorothy's plan. "Would you like to walk down to the dock, K. C.? I mean... Kel."

"Absolutely." He followed her example and licked his fingers clean of any remaining sugar granules before wiping them on the cloth napkin he'd placed in his lap at the start of the meal. "Thank you, Dorothy. That was the best meal I've had in ages."

"You're quite welcome, Kel. Feel free to join us again." Dorothy smiled.

Joy swallowed a giggle and pushed away from the table. "Come on. We can catch the sunset over the water." Up to the arrival of the turnovers, Kel's table manners had been impeccable. But if he did happen to be some sort of high-priced attorney, that finger-licking move had just ruined his polished image.

Kel jumped up to follow her off the deck, catching up to her in a couple of strides then slowing to match her speed. "That meal and the company were fantastic. Thank you for inviting me."

"Even with Victor trying to pull your life story out of you every chance he got?" JoyAnne shot him a teasing smile.

He returned it. "Even with." They walked side by side down the gravel path toward the water. "What did I do, though? You'd think I was the defendant and Victor the prosecuting attorney."

"Oh, that's just his way. He's a little protective."

"Yeah. I picked up on that."

JoyAnne grinned at his sarcasm but didn't reply to it. She wanted to talk about Kel Davis not Vic. "Can I ask you a question?"

"Sure. If I can ask you one."

"Deal." She reached the end of the dock, kicked off her sandals, and plopped down to dangle her legs over the edge, relishing the refreshing coolness on her tired feet.

Kel toed off his leather loafers, rolled up his pant legs, and joined her. He looked especially sharp tonight with his Ralph Lauren polo shirt tucked into his dark wash jeans. He could have stepped out of a men's designer clothing catalog. But it was the fact he'd chosen to wear red that made her heart give a little kick. Because he'd been thinking of their earlier conversation. His grin when she'd mentioned his color choice had told her that.

He swished his feet through the water. "So what's your question?"

"Are you a lawyer?"

His eyes flew to hers with a startled bark of laughter. "What made you ask that?"

"I don't know. I guess I've been around Victor too long. Your swanky car and the—"

"Swanky?" Kel laughed.

"Yes. Swanky. And the way you deflected Vic's cross-examination reminded me of some of his attorney friends and the lawyers who argue cases before his bench."

He grinned. "Victor needs new friends."

Laughter bubbled out of JoyAnne. "I'm gonna tell him you said that. I take it you're not a lawyer then?"

"Ugh! No." He shuddered. "But don't tell Victor. I don't want him to beat up on me. Where did he get those muscles anyway?"

Her shoulders shook. "He works out his frustrations at our justice system in the weight room."

"Remind me to never make him frustrated."

Joy grinned and was silent for several seconds, swishing her feet through the water. "Kel?"

"Yeah?"

"Don't make Vic frustrated."

He blinked then his eyes began to twinkle as he gave her a patently false smile. "Gee, thanks. You're a lot of help, JoyAnne."

A giggle escaped. "If you're not a lawyer, what do you do?"

His mouth flattened slightly, and he stared out over the water. "I… I'm involved in… public relations and spend a lot of time traveling."

"Oh. Guess that explains the nice car." And told her less than nothing. She recognized an evasion when she heard one.

"But I don't want to talk about work. I'm on vacation, remember?" His smile revived, and he twisted toward her. "Besides, it's my turn to ask the questions."

JoyAnne sliced her foot up and out of the water, sending droplets flying, shimmering in the dying sunlight. "Ask away." If she stopped to think about it, this might feel like a first date. Good thing she'd had lots of practice confining her thoughts to the immediate present.

"What's the deal with you and the Barretts? You all act like family, but… are you? Come to think of it, I guess I don't know your last name, either."

She really should have expected a question of that sort, but she hadn't. It took her a second to regain her bearings. Locals all knew the relationship between her and the Barretts, but the situation must look strange to anyone who didn't know the details. "We're family by marriage. My own folks are gone now, and since George and Dorothy are the closest relatives I have left, they're sort of stand-ins for my parents. And Victor's my bossy-but-lovable older brother." There was so much more to the story, but he hadn't asked for the whole blow-by-blow tale, and she wasn't ready to share it. Yet.

Her name was a much easier topic. "As for my name, it's JoyAnne Daye. The Anne and Daye both end with an e."

(17)

*J*oyAnne *Daye.*

Kellan stared at the hazel-eyed woman beside him. Who would've thought it?

"What?" JoyAnne squinted at him.

His grin widened. "Your name fits you." Better than she knew. She'd put him in mind of a pretty and tomboyish Doris Day when he'd watched her from the stage in St. Louis. In real life, however, she was better than a silver screen actress. She was the real deal. Not some Hollywood fabrication. And the more he was around her the more he liked her and her down-to-earth manners.

"Well, thanks. I'm rather partial to it." A twinkle replaced the suspicious look. "It was a gift. My parents gave it to me for my birthday."

The laugh started in Kellan's toes. It tickled every nerve on the way up, left his mouth in a shout, and echoed across the surface of the lake, startling a pair of ducks who took off with noisy protests.

"Now look what you did. Frightened those poor birds out of their wits." JoyAnne tried to squish her grin into a scolding expression and failed endearingly.

Kellan caught his breath. When had he last laughed like that? "You have the goofiest sense of humor I think I've ever encountered."

She cocked her head and shrugged modestly. "I hate to brag or anything, but I am talented that way."

"I can tell." He nodded.

The fake seriousness lasted two seconds before they grinned at each other again.

JoyAnne leaned back on her hands, swinging her feet through the water as she looked up at the fading colors of the sunset. "This place is good for what ails you."

Kellan studied her profile. He'd caught a brief glimpse of sadness in her long-lashed eyes a couple of times now, but it never lasted long before the disposition that matched her name took over. She sounded as if she spoke from personal experience, though. Did it have something to do with the loss of her parents?

"Don't you think?" She glanced over at him.

He nodded quickly then swept a glance over the silvery water before returning his attention to the person who made him feel much more alive than the scenery did. "Yes. It is."

"You look a lot more relaxed than you did a week ago." She teased.

"You saying I'm uptight?" He squinted at her.

She shifted her weight, lifted her hand, and held her thumb and forefinger a half an inch apart.

"I had a cold." He defended himself.

"Mmm hmm. I think it's called stress." She raised one eyebrow before facing the lake again.

How was it possible to feel so comfortable with a woman he'd met only about a week ago? They knew next to nothing about each other, but he felt like they were already friends. The old-fashioned sort. Not the social media, status-updating kind. She even teased him like she teased Victor.

Although, now that he thought of it, he didn't want JoyAnne treating him like she did Victor. Whatever Victor's feelings were toward JoyAnne, she treated the big man like a brother. The feelings she stirred in Kellan, however, were not the least bit brotherly.

JoyAnne pulled her feet out of the water and propped them on the dock's edge. "Sunset's fading. We'd better head back toward the house."

He liked the feeling of being the only two people on earth and wasn't ready to leave it yet. "Can I ask you another question first?" He dove in with both feet.

She wrapped her arms around her knees and looked over at him. "What?"

"You mentioned your parents were gone."

She laid her cheek on her knee and nodded, eyes somber. "Car accident."

"Was it recent?"

"No." She inhaled deeply. "It's been... five years now."

"So you weren't real young then." The thought relieved him. He knew what growing up without parents was like and was glad she'd been spared that early loss at least.

"No. I *really* wish I could have had them for another thirty years or so, but I'm blessed to have had them for the first thirty." She stared out over the lake. "Some people don't get *that* much."

Kellan blinked and did a quick mental tabulation. "You're thirty-five?"

She lifted her head and rolled her eyes. "Good grief. Say it a little louder why don't you. I don't think the far end of the campground heard you."

"I'm sorry. I just... how is that possible? You don't look a day over..." he studied her in the dimming light. She looked younger than Trev and Ty. "Twenty-five. If that."

A pleased smile curled her lips. "I'll have to pass that compliment along to my make-up supplier."

"If you've been wearing any when I've seen you over the past week, I'll eat my hat." She wore a trace of it this evening, though—which made him wonder if it was for his benefit. It emphasized her pretty eyes, making it even harder to look away from them.

JoyAnne ducked her head, her smile a combination of embarrassment and pleasure. "Thank you. That's the nicest compliment I've had in a long time."

He was still struggling to wrap his head around something. "How are you not already married? Are the guys around here idiots?"

The question bounced off JoyAnne, who'd gone suddenly rigid, and tumbled to the weathered boards of the dock.

A crunch of gravel behind them shattered the abrupt, awkward silence, and JoyAnne shot to her feet.

"Mom's got coffee on for those of us with more sophisticated tastes." Victor strode onto the dock.

Kellan stood, keeping his gaze on JoyAnne's stiff face.

"That sounds good. I'll go help her." Her voice brittle, she brushed past Victor and bolted up the gravel path.

Victor stared after her for two seconds before rounding on Kellan. "What did you do?"

The harsh accusation pushed Kellan backwards a step. "I didn't do anything."

"She said coffee sounded *good*. JoyAnne doesn't like coffee. And she looked like she was going to cry. And I don't like it when she cries." Victor advanced.

Kellan held out his hands, palms forward. "All I did was ask a question." A flattering, teasing one. Or so he'd thought.

Victor's eyes narrowed. "What question?"

Kellan eased backwards until he felt the edge of the deck under his heel. "I only asked what was wrong with the guys around here that she wasn't already married?" He voiced the statement like a question.

Victor stared at him a full five seconds before his shoulders dropped and he scrubbed his hand over his face.

"What is it?" Kellan's stomach tensed.

The big man sighed and turned, looking through the twilight to the warm glow coming from the windows of the log house. "She *was* married. To my cousin."

The spurt of jealousy surprised Kellan almost as much as Victor's sparse, monotone explanation. "Was?"

"Yeah." Victor shuffled off the deck.

"Wait. You can't leave me hanging like that." Kellan caught him by the elbow.

Victor stopped but didn't look at him. "It's not my story to tell." He paused, his jaw flexing. "But I don't know that you'll get it from her, either. She barely talks to us about it and we're all the family she has left."

"What happened?"

"Micah was killed in Iraq. By blood, he was my cousin, but in every other way, he was my brother. He moved in with us after his folks died when he was little. His death devastated me and my parents, but it nearly killed JoyAnne. Her parents had been killed in a car accident six months before Micah went missing..." Victor's thick voice choked off.

Gray shadows settled around them and they headed toward the house in silence.

When they reached the patio deck, Kellan paused. "Victor?"

The man turned toward him, the bright porch lights at his back effectively hiding his expression.

"I am truly sorry for your loss. I know what it feels like to lose a family member. It was never my intention to hurt JoyAnne by bringing up painful memories."

Victor shoved his hands in his pockets. "You didn't know." He sighed. "And maybe it's time we stopped tiptoeing around it."

Kellan dug his key out and fiddled with it but couldn't come up with anything remotely intelligent to say. "Thank your parents for their hospitality to me."

"Sure."

Kellan headed toward his car and finally took a full breath when he turned off the private drive onto the campground road. He understood why they all tiptoed around a subject like that one, but they should post warning signs. He'd walked blindfolded into that land-mined field and triggered an explosion that had left casualties in its wake.

He'd made a complete idiot of himself and made JoyAnne cry. But how could he have guessed that her cheerful attitude hid such wounds. JoyAnne had lost her parents and then her husband. After his stupid foot-in-mouth comment, she probably hoped to never see him again.

And he couldn't blame her.

(18)

"*Y*ou want to talk about it?"

JoyAnne flinched, dropping the toast she was shredding rather than eating, and jerked around in her chair. Dorothy leaned against the counter by the coffee maker, sipping on a mug. Joy hadn't heard the woman enter the room, much less pour herself a cup of the black brew.

"You're up early." JoyAnne brushed her hands off over her plate and pushed away from the table to dump the mess in the trashcan.

"I didn't sleep well." Dorothy calmly observed JoyAnne's actions.

"I'm sorry." JoyAnne drank the last of her orange

juice then immediately wished she hadn't added more of the acidic juice to her already-troubled stomach.

"I was worrying about my girl."

Joy forced a smile to her stiff lips. "You've told me many times that worry's not productive."

"Stop it, Joy." Dorothy commanded gently. "You don't always have to live up to your name. It's okay to be sad."

The deep breath burned past Joy's tight throat, and she stared unseeingly out the window above the kitchen sink. "I got heartily sick of that emotion a long time ago."

Dorothy softly slid her arm around JoyAnne's waist. "I did too, Honey. But we all knew this week would be hard. You don't have to hide behind humor to try and make it easier on the rest of us. We hurt, too. But it's okay to feel that pain. Jesus will help us carry it if we let Him."

A tear slipped down Joy's cheek. "I tried so hard to forget what date was on the calendar. I was glad for the storm the other day because it kept me too busy to think." And she'd sort of used Kel as a distraction, too. She slapped the edge of the counter hard enough to make her palm sting. "It's been four years! When does it get easier?"

"Grief takes the time it takes. And we've only known for sure Micah was gone for three years." Dorothy's voice broke and she squeezed JoyAnne tight. "I am so thankful we have you, though. It's like a part of him is still with us."

Joy hugged Dorothy but tilted her chin up to keep further tears at bay. "I really, really don't want to cry and mope around all day. I have too many things to accomplish."

Dorothy released Joy and retrieved her coffee mug. "You don't have to worry about that. George is handling the campground today. He left an hour ago. All you have to do is hang out in the hammock, read a book, or sleep."

"No. I need to stay busy. There are still a lot of trails to check after that storm. Work kept my mind off things Saturday and Sunday, maybe it can do it again today." She'd felt guilty for not taking time to go to church yesterday, but she hadn't been up to facing the pitying glances of those who remembered the family's painful anniversary, or the curious what's-wrong-with-you looks of those who didn't.

Dorothy eyed Joy over the rim of her cup. "Is that why you invited Mr. Davis here Friday night? As a diversion?"

Joy nodded slowly. "Subconsciously, I guess. I can hardly believe it, but when I asked him, I wasn't thinking about today's date. I'm sorry." It felt slightly traitorous to be glad Kel had shoved the anniversary of her husband's disappearance to the back of her mind for once. But his presence had prevented another painful it's-almost-that-time-of-year mealtime of forced cheerfulness.

"I'm glad you invited him. It made the evening easier on all of us. But what happened later? You ran through here like the headless horseman was behind you, then Victor stomped through like he wanted to murder someone, and all I could get out of him before he left was the mumbled assurance he hadn't done any bodily harm to Mr. Davis. And then I barely saw either of you all weekend."

Joy groaned as embarrassment layered her grief. She'd worked on the farthest edges of the property the past two days to stay out of sight. "I made an idiot out of myself. We were watching the sunset and chatting and suddenly he asked why I wasn't married. To say I didn't handle it well is an understatement." She dropped her head into her palms. "I suppose I owe him an explanation, too."

Dorothy pulled JoyAnne's hands down. "You don't owe anybody anything. Especially a campground guest." She paused. "Or… is he more than a guest? You two looked pretty cozy sitting on the end of the dock."

"I honestly don't know." Dull heat climbed Joy's cheeks. "He's the first man I've even looked at twice since Micah. But how can I be remotely interested in him when I still miss Micah?"

"Because our hearts are big enough to love more than one person at a time."

"Who said anything about love?" Joy squeaked.

"Micah is gone, Joy. And if God brings a man across your path for you to love and be loved in return,

I pray you snatch the opportunity with both hands. Maybe it's not Mr. Davis. Maybe it is. You'll never know if you push him away before you give each other a chance to find out."

"I don't think he's from around here and before long, he'll leave." And Joy was done with jaunting around the world. She'd been there, done that, and had the baggage to prove it.

"So? I love having you close and would love nothing more than for you to stay here the rest of your life, but it might not be what *God* wants for you. Nor does staying here guarantee you a life free from further pain." Dorothy's gentle words hit Joy with the force of a sledgehammer.

Joy grimaced and tried to joke it off. "If I'd known we were going to tackle such a heavy topic this morning, I'd have eaten a bowl of Wheaties."

Dorothy smiled sadly. "All right. I won't badger you anymore today. Why don't you go exercise Ladybug for a while since you have the day off?"

"I think I will." Escape sounded good. If only she could leave the memories behind as easily as Dorothy's soft lecture.

"I love you, JoyAnne."

Joy gave the short woman a quick hug. "I love you, too, Aunt Dotty."

"Promise me you'll think and pray about what I said."

"I will." JoyAnne shook her head ruefully. "You're

as bossy as Victor."

"Where do you think he learned it, Honey?"

The two women parted and JoyAnne's mood sunk lower as she drove toward the barn. She really did need the distraction of doing something today, but she knew George well enough to know that if he caught her working around the grounds, he'd send her home. So she would check trails for storm damage while she was riding Ladybug. If there were limbs down that needed to be moved, so much the better. The task would also keep her out of sight of K. C. Davis until she figured out how to explain her behavior the other night.

Thankfully, the lakeside trail gave her plenty of work to focus her attention and energy on, forcing old memories to the background where they couldn't overwhelm her. Before she knew it, the sun stood directly overhead and trickles of sweat ran down her temples as she worked. But sweat was better than tears.

Joy picked up an armload of small limbs and carried them well off the path. Ladybug had helped her pull the bigger pieces of dead wood off the trail, but this big old limb had shattered when it landed leaving a nice mess.

Ladybug jerked her head up from the tuft of grass she'd found to nibble on. Joy followed the direction of her attention and caught her breath at the familiar figure walking down the muddy trail toward her.

Her jaw tightened. Gone was the easy camaraderie she'd felt on their previous meetings.

She hastily brushed at the bits of wood and dirt that clung to her shirt and jeans as Kel approached. "Hi." He didn't respond to her croaked greeting. "I haven't been down the rest of this trail so you might encounter some obstacles."

He stopped a few feet away. "I'm not interested in hiking trails. I've been looking for you. Took me three days to track you down."

"Well, here I am." She spread her hands, grimaced at her muddy gloves, and started pulling them off.

He didn't return her crooked smile. "I owe you an apology."

She stilled at his quiet seriousness. "No. You don't."

"I'm sorry, JoyAnne. I didn't mean to bring up such a painful subject."

Joy lifted her chin. *Victor and his big mouth.* She'd wring his neck next time she saw him which is probably why he'd been out of sight all weekend, too. "What did Vic tell you?" She hated pity.

"Not much, but enough to make me see how far I'd stuck my foot in my mouth." His chocolaty eyes held remorse but not a trace of pity.

She knuckled a loose strand of hair off her cheek, opened her mouth to reply, and couldn't find any words.

"Are you okay?"

Her throat ached, and she swallowed hard before shrugging her shoulders. She rarely talked about what had happened. But the man standing before her had blindly slammed into her past Friday night and deserved some sort of explanation. Especially since he was apologizing for something that was in no way his fault.

She walked toward Ladybug, stuffed the grimy leather gloves into a saddle bag, picked up the trailing reins, and headed further down the trail.

Kel stayed glued to her side, eyeing her with concern but not trying to fill the silence.

His restraint finally made the words tumble past her numb lips. "Today is an anniversary I dread every year."

(19)

*A*fter that one cryptic sentence, JoyAnne had gone silent again and continued leading her horse down the trail. Had she'd forgotten his existence?

A medium-sized limb lay across the path and Kellan jogged forward to move it. When he straightened after dragging it off the path, he found his silent companion staring blankly at him. She *had* forgotten he was along.

"JoyAnne, you don't—"

"My husband and his team were ambushed while on patrol in Iraq." She spun toward the horse, stroking its neck and hunching a little as if protecting herself from a blow. "Three of his teammates were killed, but Micah was captured by insurgents. I found out about it four years ago today." No emotion colored the stark words. "The day the chaplain knocked on my door with the news, I already knew something was wrong. It was our fourth wedding anniversary and I hadn't heard anything from Micah in over forty-eight hours."

Kellan felt frozen in place.

JoyAnne licked her lips, her fingers curling into the long strands of the horse's mane. "One year later, again on our anniversary, we finally buried Micah's remains."

The breath left Kellan's chest. *Lord, why? On the lady's wedding anniversary?*

"I kind of hate this date." Pain dulled the hazel eyes that flicked toward him.

Kellan's hands fisted. "How did you survive?" The whispered question popped out before he could catch it.

Her brow knotted up before she pressed it against the horse's neck. "I don't know that I did. That first year of being terrified for Micah and hoping and praying he'd be found is still pretty hazy. After the funeral, the Barretts dragged me up here because they were afraid I'd walk off a bridge or something."

Kellan's stomach lurched. "No."

She shook her head at his ragged denial. "Not on purpose. I was so spaced out in the days before the funeral that I nearly walked in front of a car because I flat didn't see it. Victor didn't ask permission. He hired a moving crew, packed up all my stuff, and hauled me north, telling me every ten minutes that with Micah gone and Alyce and Jordyn living in St. Louis with their own families, they needed me up here." She turned her head toward him, her eyes swimming in tears. "But *I* needed them. They're all the family I have left."

Her whisper punched Kellan in the throat. *Why*

couldn't he find any words to tell this woman how deeply he hurt for her?

"George and Dotty raised Micah after his parents died when he was five and he and Victor were closer than some siblings. Being here made me feel closer to Micah." She took a breath and gave him a faint shrug. "I thought it was finally getting easier this last year. I actually had days where I didn't think about it. I should have been expecting it, but today snuck up on me. And the other night you caught the backlash of that. I'm sorry."

"No!"

Joy flinched.

"Good grief, woman." Kellan scrubbed a hand over his scalp, faintly registering the odd sensation of recently shorn hair. "Most people, me included, would likely wind up in a psych hospital if we experienced what you went through. You are not allowed to apologize to me for getting upset because *I* stuck my foot in my mouth."

The rigid cast of her features softened. "Now you're starting to sound like Victor."

"Does that mean you'll listen to me and stop apologizing?"

"Probably not. I don't like being bossed around." The woman actually tried to smile at him.

It made him long to pull her in his arms and shield her from the pain. But how did you protect someone from memories? "Then I'll extend it as a request. Please don't ever apologize for those emotions. Not to me."

She held his gaze then lowered her lashes. "Okay. But only if we can talk about something less depressing now." She grimaced.

"Certainly." His heart ached for the sadness darkening her gold-green eyes. She'd camouflaged it well with her bright smiles and quick wit, but now that he'd seen past them it could no longer hide.

Snagging the reins, she started walking again. Her stride long and fast as if to escape the conversation.

JoyAnne Daye was one impressive woman. And the strongest one he'd ever met.

"Hey."

"Yeah?" He jerked to attention.

"You're not holding up your end of the bargain." A hint of desperation weighted the light accusation.

"What bargain?" Kellan had not only lost the train of conversation, he'd fallen off and been run over by it.

"You're supposed to be talking about something happier."

"I am?" How could he drag her out of those harsh memories when the realization of what she'd lived through was still dawning on him? His own father had died in a plane crash, but he'd died immediately. After losing both her parents, Joy's husband had been captured by terrorists who excelled at torture. Thinking about what that American soldier must have endured sickened him. And must have driven JoyAnne crazy.

"Yes. Now get talking."

"Yes, Ma'am. Let's see…" He scrambled for something—anything—to say. "Uhh… Do you have a favorite topic?"

Long moments passed before she answered with calm determination. "I like the liquid chocolate that hardens when you pour it over the ice cream."

Kellan squinted at her, completely lost. "Huh?"

"My favorite topping—that liquid chocolate that

gets hard when you pour it over cold ice cream."

Yep. The woman impressed him. All the way to the ground. She was trying to make *him* smile. He bumped her arm with his elbow. "You're nuts, you know that?"

"I prefer chocolate shell rather than nuts on my ice cream."

Kellan silently cheered on her determined humor. "Am I sensing a theme here?"

"That I want ice cream? Took you long enough to guess. You're a little slow, K. C. Davis."

A way to distract her suddenly appeared. "Are you on the clock?" He very much doubted her employer in-laws were making her work today.

She frowned. "No."

"How far are we from the cabins?"

Joy pointed the direction they were heading. "About a... quarter of a mile, I think. What's wrong?"

"Nothing. But I have an idea. How do you feel about a race?"

"A race?" She blinked at him, her face losing some of its tension.

"The kind where the loser buys ice cream for the winner?"

The green flecks in Joy's eyes brightened. "Go on..."

"Didn't I see an ice cream parlor advertised in the campstore?"

"Yes. There's a new place on the other side of the lake."

"Then I'll race you. You take your horse back to the barn and I'll go get my car. The first one to the campstore porch has to buy the ice cream." The plan was half-baked and leaving her alone might mean she'd disappear on him again, but the interactions he'd witnessed between her and Victor said she was competitive. And a little healthy competition might be just the thing to divert her attention from her memories.

The light in her eyes faded. "I don't know."

"What? Chicken? Think you can't make it? You'll have the advantage of horse power to get back, but I'll be limited to leg power."

She drew herself tall, her eyes narrowing. "But you're closer to your cabin."

"Are you forfeiting the race?" He taunted her, relieved when she shook her head.

"I didn't say that."

"Then on your mark…"

"I didn't agree to this."

"Get set…"

"Are you sure you want to—"

"Go!" Kellan took off down the trail, hollering over his shoulder. "Get your wallet ready. I want a triple scoop." *Follow me, JoyAnne. Please follow me.*

"We'll just see who's buying the ice cream."

Kellan glanced back in time to see Joy do a flying mount and her horse take off. Directly toward him. He jumped out of her way and watched her gallop past on her horse before following more slowly, his mouth setting in a grim line. If her family hadn't realized she desperately needed a diversion today, he did. She would win the race with her horse power—he would see to that—but he had over 400 horsepower sitting in front of his cabin.

And he intended to use every bit of it to make her forget today's date.

(20)

What'd you think you're doing? This is a bad idea, Joy.

She flung Ladybug's saddle on its rack and ran a hasty brush over her back and belly to rub out the sweaty marks left behind from their ride before turning the sweet mare into the pasture with a pat on her face. "Thanks, girl."

Joy rushed through the barn and jumped onto the golf cart she'd left there earlier that morning. Going for ice cream with the handsome Kel was a bad idea. It could be construed as a date. And she wasn't ready to date. To move on.

The very idea of moving on terrified her. She'd found a safe spot, had hunkered down to survive, and had no intention of leaving it.

But she'd go tell him she'd changed her mind, since running back to the house to hide without a word would be rude after he'd allowed her to figuratively cry on his shoulder. But if she didn't hurry, she'd lose the race and be obligated to go with him to pay for his ice cream. So she had to win. And then she could tell him to forget about it and go fishing or something.

Except... The thought of the ice cream served at The Dogwood Creamery was making her mouth water. She had fallen in serious like with the frosty treats served there. Food might not solve all problems, but ice cream certainly went a long way to making a hard day a tad more bearable. Although somehow K. C. Davis had managed to do that already. Because now instead of the overwhelming sadness this day started with, other more confusing emotions were vying for center stage.

Joy stomped the accelerator of the golf cart to its maximum speed of half-past crawl. Why hadn't she driven her car to the barn instead of this pokey old thing? She owed the man that triple scoop cone he wanted for putting up with her rotten mood this morning, and she'd definitely be buying it for him at this rate. The only thing that might make the difference was the fact she didn't have to stay on the blacktop to get to the finish line.

She turned onto a narrow gravel path and rolled past the playground. The back of the camp store was in sight. Joy willed the machine faster. Maybe she should take up running.

"This is a dumb idea."

The low growl of an engine reached her ears but the camp store hid the automobile from view. Was it Kel?

She braked hard in the small parking lot behind the store, the low-power machine actually managing to spit a couple pieces of gravel as she squashed the brake, killed the engine, and launched herself around the building. Frantic nervousness spurred her on as she spotted the sleek Mercedes nosing between the yellow stripes of a parking slot.

Joy jumped onto the edge of the campstore porch, vaulted over the railing, and plunked into one of the wooden lounge chairs with a triumphant grin.

Kel jogged up the steps then propped his hip on the railing, crossing his arms as he studied her from behind his sunglasses. "I thought for sure I had won because I didn't see you anywhere. Then you exploded around that corner and sailed over the railing like a track and field athlete. I thought you didn't run."

Joy caught her breath. "I don't."

His crooked smile turned skeptical. "Uh huh. Sure you don't. Guess I owe you an ice cream cone."

She tamped down the exhilaration of beating him by a hair's breadth and grabbed for a fistful of common sense. "You don't owe me anything. Since I won, I absolve the debt."

"Oh no, you don't." He strode toward her, plucked her hands off the arms of the chair and hauled her to her feet. "I don't welch. Come on. I need something to sooth my pride after losing so ignominiously."

Common sense trickled through her fingers like water, and she followed him across the porch, down the steps to the passenger side of the sleek black car.

"Hop in." He held the door for her, and she climbed automatically into the automobile. While he walked around the front of the vehicle, movement from the campstore window caught Joy's attention. Tayleigh watched them through the clean glass, grinning like a monkey with a fresh banana instead of a squirt bottle and roll of paper towels.

Great. The news of this little outing would be all over the grounds before they'd reached the main highway.

Joy's hand went to the door latch but before she could make up her mind to leave, Kel had shut his door and stuck the key into the ignition.

"Which way?"

She slouched into the buttery luxury of the seat. "Toward the dam. Did you cross it on your way into the campground when you arrived?"

"No." He backed out and turned toward the blacktop drive.

"Then turn right when you reach the highway at the campground entrance."

"Gotcha."

Joy busied herself with the seatbelt, trying to think of something else to talk about.

"Would you like to be the DJ for this trip?" Davis shot a brief smile her direction.

"Sure." She jumped at the chance to have something to listen to besides awkward silence or stilted conversation. "I promise not to blow your ears out this time, too."

He grinned. "I'm not worried."

It took a second to figure out the high-tech radio, but she soon had it on and scanned the stations before settling on one playing a Michael Bublé song.

"Good choice. I like his music."

"Me, too."

They reached the highway and rode in silence until the song changed. Kel's presence definitely distracted her from sad memories, but it had also tangled her tongue.

A musical jingle came from the smart phone that lay in the console between them.

"You can get that. I don't mind." She prompted when he made no move to pick up the device.

"It's not a phone call. That's a message alert. And even if it was a call, I'm busy driving."

The phone went silent then began to buzz. Then it jingled again. And again.

"I think someone really wants to talk to you."

"No. It's been turned off so I'm just now getting my messages."

"Yeah. We don't always have the best cell phone reception around here. Drives some people crazy."

"Not me. I appreciate the break from my electronic leash." He reached down and pressed the side of the device and the noises stopped.

Joy glanced around the interior of the automobile. It was luxurious, smart-looking as his phone, and very clean.

She sniffed the air. "It even smells new."

"It is. And in your honor, I took a second to empty it out so you wouldn't have to ride with all my gear."

"I wouldn't have minded. And if you hadn't, you might have won the race."

He smiled again. "I think I like this arrangement better. Am I still heading the right direction?"

"Yes. The ice cream parlor is on this road in about another five miles. It's right before the dam. You can't miss it."

Conversation lagged again until the elegant sign for The Dogwood Creamery came in sight.

He slowed to pull in the crowded parking lot. "Popular place."

"Yes. It opened last summer and already it's the go-to spot around here. It won the best new business award from the county newspaper, too."

They exited the car, and Kel looked across the parking lot to the 2000-foot-long hydroelectric dam that stretched across the Langhorne River, creating Dogwood Lake. "Sitting right next to the dam, I'm surprised this shop doesn't have a different, more colorful name." He grinned and they walked toward the front door of the creamery.

"You're not the first one who's said that, but nobody's been able to make the nickname stick because the owner will charge you double for cussing if she hears you call it that."

"Thanks for the warning. She sounds like a hard woman."

Joy chuckled dryly, picturing the petite proprietress. "Nope. Merely opinionated."

They walked into the small dining room decorated like an old-fashioned soda shop and joined the line to the counter.

"All the ice cream is made on site with milk from a big dairy in the northern part of the county. It's absolutely delicious."

Kel glanced around at the full tables. "I can believe it." He stuck his sunglasses above the brim of his hat and checked the menu behind the counter. "I don't know about you, but I missed lunch and want something else besides ice cream. Do you like corn dogs?"

"Are you kidding? Even though this place batters and fries their own, I doubt those things have any nutritional value whatsoever."

He glanced down at her. "So you don't like them?"

She smiled. "I love them. It's another excuse to eat ketchup so I'll take two. And a glass of tea and a double scoop of mint chocolate chip in a sugar cone since you're buying, Mr. Loser."

"Coming right up." He stepped to the counter. "We'll have two sweet teas, five corn dogs, one double-scoop of mint chocolate chip in a sugar cone, and a scoop of vanilla, a scoop of chocolate, and a scoop of strawberry in a bowl, if you please."

The short woman behind the register nodded and smiled. "Absolutely." She rang up the order and announced the total. After Kel paid her, she nodded toward the seating area, "Grab a table and I'll bring out your order in just a sec."

JoyAnne led the way to a vacant table in the corner. "That was the owner."

Kel looked over his shoulder at the diminutive brunette with the pixie haircut. "*She's* the one who doesn't want this place called—"

"Shh! She'll hear you." Joy warned with an exasperated smile.

"Aww. She doesn't look so tough."

"Bigger men than you have tried to get away with it and failed. Not only does she have a black belt in karate, she also participates in firearm competitions. I would not mess with her were I you."

"Yes, Ma'am." He eyed the woman bringing their tray of drinks and food.

"I'll have one of the other girls bring your dessert when you've finished these." The petite lady set the tray on the table. "I don't want it melting on you. Good to see you, JoyAnne. Who's your friend?"

Joy swallowed a groan at the curiosity gleaming in the ice cream shop owner's eyes. "Libby, this is Mr. Davis, a guest at the campground. I'm showing him around the area. Kel, Libby Larkin, owner of The Creamery."

The woman smiled politely at Kel. "Nice to meet you. JoyAnne's never brought a campground guest here. Are you planning on relocating to the area or something?"

"Oh, I don't know. Right now I'm simply enjoying a vacation."

Joy's heart ka-thumped at the thought of the man being around permanently.

"Well, it's nice to meet you, Mr. Davis." Her gaze narrowed and she cocked her head. "Has anyone said you look a little like… oh, I can't think of his name, but he—"

"It's nice to meet you, too, Libby This is a really nice place you have here." Kel cut her off and tugged on the brim of his cap. "Being this close to the dam, I'm surprised you don't call your shop by another name."

Joy's mouth dropped.

Libby's fists shot to her aproned hips. "Do you still want that ice cream you ordered?" Her voice was low, measured.

Kel nodded cautiously, eyes shadowed beneath his ball cap. "Uh, yes, Ma'am."

"Then don't you dare finish that remark." The short brunette spun on her heel and stomped back to the counter, giving him another glare when she reached it.

Joy picked up a freshly-fried corndog, dipped it into the container of ketchup then dipped it into the mustard. "What part of 'don't say that to her' did you not understand?"

Kel snagged the end of a wooden skewer from the paper-lined plastic basket. "I couldn't believe someone that small would be so picky about it. Guess she proved me wrong." He bit off the end of his corndog.

"Told you so." Joy grinned at his sheepishness. If that's what it was. He'd almost looked relieved when Libby stormed away.

She took a bite of her own corndog and glanced over at the woman who'd retreated behind the front counter. The shop owner threw a glance at Kel but it was more speculative than peeved.

Joy rolled the corndog stick between her fingers as she chewed. A couple of times K. C. Davis had done or said something that had registered as faintly familiar, but she'd brushed it aside as a side effect of seeing so many people come through the campground. After a while, they all started to blend together. But Libby had thought him familiar, too.

She studied him surreptitiously as she ate. The man was definitely easy on the eyes, but she couldn't figure out why he sometimes seemed familiar. And it didn't help that she'd been around him enough now that the sensation was fading.

Kel's gaze met hers, and she ducked her head to dip her half-eaten corndog into the generous dollop of ketchup and mustard she'd squirted onto the red-and-white striped waxed paper. Whatever else he was, he was a man she could easily like a little too much.

(21)

*H*e hadn't had a corn dog since his days of playing county fairs before KWESTT. And since these were hot and fresh, rather than tasting of old grease and freezer burn, they should have tasted better. But the cornmeal coating turned to sawdust in his mouth with every narrow-eyed stare he intercepted from the miniature battle axe behind the counter.

If she put a certain name to his face and told Joy, his vacation would be shot.

A braces-wearing adolescent female delivered their ice cream with a cheerful greeting before hurrying away to fill another order.

Kellan snatched a couple of napkins off the table and picked up his waxed paper bowl and plastic spoon. "It's too nice a day to eat our ice cream in here. Why don't we go outside?" The noisy place made it difficult to talk, and Joy had grown quiet as she'd nibbled her impromptu meal.

She ran her tongue around the top of her sugar cone to catch a couple of drips. "All right."

After clearing their table and exiting the building, Joy pointed to the sidewalk that ran across the top of the dam, separated from the two-lane highway by a waist-high concrete barrier. "Want to go take a look?"

"Sure."

They strolled onto the dam side by side, silently eating their cold, creamy treats. The ice cream was delicious and worth the drive, and if the owner didn't run off customers with her prickly aversion to teasing, the shop should do well.

Kellan dug a bite of real strawberry out and watched Joy lick her chocolate-flecked scoops. She looked more relaxed than when he'd found her working beside the lake trail, but a faint melancholy still lurked at the edges of her expression.

He stopped halfway across the dam and stared down at the large body of water held in by tons of steel and concrete. If you stood in front of the dam, all you would be able to see was a small river running out of an opening in a massive wall. It was only when you stood on the top that you realized the tremendous forces hiding behind that wall.

It reminded him of the woman beside him.

On the outside, she appeared happy-go-lucky with nothing to worry about beyond a few normal everyday problems. Until you looked past the surface. And discovered the tremendous pain she'd lived through.

Survived.

He felt like a wimp beside her. He'd gone whining into his vacation because he was tired. Worn out. From doing something he loved. But hearing Joy's story had made his career dilemmas fade to the background nearly forgotten. Until the ice cream shop owner had abruptly reminded him who he was. And all the guilt of hiding who he was—practically lying about what he did—rushed back at him.

But he didn't want to be Kellan Campbell right now. He wanted to be Kel Davis. The man Joy trusted enough to share her pain with.

"You've gotten awfully quiet." Joy leaned her shoulder against the tall metal fence that allowed one to appreciate the view off the dam without fear of falling.

"I was thinking the same thing about you." He gladly shoved aside his guilty conscience to concentrate on Joy.

"Yeah. I'm real good company." She grimaced. "Today hasn't been one of my better days."

"I'm not complaining."

Her eyes lowered. She put the last bite of cone in her mouth, wadded up the paper wrapper, and rolled it between her palms as she started walking again. "We've talked enough about me, today. What's your story?"

The plastic spoon cracked between Kellan's teeth and he yanked it out and dumped it and his almost empty bowl in the trashcan at the end of the dam's walkway. "I'm a boring subject." *Liar.*

"Only because I know hardly anything about you. Beyond the fact you're terrible at putting up a tent."

"Hey now. I got my tent up fine, thank you very

much. It was setting tent stakes with a throbbing head that was the problem."

"Excuses, excuses."

Her singsong ribbing made him laugh in spite of his wounded pride and stinging conscience. She had every reason to view life with a grim outlook. Especially today of all days. But she didn't. He admired the way she saw the humorous side of things and didn't take herself too seriously. She didn't take *him* too seriously, either. That in itself was one of the things he most enjoyed about being around her.

It was a novel experience being incognito with someone who liked his group's music but didn't recognize him as part of it and treated him as a normal human being. He understood her wanting to know more about him, but he didn't want to spoil whatever was growing between them by bringing his alter ego into the picture. Not yet. Not until she knew him a little better.

And exactly how is she supposed to get to know you better when you won't tell her who you are?

"Where are we going, by the way?" He changed the subject.

She pointed to a log-and-glass structure overlooking the lake. "The visitor's center. You can pick up a souvenir if you want and see pictures of the construction of the dam."

Kellan eyed the steep drive up to the building. "Why don't we go back to the car and drive up there?" He wasn't interested in souvenirs, but he *was* interested in stretching out the time he got to spend alone with her.

"Because we should walk off our dessert."

"Walk? That's not a walk. That's a climb." He

teased her.

"Pssh." Joy blew air between her pursed lips. "What happened to the idiot who ran a mini-marathon in the rain?" She started up the driveway.

"Did you just call me an idiot?"

"Yep. I calls 'em as I sees 'em. And running in a thunderstorm is pretty idiotic."

"That's not a nice thing to say to the man who bought you ice cream, JoyAnne."

She studied the ground they were climbing. "No. It's not. I'm sorry."

Shoot. He hadn't meant to make her sad again. "Hey. I'm only teasing."

Her head popped up. "I know. So am I, Kelso Conner."

Kellan elbowed her. "Brat. Try again." He was going to miss her crazy guesses when he finally told her his full name. If she was still talking to him afterwards.

She laughed. A light sound that made him hope she was forgetting about other more serious things. "Okay. Let's start with something easy. Where do you live?"

"California." She caught him off guard, and the answer escaped before he had time to evaluate it.

The ground leveled off as they reached the top of the hill. "Ooh. A surfer boy, huh? I'll have to think of some surfer-sounding names."

His grin returned. He couldn't wait to hear what she came up with. "I surf. Some."

"Some?" Joy turned toward him, walking sideways as she gave him the once-over. "I bet you do more than some, but I can't picture you as the beach bum type. You're too clean cut."

"Thanks. I think." He swallowed a laugh.

"You're welcome. I think." Her grin mocked him as they approached the entrance to the visitor's center. "Do you have family out there?"

He held the door open for her to enter the building ahead of him. "No. I only have distant cousins left and they're scattered all over the country."

She led him to a gallery showcasing the construction of the dam and lake. "No folks?"

"They're already gone."

Her hand touched his arm. "I'm sorry."

He shrugged. "It was a long time ago."

"That doesn't make it any less hard." Her eyes held compassion and understanding.

And they warmed him to the bone. She understood what it was like to be the lone survivor of a family. "Thanks." His tight throat prevented anything else.

She smiled softly and turned toward the exhibits and they browsed in silence for several minutes, Kellan pretending to read the explanations under each picture as he searched for a suitable topic to distract her from the current conversational trend. How did you go about getting to know someone when you didn't want to trigger any more bad memories on their part and you didn't want to suddenly announce you were a member of a prominent musical group?

"I guess I don't know a lot about public relations work. What exactly does your job entail?"

"Well…" Kellan studied a large table diorama, playing for time. The decision was a simple one, but simple didn't mean easy. Either he told her the truth, or he lied. Again.

"Wait. Hold that thought." Joy dug in her jeans pocket and dug out a flip-style cellular phone.

"What's wrong?"

She grimaced and walked toward the wall of windows overlooking the lake. "I've got three missed calls. I'll probably have missed texts, too, whenever they finally decide to load."

Kellan drew a breath. Saved by the cell.

(22)

*J*oy punched in the code to her voice mail and waited for the first message to play.

Victor's voice barked into her ear. *"Joy, where are you? You need to call me."*

Her brow scrunched. She should have texted someone her whereabouts—if her phone had decided to cooperate—but she'd assumed Tayleigh would spread the news of her departure with the handsome campground guest.

"Something wrong?" Kel joined her beside the large plate glass window.

"Victor's looking for me, and since my phone is contrary, I'm just now getting his message. Thirty minutes after he first called." She punched a button to hear the second message.

"Call me, Joy. It's serious."

Joy's fingers trembled as she went to the third message. Vic's tone of voice...

"Joy, you need to call me. Now. It's... it's Dad."

She nearly dropped the phone in her rush to disconnect from voice mail and dial Victor. But the useless piece of technology beeped at her, and a *No Service* message mocked her from the tiny screen.

"Joy. What's wrong?"

"I don't know. This stupid thing won't work. I need to call home. Right now." Terror blazed through her, robbing her of coherent thought. *Please, Lord, no. I can't handle any more loss. Especially not today of all days!*

"Here. Use mine." Kel tugged her phone from her tight fingers and held his out to her.

She grasped it like a life line. And then stared at it. "I don't know how to work one of these." Why hadn't she given in to her friends' nagging and bought a better phone before now?

He took his phone back without laughing at her. "Tell me what to dial." He tapped the numbers she gave him into the device and handed it back to her.

She stuck it against her ear, pacing in small circles until the call went to Victor's voice mail. "He doesn't answer."

Kel laid his hand on her shoulder, halting her agitated movements. "Calm down. Who else can you call?"

"I don't know. Victor said something was wrong with George. Try the house." After he'd dialed the next set of numbers she rattled off, JoyAnne paced off the agonizing seconds waiting for someone to answer.

Nothing. She thrust it back at Kel. "Call the campstore. Maybe Tayleigh knows what's going on."

Joy's stomach heaved when no one answered that phone, either. "Something's really wrong." Her arms wrapped around her middle and she hunched over them. "I don't know if I can face... bad news again."

"Hey. Breathe. Let's not jump to conclusions. There might be a very simple explanation. After all, Victor couldn't get ahold of you either but you're okay." He slid an arm around her shoulders and squeezed her to his side. "Do you want to wait here and keep trying to reach him while I go get the car?"

"No. I'll go crazy." Kel's touch grounded her enough she could draw tiny breaths past the fear wrapping its skeletal fingers around her throat.

"Come on then." Kel grabbed her free hand and they hit the visitors' center doors at a jog.

Why, oh why did I have the brilliant idea to walk up here? This wasn't a date with a cute guy. This is the anniversary of losing my husband! I should have stayed home where I belong. Joy lashed herself all the way down the hill and across the dam.

She was gasping for air by the time they piled into the car, but he wasn't even breathing hard.

"Hand me the phone a second, and I'll show you how to use it so you can keep calling while I drive."

She focused on his instructions and when he pulled out of The Creamery's parking lot, she dialed again. "Come on, Vic. Answer. Please." She muttered under her breath.

"Nothing?" Kel glanced at her when she lowered her hand after several attempts and one voice mail message later.

Joy shook her head, fighting to remain calm. "What is so wrong that he's not answering his phone?"

"Didn't you say something earlier about poor cell reception around here?"

Her rigid muscles softened enough to let her draw a fuller breath. "Yeah. Maybe that's it." *Dear Lord, please…*

She nearly jumped out of her seat when the phone trilled and buzzed in her hand. She recognized the number on the screen. "It's Vic! How do I answer it? You didn't show me that."

"Touch the green circle on the bottom right of the screen."

Duh, Joy! "Vic! It's me. What's wrong?" As she listened to him, tremors began to rattle through her. "Okay. We'll be there as soon as we can. We're over by the dam. Tell Dotty I'm praying." Her voice broke, but Vic had already hung up.

She lowered the phone to her lap and covered her mouth with her left hand, holding in a desperate sob. Kel's presence was keeping her rising panic in some semblance of control.

Then again, if she'd been working, doing her job like she was supposed to instead of hiding in the woods and then taking off with Kel for a *date* none of this would be happening.

"JoyAnne! What is it?"

"George… They think… he had a stroke." Tears flooded her eyes but she fought them back and gripped her knees.

Abandoning his ten-and-two driving style, Kel reached over and tugged her hand down to wrap it in his firm grip. "Where do we need to go?"

She held on tight. *We.* It had been so long since she'd been the other half of a *we.* "The ER. They're waiting to hear from the doctor."

"I'll need directions. Can you do that or do you want to give me an address to program into my GPS?"

"I'll tell you. I know the shortcuts." And maybe it would keep her mind from falling off the precipice of worst-case scenarios.

Joy willed the miles away as she gave Kel instructions, and he pushed the speed limit while retaining his grasp on her hand.

Five minutes out from the hospital, the phone rang again and she dropped his hand to punch the green circle.

"Yes?" She'd forgotten to read the caller's id on the shiny screen.

"Who is this?" The female voice on the other end snapped.

Joy jerked the phone away from her ear. She must have inadvertently hit a volume button or something. The sound level was downright painful. "This is Joy Daye. Is this about George Barrett?"

"Who? Where is Kel?"

The slender electronic device disappeared from her fingers and she blinked at Kel who slammed it to his ear after pressing a button on the side. "Patricia, K. C. here. This isn't a good time… No. I'm in the middle of an emergency. I'll call you back later." He handed the device back to Joy. "If her name pops up again, hit the red *Decline* icon."

"I'm sorry for tying up your phone." She dug in her pocket. "Mine might be working now."

Davis touched her arm. "Don't apologize. It's just

work stuff, and she's *not* supposed to be bothering me on vacation. I'll deal with it later."

"Is Patricia your boss?"

"No. Is this where I'm supposed to turn?"

Joy jerked her attention back to the road and saw the blue sign indicating a hospital at the next exit. "Yes. At the top of the overpass, turn right and then take the next right. That road will take us directly to the ER entrance."

She vaulted from her seat when he pulled under the ER canopy. "Thank you, Kel."

"Not so fast. I'm going with you." He slammed the vehicle into park and jumped out, hard on her heels as she raced through the automatic doors.

"Joy!" Victor waved them over to the corner of the waiting room.

"Vic. Dotty. What's happening?" *Lord, help us through this.*

Dorothy wiped her face and hurried toward Joy. "It's okay. George'll be okay." She pulled Joy into a hug. "They just gave us an update. They've done a CT scan and have started him on clot buster meds and are moving him to ICU but they said his speech is already improving. It might have been only a mini stroke, but they'll know more after some additional tests, and we should be able to see him in a few minutes."

"I'm so sorry I wasn't there, Dotty." Joy hugged the short, round woman hard. Guilt hitting her squarely in the gut. "If I'd been working, George wouldn't—"

"None of this is your fault, Joy. He had just come in for lunch complaining of a severe headache when he started having difficulty speaking. You being there wouldn't have changed a thing. George struggles with this day, too, and he would have been outside working regardless of what you were doing."

Victor wrapped his arms around Dorothy's and her shoulders and Joy felt the tension in his arm. This had scared them all. And though the diagnosis might not be as black as she'd first feared, worry still coursed through her. A stroke of any kind wasn't good.

A hand settled on her other shoulder. "Heavenly Father," Kel's calm, low voice slid over her like a warm blanket on a cold day. "Give this family peace as they wait for information, and as the Great Physician, lay your healing hands on George. Give the doctors and nurses wisdom as they diagnose and treat him, and restore George to full health. I ask this in the name of Jesus Christ, Amen."

"Amen." Dorothy turned and hugged him. "Thank you, Kel. That's exactly what we needed."

"Excuse me?" A nurse approached them. "Mr. Barrett is in his room now and two of you may visit him for a couple of minutes. But only two of you."

"Vic, take Dotty." Joy shoved Victor forward.

He looked between his mother and her, his brow furrowing deeper. "Will you be okay for a few minutes?"

"Go. I'll be fine." Joy held herself stiffly erect as they walked away, but when they disappeared behind a set of swinging doors, her spine wilted.

Blindly, she spun to find a chair, but a pair of hands pulled her into a firm chest. Her arms automatically wrapped around Kel's waist as his encircled her. The tears came full force. "I was so scared. I still am. What if he has another stroke?"

"I know. I know." His hug shored up her collapsing

composure, giving her a safe place to let go for a second.

She'd missed this part of being a couple. Having someone to lean on. Yes, she had the Lord, but a pair of strong human arms sure felt good during a crisis.

Don't get used to it. He's leaving next week, and you'll probably never see him again.

(23)

"*Y*ou don't have to hang around here. You should go. It could be late before we're ready to leave." Joy spoke so quietly she didn't disturb Dorothy who looked to be dozing against Victor's shoulder in the corner of the small second-floor waiting room they had to themselves.

Kellan shifted in the uncomfortable, short-backed chair. "I'd rather wait and hear what the doctor has to say if you don't mind." He wasn't about to bail on Joy. Victor's face was set and emotionless, but the tick in his jaw said otherwise, and although Dorothy appeared to be handling the crisis with graceful strength, they might need someone who wasn't listening through a fog of panic if the doctor brought bad news.

"I don't mind. But it's already been hours and you

have to be bored out of your skull." JoyAnne twisted a tissue between her fingers, eyes fastened on the door to the waiting room.

Thankfully, she'd only needed them to keep her hands busy for the last couple of hours. She hadn't cried since he'd held her in his arms, but he wouldn't mind a few more tears if it meant he got to hold her again. Music had been his life for so long. His purpose. And when he'd started questioning that, he'd felt lost. Until he'd held Joy in his arms.

"Nope. I'm not bored." Not with new possibilities for the future whirling through his brain.

JoyAnne sprang to her feet and Kellan twisted to find a nurse entering the room.

"Are you the Barrett family?"

"Yes." Victor kept a hand on his mother's back as they stood.

"Mr. Barrett is ready for visitors. The neurologist will meet you there in a few minutes."

"Oh, thank you! Can we all go?" Dorothy slipped the strap of her purse over her shoulder.

"If you're all family, yes." The woman smiled and turned to exit the room with Dorothy, Victor, and JoyAnne following her.

Kellan sat down to wait.

JoyAnne jerked to a halt and spun toward him. "Aren't you coming?"

"I'm not family. I'll wait here for you."

She hurried over and pulled him up. "Tonight you are. Right, Aunt Dotty?"

"Absolutely." Dorothy nodded emphatically.

Victor didn't look nearly as enthusiastic but he didn't protest, so Kellan allowed JoyAnne to lead him through the door, suddenly having to swallow hard a couple of times. "Thanks. I'll stay out of the way."

Family. He wouldn't mind being a part of this family for much longer than the length of a hospital visit.

The yearning worked its way deep into his heart as he hung out by the door of George's tiny ICU room and watched the man's family hug him, scold him lovingly, and shed a few more tears.

"Knock, knock." A white-coated woman entered on silent rubber soles, bringing the sharp scent of hand sanitizer with her. "How are you feeling, Mr. Barrett?"

"Worn out. If I'd known... how many tests you would give, I'd've studied harder. Did I pass?" George smiled, but his eyelids drooped, and his words came slowly.

The tall, blond physician laughed. "You did very well. I wish all my patients were such good students."

Kellan felt the relieved breaths that puffed from the standing members of the Barrett family as the doctor gave the results of the tests.

"Mr. Barrett, you didn't have a stroke or even a blood clot. You had hyponatremia."

"What is that?" Dorothy frowned, holding George's hand.

"Abnormally low sodium in the blood. Mr. Barrett told us he'd gotten very thirsty working outside today and drank more bottles of water than he normally would. Unfortunately, it is possible to *over*hydrate and cause the body's sodium level to drop to dangerous levels. And that's what happened here, causing stroke-like symptoms. The first CT scan showed some abnormalities on one side of Mr. Barrett's brain so clot medication was administered. However, the MRI shows that there was no stroke or blood clot, Mr. Barrett has veins on one side of his brain that are a little larger than the other side, but he was probably born with that abnormality."

"So now what?" George asked.

The doctor smiled. "Now you get to spend the night with us, Mr. Barrett. Your sodium is still low and the clot medicine you were given can cause side effects like bleeding in the brain, and we don't want you up and moving around for the next twenty-four hours to prevent a fall. Tomorrow afternoon, we'll do another CT scan to check for any bleeding, and if that looks good and we have your sodium back up to normal levels, we can start talking about sending you home. But then you'll need to take it easy for the next week or so."

"I'll make sure he does." Dorothy stiffened like a sergeant getting orders from a commanding officer.

"I believe you will." The physician chuckled and jotted down information from the machines that monitored George's vitals before tucking her clipboard under her arm. "I'll see you in the morning, then, and try to get some sleep. Visiting hours will be over in about fifteen minutes, but Mrs. Barrett, you may stay with him in the room tonight if you like." The door closed behind her with a quiet whoosh.

George pushed himself higher in the bed. "A week? I've got too much to do to lie around the house."

"Now, George. She didn't say you had to lie around the house just that you were to take it easy."

"She might as well have. I see that look in your eye. The holiday weekend is nearly here. There're damaged trees that still need trimming, cabin five needs plumbing repairs, I haven't gotten all the stuff I need for our annual fireworks show—"

"You let me worry about that, George." Joy patted the man's arm. "That's what you pay me the big bucks for."

"You're gonna have enough to do without worrying about getting the grounds mowed and trimmed and the rest of the trails checked." George took a breath, seeming to run out of his brief burst of steam. "We don't even have all our summer staff yet."

"I'll help her." Victor joined the discussion.

"When? You told me... you've got a full court docket the next couple of weeks." George frowned, fretting. "Of all the fool times to have a stroke—."

"Hyponatremia, Dear. Not a stroke."

"Potato pahtahto. It won't hurt me... to sit on the tractor and ride around."

"No!"

George flinched at the outburst from his family. "You don't have to yell."

"I'll help out in the evenings after court. We'll get it taken care of, Dad."

"Thank you, Vic, but our staff and I can handle it. We'll get everything in tiptop shape before the big weekend." JoyAnne crossed her arms, the light of battle gleaming in her hazel eyes.

"That's enough!" Dorothy's eyes flashed. "We should be thanking the Lord George didn't have a stroke instead of worrying about cutting grass! I don't want any of you trying to kill yourself to get the campground ready. If the grounds aren't up to George's nitpicking standards for one year, it won't hurt us. I think they already look pretty sharp."

Kellan grinned at the mutinous look on Joy and George's faces. They didn't like Dorothy's opinion. At all. It was his turn to take a hand in the game.

He walked to the end of the bed. "I'll help."

Four pairs of eyes swiveled toward him.

JoyAnne shook her head. "You can't. You're a guest. And we already owe you for your damaged tent."

"You ever run a tractor, Son?" George eyed him, a gleam dimming the fatigue in his eyes.

"Yep. Grew up on a small farm and ran a brush hog many times."

"You're hired."

"George. I can handle it." JoyAnne protested.

"I know. Especially with his help."

JoyAnne turned to Kellan. "You're planning to leave in a few days. Not to mention you're on *vacation.*"

"I have plenty of vacation time left and was already thinking about staying around this area instead of looking for new ground to explore, but I'm bored. I need something to do. So put me to work."

"Why?" Suspicion hardened Victor's face.

Kellan lifted one shoulder. "Because you all have been kind to me and I'd like to lend a hand."

"That's good enough reason for me." George settled into the pillows behind him and smiled. "I think I can rest now. You all take Dotty home so she can get rest, too."

"I am staying here tonight. The doctor said I could." Dorothy held up a finger to hush her husband. "You three go on home. We'll call you in the morning with an update."

JoyAnne and Victor protested, but Dorothy shooed them out of the room and closed the door behind them.

After a few seconds of indecisive silence, Victor slapped the side of his leg. "I don't know about you two, but I'm hungry. Let's go find some pizza and plan our strategy for keeping George under control until the doctor gives the all-clear."

"Look out Black Jack's Pizza, 'here come de judge!'" JoyAnne grinned weakly, but Kellan was happy to see some of the strain that had stooped her shoulders fall away.

"If it hadn't been such a long day, Squirt..." Victor looked over at Kellan. "I hope you know what you're getting yourself into. I wouldn't work for this woman if you paid me."

JoyAnne grabbed Kellan's arm and marched him down the hall. "Don't you listen to him, K. C. He's so used to being in charge and banging his little wooden mallet to get his own way he doesn't know how to handle not being the boss. Ack!"

Before Kellan realized what was happening, Victor had grabbed JoyAnne around the legs and tossed her over his shoulder.

She thumped his back with her fists. "Put me down, Bam Bam!"

Victor bounced her, eliciting a grunt as he punched the elevator call button. "Shh! You're in a hospital."

JoyAnne levered herself up until she could see Kellan, an annoyed frown slanting her mouth. "Do you see the abuse I have to put up with from this big lug?"

Kellan grinned, enjoying the verbal sparring. Yeah. He could easily envision being a part of this family. And helping them would give him the chance to get to know all of them on a more personal basis than as a paying guest. He only hoped there were no rules about fraternization between the boss and employees.

Because he *definitely* wanted to fraternize with his cute new boss.

(24)

JoyAnne had always had a soft spot for a man in uniform. She'd fallen in love with a man in one and married him. And then his abduction, death, and closed-casket funeral had shredded her heart. However, the man riding the tractor in the early morning light was making that scarred organ beat like it had never been damaged. His ball cap, sleeveless shirt, cargo shorts, and grass-stained tennis shoes were as far from a uniform as a guy could get, but he didn't need a uniform to be a hero. The man had faced her painful past and subsequent family emergency head on, and his compassionate support had strengthened her when she'd needed it most.

The big riding lawnmower turned toward her and she waved, catching Kel's attention and motioning him over to the golf cart.

He waved back and nodded.

JoyAnne watched him approach. She'd hesitated when he'd offered to lend a hand after the scare with George, but she'd secretly looked forward to the chance to spend more time with him. There was more to the man than his looks—which she fully appreciated—but his work ethic had been about the only additional information she'd found out about him since George's emergency. She could count on two hands the amount of minutes they'd had alone together since the evening spent at the hospital. They were always going in opposite directions. She was used to the work it took to keep a campground looking neat and running efficiently, but even she was dragging from the effort to have everything so shipshape George wouldn't be tempted to try and take a hand as he recovered his strength.

Thank you, Jesus, that Uncle George is recovering so well and for protecting him from any permanent damage!

Kel had a standing invitation for Dorothy's home-cooked suppers now, but he tended to let the rest of them do the talking, content to watch, listen, and relax. He seemed to enjoy her family, though, and she liked hearing him laugh at George's stories and her family's back-and-forth teasing. If his lingering glances in her direction were any indication, he might be thinking about hanging around longer than a few weeks to help out.

Her heart raced just thinking about that possibility.

Kel shut off the lawnmower blades, pulled the machine beside the golf cart, and killed the engine.

"Morning, JoyAnne. What's up?"

She really liked how he said her name. Now if only she could make him spill about his full name. "Good morning to you, too, Kel. You're the one who's up. Before the sun."

"I noticed there wasn't a lot of dew this morning, so since this section was empty and I wouldn't be disturbing anyone, I thought I could get it mowed before the next wave of campers hit." He took off his hat and ran his fingers through his chocolatey-thick hair before repositioning the cap.

"You're as bad as George. The two of you act like you have a personal vendetta against tall grass."

Davis laughed. "No vendetta. But I had forgotten how much I liked doing this job. It gives a man time to think. Or not think if he doesn't want to."

"Maybe this will help." She picked a tall, insulated mug off the seat and handed it to him.

"Coffee?" He opened the lid and sniffed before taking a long drink and closing his eyes on a satisfied swallow. "You are my hero. How did you know I had to make do with a bottle of cold tea for my caffeine fix this morning?"

"'Cause Dorothy said she hadn't seen you up at the house. I heard you mention yesterday that you'd run out of coffee grounds, and the campstore's coffee machines weren't going yet." She ticked the reasons off on her fingers, enjoying the chance to sit and talk. And watch him.

He lowered one brow. "What are you? A detective?"

"I have to be to find out anything about you. You're as closemouthed as the stone turtle in Dorothy's flowerbed." But she really wasn't quite ready to push him about his life outside Wad-A-Wa Campground. Because then she'd have to think about him leaving and going back to it instead of imagining him as a permanent fixture in her life.

A strange expression flickered through his eyes then disappeared. He took a quick sip from the mug and groaned. "For a woman who doesn't drink it, you sure brew a mean cup of joe."

"Thank you. Micah taught me how." She was a little proud of the fact she could make coffee that other people liked when she couldn't stand the taste of it herself, but the ease with which Micah's name entered the conversation surprised her. And for a change, it didn't sting.

"He taught you well." Kel didn't flinch at the mention of her husband. "So tell me. How do you manage to be so bright-eyed every morning if you don't drink this stuff?" He raised his mug.

"Good, clean living, Kelton Christopher." Joy lifted her nose in a haughty pose. "Early to bed and early to rise means I don't have to depend upon stimulants like the rest of you poor, unenlightened folks."

Kel took another long swig, but she caught the smile he tried to hide with it. "Wrong again, Brat. And insulting the hired help is never a good option. We can vote now, you know. And I'm getting inclined to vote for Victor to give you that swimming lesson he promised you the other night. I might even help toss you in for coming up with such *awful* names. And then I'll find whatever name book you're using and toss it in after you."

A thrill shot through JoyAnne at the thought of his strong, corded arms picking her up. She shook her head, grinning. "Won't happen. Victor's been threatening me with a dunking for years. It's all show. Besides, we've got too much work to do to be playing around."

"But all work and no play makes Joy a dull girl." He teased and took another drink.

The remark stung her. Jordyn and Alyce had leveled that same accusation at her on more than one occasion. But they didn't understand dull also meant safe.

And dull would never catch the attention of a mysterious man like K. C. Davis.

She forced a smile and started the golf cart. "Guess I'll have to be dull, then. Enjoy your stump water."

Kel reached over and touched her forearm before she could drive off. "Thank you. I really appreciate you taking time to bring me this, but I enjoyed getting to talk to you more. You're not dull, JoyAnne. You couldn't be if you tried."

Her cheeks heated, and her smile felt as sloppy as it probably looked. "I don't think you're dull, either."

"Then the feeling is mutual." He grinned and handed the empty mug back to her. "Would you care to share your lunch break with me? We both have to eat."

"Yeah. I'd like that." Butterflies she'd thought long dead began to compete with each other on a newly installed trampoline.

"I'll see you later then."

"Yeah. Later." JoyAnne touched the accelerator and zoomed away from the smiling man who'd tied her tongue in knots. Again.

The ice cream parlor outing couldn't really be

considered a date since he'd only taken her there to distract her. But this... this invitation felt like a date. And she was dangerously close to falling head over heels in very-intense-like with the man. If he walked away in a few weeks and didn't look back, her battered heart would take another beating.

(25)

Kellan whistled a classic old tune as he scrubbed away the signs of the day's toil in preparation of seeing JoyAnne again at supper. Lunch had been a rushed affair consisting of sandwiches eaten at a picnic table behind the campstore building with several of the teenage summer staff. Nothing romantic about it at all. Except their shared smiles at the juvenile text-speak floating around them.

The almost foreign language would have made him feel old if he hadn't been entranced by a pair of laughing hazel eyes across the table.

Cliché it might be, but the classic old lyric running through his head described his feelings exactly. JoyAnne made him feel young—almost as young as the summer staff. Made him feel there were songs to be sung--songs he hadn't written yet. He'd been in a dry spell so long the fear he'd never write again had wormed into his soul and frozen it. But while clearing trails, cutting grass and brush, working in the fresh air and sunshine, and catching glimpses of a certain bouncy, brown ponytail, he'd found himself humming snatches of new tunes. Hearing new lyrics. Until his fingers itched to grab his guitar and a pen.

Moving into the cabin had worked out great. He had more privacy and he'd been able to work on capturing those new tunes and lyrics in the evenings before crashing and sleeping like a log. It felt good to play and sing for the sheer joy of creating a new piece.

If you're serious about JoyAnne, you have to tell her who you are. Sooner rather than later.

"I know. I know." He tried to silence his nagging, persistent conscience in vain.

As nice as it was to be plain ol' Kel Davis, JoyAnne deserved to know all of him. The songwriting and performing side of him had needed this escape and change of pace, but they were as big a part of him as the fishing, camping, mowing, and laying-low side of him.

"Tonight, however," he pointed at his reflection in the mirror, "is not the time for that surprise. We're celebrating accomplishing JoyAnne's and George's lists in time for the holiday weekend."

The jingle of his phone stopped him on the way out the door. He glanced at the screen then answered it. Ignoring her wasn't working so he'd try something else. "Patricia, you need to learn the meaning of the word *vacation*. You have either called or texted every single day of mine."

"Kellan," the bossy female voice on the other end

warned, "if you expect me to take your career to the next level then we have to talk."

"We can talk when I get back."

"But things are happening now."

"Like what?" Kellan flopped into the cabin's lone easy chair and eyed the ceiling. His agent had been extremely instrumental in getting him where he was in his career and definitely earned her paycheck, but lately her nagging persistence grated on him. Thank the Lord his brains had kicked in before his emotions had gone off the deep end with her.

"Like how would you feel about a solo career?"

He sat straight up. "What are you talking about?"

"I'm talking about a new contract with the biggest record label in Nashville and headlining your own shows. I'm talking about more digits before the decimal on both our paychecks."

Kellan could almost see her rubbing her ring-bedecked fingers together. "I'm not exactly hurting for money, Patricia, and I've been part of KWESTT from the beginning. All I'm asking for is a little more say in the decision-making process and permission to do a solo album of my own music every couple of years."

"Kellan, *nobody* turns down the chance for extra fame and money. And since your current contract doesn't allow you to do solo albums, I went shopping."

"That's why you're supposed to be negotiating a new contract with our current label." KWESTT had been put together by a record label company and had proven to be a successful, award-winning concept. Because of those beginnings, however, creative control rested largely in the hands of the record execs instead of the performers. And after ten years, it had become stifling.

"They won't budge. But I found as sweet a new deal as I hoped for."

"A deal I'm not giving you permission to make."

Her voice hardened. "You're too sentimental, Kellan. All groups break up eventually and move on to greener pastures. You need to snatch up better options while you're still at the top. You won't find this kind of offer when KWESTT is no longer hitting the top of the charts."

"Since when are we in danger of that?" Kellan rubbed his forehead, the old, familiar tension headache returning with a vengeance at her strident words.

"You're only as good as your latest album."

He pinched the bridge of his nose. "What did they think about the new songs I gave you to pitch to them?" They'd used a couple of his songs before and they'd been well received by their fans.

"They weren't interested. You can do better for yourself. So think about what I said and get back with me. This offer won't be on the table for long." Patricia's voice softened. "I'm only looking out for your best interests, Kel. It's what you pay me for."

He closed his eyes and rubbed his forehead. "All right. I'll think about it. But let me do it in peace. Okay?"

A rapid tapping came over the line. The woman drummed her red polished nails against her desk when she was about to accept an offer. "Fine. You've got until Tuesday. But I need an answer then by the end of the day." The dead air that followed indicated she'd hung up on him. If she'd had an old-fashioned phone, she probably would have slammed the receiver down.

Kellan resisted the urge to toss his own phone across the room. He shouldn't have answered it. The thought of leaving KWESTT...

Those guys were his friends. They'd been together nearly a decade. They were as much family as band mates. Yeah, he'd been exhausted and ready for a break, but he'd never intended to quit. Had he?

The new offer was a good one. It could potentially give him more creative control and license. The early years of his singing career before KWESTT had been hard and nearly hand-to-mouth, but he'd loved writing and performing his own work. With the name recognition he had now, going solo again should be easier but with the added challenge and excitement of making good with his own stuff.

Kellan dropped his head against the chair. Patricia had been right to tell him of the new offer. He had a big decision to make.

Changing labels was a risky business move, though. Leaving KWESTT could jeopardize not only his own career but his buddies' careers, too. They'd all been successful because of each other. Breaking up that combination shouldn't be done lightly.

The pros and cons whipped through his thoughts, each one outweighing the other. He shot to his feet. "I have until Tuesday. She can't do anything until after the holiday weekend."

He tossed the phone on top of his duffle bag then locked the cabin door behind him. Tonight the only things getting his attention were JoyAnne, the Barretts, and a good meal. In that order.

Kellan enjoyed every moment of the laid back evening. George and Dorothy had welcomed him from the first, but now they treated him like family. Even Victor had mellowed and seemed to grudgingly accept him.

"You about done in here?" JoyAnne stuck her head through the open sliding patio door. "Victor's ready to light some fireworks for our own private Memorial Day salute."

"We're coming." Dorothy took the dishcloth from Kellan. "You run ahead and make sure George isn't doing something he shouldn't. I'll be right behind you as soon as I start the load of towels in the washer."

Kellan followed JoyAnne to where George lounged in a chair in the yard, watching his son set up fireworks at the far edge of the dock. "Is it legal to shoot fireworks this time of year?"

"Yes." JoyAnne plopped on the ground beside George. "Judge Victor can attest to that. We're on private property, and since he's shooting them over the water, our surroundings should be in no danger from Mr. Pyromaniac. Unless of course, he burns the dock down."

"I heard that, Squirt." Victor tossed a glare at JoyAnne. "Keep it up, and I'm going to make you shut that smart mouth of yours."

JoyAnne smirked at the big man, and George chuckled. "You're crusin' for a bruisin', girl. You know he'll eventually retaliate if you keep picking on him."

"Somebody's got to keep him humble. Whacking that gavel every day does terrible things for the size of his head." JoyAnne muttered the words under her breath. Apparently she had a sliver of caution about teasing her massive cousin-in-law too much.

Dorothy arrived and Victor set off his short but

fairly impressive pyrotechnic show. The women oohed and aahed, and they all applauded when it ended.

Kellan stood and brushed off the seat of his britches. "I'll help him clean up." He joined Victor down on the dock. "How cold do you think that water is?"

Victor stuffed a handful of blackened cardboard tubes into the trash bag. "It's been running in the upper sixties, so still pretty chilly."

"Too cold for a quick swim then?"

"Not if you're a polar bear." Victor laughed.

"What if you're a fellow who thinks it's time a certain 'smart mouth' female got a little payback?"

Victor straightened slowly, his narrow-eyed gaze pinning Kellan in place. After a second, a sly smile formed. "Now that you mention it, Davis, the water might be precisely the right temperature for that kind of swim. She's been talking behind my back again, hasn't she?"

"Yep. And picking on me about my coffee."

"That's a given. Anyone she likes is fair game." Victor stuffed another handful of spent fireworks in the plastic sack, eyeing the water thoughtfully. "How're we going to work this?"

Kellan kept his back to the shore and his voice low. "Kind of thought we might just grab her and toss her in."

"Nah. Too clumsy. It needs more... finesse." Vic cast a measuring glance at Kellan then turned. "Hey, JoyAnne?"

"Yeah?"

"Give us a hand out here, would you?"

JoyAnne stood and applauded, throwing her head

back to utter the same ear-piercing whistle that had caught Kellan off guard in the theater the last night of KWESTT's tour.

He snickered. The woman didn't need coffee. She was already wound so tight she'd be downright dangerous on caffeine.

"Very funny, Squirt. That's not what I meant. Get over here."

She laughed all the way to the dock. "I'm coming, I'm coming. What's so difficult that you need a woman to solve it?"

"It's Davis's problem."

Kellan blinked. "It is?" The guy should have let him in on whatever plan he'd hatched.

"You wanted to ask her something?" Victor winked behind JoyAnne's back as she twisted to face Kellan in the early twilight.

This was Victor's idea of finesse? "Uh…"

Victor chuckled and shifted to lean slightly between them and point across the darkening lake. "Oh, wait. Do you see that over there?"

Kellan turned to follow his pointing finger even as a sudden suspicion raced through his brain. Before he could react, a large hand landed between his shoulder blades and pushed. The trap he'd walked into registered as he fell. He heard JoyAnne shout before cold water enveloped him and drowned out any sensation but shock.

Cold, *cold* shock.

(26)

*C*old! *Cold! Cold! Cold!*

JoyAnne broke the surface of the frigid lake, spitting water and swiping plastered strands of hair off her face. "Victor!"

Her cousin-in-law gripped his knees and howled. The water was absolutely freezing, and she should be thoroughly ticked off. Except Victor hadn't laughed like that since before Micah's death.

Not that she intended to let Victor know she wasn't mad. He deserved to sweat about retribution for a few days, but if someone had told her any of them would be able to laugh so wholeheartedly this month, she'd have said they were out of their heads.

A sputter and splash made her jerk around in the water. "Kel! Did he push you in, too?"

"No. I took my goldfish for a walk." He shook his head like a wet dog, spraying her grinning face.

"Hey!" She slapped the water and splashed him back. "I'm not a goldfish, and I'm wet enough already."

The fading light did nothing to hide the challenge on his face. "I don't think you are."

JoyAnne backpedaled. "I promise you I am. And this water's freezing. I'm getting out. Kel... What are you doing?"

He disappeared under the water, and JoyAnne grabbed for the dock, scrambling to get away from another dunking.

Arms grabbed her around the legs and tugged her under.

When she found her way to the top again and wiped the water out of her eyes, she saw him sitting on the edge of the dock laughing with Victor. *The traitor.*

JoyAnne swam to the dock, ignored both men's offered hands, and pushed herself up on it and glared at the hyenas grinning back at her. "Why do I get the feeling you two ganged up on me?" She crossed her arms to control the attack of shivers in the evening air.

"I always did say you were smart. A smart mouth." Victor smirked. "But it was his idea." He pointed to Kel.

Kel's unrepentant grin met her surprised glance. "You've been raggin' on us for days. But look at it this way; it took two of us to get you back. Although I'm not sure why I went for a swim, too." He frowned at Victor.

"Because I hate to see anyone suffer alone, and no one picks on JoyAnne without my permission."

"Thanks, Vic. Your chivalry astounds me."

JoyAnne glared at the unrepentant prankster, then a slow smile formed. "By the way, Kel. Have you ever wondered about the name of this place?"

"JoyAnne..." Victor growled, no longer grinning.

"You mean Wad-A-Wa? Sure I have. I figured it was some kind of old Indian word."

Joy laughed as Victor's warning glare strengthened. "Nope. Not an Indian word. A Victor word."

"Joy... you're gonna get another bath."

She scooted out of reach. "Uh uh. You started this."

"Fine. Get it over with then." Vic crossed his arms, a pained expression replacing the glare.

"Care to let me in on the joke?" Kellan's smile was confused.

"As a kid, Victor had a little trouble pronouncing certain words, and he loved playing in water. Didn't matter if it was the bathtub, a creek, or a mud hole in the back yard. The first time he saw Lake Dogwood, Dorothy says he got very quiet and had the most amazed expression on his face. Then in a voice of quiet awe, he said, "Wow! Wad a wa hole!""

Giggles spurted out of JoyAnne as Victor grimaced and realization dawned on Kel.

"What a water hole. Wad-A-Wa. I get it now." Kel chuckled, clearly enjoying Victor's discomfiture.

"Yep. I think Vic cringes every time he has to say the name of this place." JoyAnne laughed again.

Victor huffed a long-suffering sigh. "Give me a break. I was only three when it happened. And only four when they named this place. If I'd been a little older, I could've talked them out of the ridiculous name." He turned and stalked off the dock. "I'll go get you two drowned rats some towels."

"That's true." JoyAnne conceded, snickering. "Dorothy says by the time he was five he could talk anybody into anything."

"I can still hear you, Squirt." Victor groused over his shoulder, passing the empty chairs where George and Dorothy had been sitting. They must have retreated inside, out of danger of a possible escalation in the water war.

"Good. Maybe next time you'll think twice about pushing me into the lake." Kel's laughter rang out and JoyAnne turned on him, trying to squish her grin. "I can't believe you helped him try to drown me."

He shrugged, trying to look ashamed—which was hard to do when he was grinning like an idiot. "It was rather spur of the moment, but you can't say you didn't deserve it."

"I can, too." She crossed her arms and squinted up at him. "Especially after bringing you coffee this morning." The man deserved to be dunked again, but she'd have to go about it slowly since he was probably expecting her to get even.

"And made fun of me for needing it, if I recall correctly." He lifted an eyebrow.

Yeah. She had kind of done that. JoyAnne bit the inside of her lip. "But I got dunked twice and you only got dunked once." She stepped closer.

"Oh no, you don't." Davis wrapped his hands around her upper arms, holding her away from him. "You got dunked once by Victor and once by me. I say we're even."

"That doesn't seem quite fair, Kelby Cagney." She

pooched her bottom lip out and crossed her arms.

He shook his head at her newest guess as his eyes dropped to her mouth. His smile faded.

JoyAnne's heart rate doubled as he moved closer, heat flaring in his eyes.

"How do you come up with those names?" His whisper caressed her face.

She swallowed past a thick throat. "I just try to think of names bad enough you'd only want to use your initials."

His eyes lifted to meet hers. "Remind me not to let you name any children in the future."

The realization of what he said hit them at the same moment, and they froze, staring at each other without breathing.

Something flared in Kel's eyes. He leaned in.

JoyAnne knew what was coming but couldn't look away. And didn't try to stop it.

She didn't want to stop it.

His lips touched her cold ones and liquid heat poured through her. His hands slid down her wet arms to her elbows and then back up to her shoulders in slow, mesmerizing repetition. She uncrossed them and grasped the wet folds of shirt at his waist for support as he shifted his head to deepen the kiss.

Oh, she'd forgotten how nice it was to be kissed.

She stiffened, and her eyes flew open. What was she doing? She hadn't kissed anyone since Micah.

"JoyAnne?" Kel cradled her face, his breathing ragged, his nose a fraction of an inch from hers. "Do I need to apologize?"

"N...no. It... I... you surprised me." Her lowered gaze landed on her hands still fisted at his sides. She released him like a hot potato and stepped back. "I'm sorry."

"You caught me off guard, too, Joy." His arms dropped slowly to his sides but his eyes didn't release her. "I didn't come looking for anything but solitude. But... here you are."

She swallowed. "I... I don't know if I'm ready for... for..." JoyAnne shrugged. What exactly did he want? Especially after mentioning children. He'd surely meant it as a joke, but the thought did strange things to her insides.

"We can take it slow. But don't shut me out, Joy. You... You're something very special. I'd..." His chest rose, fell. "I'd like to see where this goes."

She lifted her chin, his shaky voice giving her courage. "I joke and tease a lot, but I come with a serious amount of baggage. I'm not sure *I* know how much I carry around."

"I'm not exactly baggage free myself. Maybe we could start by talking about our separate luggage?"

JoyAnne nodded slowly. "I think I can handle that." She hoped. But she'd never know until she tried.

The sliding patio door's wheels squeaked and JoyAnne shot a look over her shoulder.

Victor. With an armload of towels.

Oh, yeah. They were dripping wet. "We better dry off before we freeze to death." She turned to head for dry land and firmer footing.

"I'm not cold." Kel's low, mellow voice rumbled through her.

She wasn't cold either. For the first time in four years.

(27)

"Spike it, Joy! Spike it!"

Kellan whooped from the sidelines as JoyAnne followed her teammate's advice and drove the volleyball to the ground on the opposite side of the tall net for the point. The opposing team groaned, scooped it up, and fought on.

Instead of following the spirited back-and-forth game, Kellen's eyes remained fixed on the owner of the curly brunette ponytail. She played as hard as she worked. It showed in the sand on her knees and the red, sequined-flag tank top that clung damply to her sides. She was a lot of fun to watch play, and he couldn't help but wish she wasn't quite such a conscientious worker.

The holiday weekend was supposed to be just that—a holiday. But when you ran a campground on a recreational lake, a holiday meant double, maybe triple, the work. He'd thought they'd been busy earlier in the week while preparing for the rush. He'd been wrong.

Friday and Saturday, the campground had turned into a zoo. On steroids. Every conceivable place for a tent, popup camper, RV, and boat trailer was full. And then there were the horse trailers. When Wad-A-Wa said they allowed pets, they meant it. Big pets. The square welded-pipe pens he'd noticed while mowing around the pasture were outdoor stalls for those who wanted to camp with their horses and trail ride during the day.

Kellan leaned back on his hands, continuing to watch the fiercely friendly volleyball game. After kissing JoyAnne on Thursday night, he'd planned to spirit her away from the holiday festivities and take her someplace they could talk in private. And he would explain who he was and why he'd kept his identity a secret so long.

His lips twisted wryly. How naïve he'd been. There hadn't been one free moment for anything besides food and sleep. Between the registration and settling in of guests and the inevitable snafus and problems to troubleshoot, there'd been daily scavenger hunts, timed hikes, swim races at the beach, water balloon wars, and volleyball tournaments. And in the evenings, hayrides and hotdog and marshmallow roasts. The activities were a long-standing tradition that brought families back year after year.

Sunday morning, a sunrise service had been held beneath a large grapevine arbor by the lake—it had been surprisingly well-attended. And tonight, the Memorial Day festivities would be concluded and crowned with a fireworks display over the lake.

He'd thought nightly runs of KWESTT shows were hard work. The Barretts, their summer staff, and JoyAnne, had proven him wrong. Wad-A-Wa well deserved the title of happiest campground in the state and had earned every rave review he'd overheard the last couple of days. And he'd have enjoyed every second if he could have spent a few more of them with Joy.

It was an exquisite form of torture to be so near her yet be unable to discuss that foundation-shaking kiss— or repeat it. His agent was expecting a decision tomorrow, and he'd been unable to spare a thought about it for wondering what JoyAnne's reaction would be when he finally revealed the other side of his identity.

Kellan nudged the brim of his ball cap up half an inch and readjusted his sunglasses. JoyAnne liked KWESTT. So finding out that K. C. Davis was Kellan Campbell would be a good thing. Right?

"You got something you want to tell me, Davis?"

Kellan flinched and jerked toward the source of the quiet question. When had Victor sat down beside him? "What?"

Steely gray eyes studied him before flicking toward JoyAnne then back to him. "What's going on between you and her?"

Kellan's heart rate slowed. "Is it any of your business?"

"Yes. She's family. And by the looks passing between you two the last couple of days, something else happened Thursday night besides a cold swim."

A smile quirked Kellan's mouth. Yeah. That might

be the understatement of the year.

"I don't think I like that look in your eyes, Davis."

"Jealous?" Kellan prodded.

Anger flared in the judge's eyes. "Micah was the only brother I've ever had. JoyAnne was his wife and is like my sister. A sister I love dearly, but a *sister!*" Victor's growl contrasted sharply with the cheers of those gathered to watch the volleyball game.

Kellan dropped his chin. "Sorry, Man. Wasn't sure where you stood."

"Now you do." Victor's jaw flexed as he focused on JoyAnne. "We've had a rough few years. We're doing better, but I want to see her genuinely happy again. Vibrant. Like she was with Micah. Not forcing the emotion to make those around her more comfortable. Maybe you're part of the solution, but what I know about you wouldn't fill two sides of an index card." He turned his hard, searching eyes back to Kellan. "If you hurt her, I'll put you away. Do you understand me?"

"Perfectly." Kellan kept his voice calm. "I fully intend to tell JoyAnne more about myself as soon as I get a chance to talk with her longer than five minutes."

Victor's jawline softened.

"And though I wish I could promise never to hurt her, it's impossible. I'm human. I mess up." He already had.

"Not acceptable." The judge's jaw was rock hard again.

"I *can* promise you this," Kellan continued as if he'd not been interrupted. "The thought of hurting JoyAnne is as repugnant to me as it is to you."

They ignored the fresh outburst of cheers around

them, neither one backing down from the challenge in the other's eyes.

"Hey! Who said you two could have a staring contest in the middle of our brilliant victory?"

Cold drops of water splashed Kellan's bare shins, jerking him out of the silent standoff. JoyAnne stood over him and Victor, eyeing them curiously as she drank from a cold, sweating water bottle.

"We're deciding who gets the honor of the opening serve." Victor shot to his feet and squished Joy in a quick hard hug. "Enjoy your moment of glory, Squirt. You play us next." He pointed a finger at JoyAnne's nose but flashed a quick glance at Kellan. "You're going down."

"Dream on, Vic. We'll wipe the sand with you."

"I believe that's what you said last year." Victor slid his sunglasses from the top of his head onto his nose and shot her a grin before heading toward the dining pavilion with the rest of the crowd to get some fresh watermelon and cookies before the final game of the volleyball tournament commenced.

JoyAnne plopped down beside Kellan and blew out a big breath. "Whew!"

Kellan twisted so he could see her better. "Running out of energy?"

She lowered her water bottle and narrowed her eyes. "Not on your life. We've got plenty left in the tank to take on you and Victor's team. It's our turn to win that trophy this year."

Kellan lifted his hands. "Save your trash talk for Victor. I'm just here to enjoy the scenery." He let his eyes run over her relaxed frame without lingering over any area in particular. He wanted her to feel admired, not leered at.

Her sun-kissed cheeks grew a little rosier and she dropped her gaze. "What was that between you and Victor anyway?"

"Nothing but a slight difference of opinion." He shrugged it off.

She raised her eyes to his. "Me?"

Kellan hesitated then quirked his lips on a sudden spurt of humor. "I think someone's having a hard time dealing with the fact I kissed you."

JoyAnne choked on another swallow of water. "He... he knows?"

"Not for sure, but I think he's suspicious." Kellan's gaze tracked past her to where Victor watched them from beneath the shade of the pavilion.

She followed Kellan's focus then whipped right back around, eyes squeezed shut. "Oh, dear."

Her delightful embarrassment increased Kellan's enjoyment of the situation. "Shall we prove his suspicions right?"

Startled hazel eyes met his. "No!" She swallowed hard and lowered her voice. "Umm... no. Not here."

Kellan's grin exploded and he bounced to his feet and grabbed her hand, hauling her upright. "Then let's go someplace else. I think the barn must be pretty quiet about now."

She pulled her hand free, cheeks flaming. "Don't be silly. The final game of the tournament is in twenty minutes."

"I admit, it's not a lot of time, but it's plenty for say... two or three kisses."

"Would you hush?" A shy grin lit her eyes even as she tried to frown at him. "I'm trying to be serious."

"So am I, Joy." He dropped the teasing and lowered his voice. "I do want to kiss you again." He inhaled deeply then released it. "But we should probably do some serious talking first."

A pleased, tentative smile played around JoyAnne's tempting lips as she nodded, eyes darting to and from his.

"How about we go for a moonlight drive and some ice cream after the fireworks tonight?" He'd noticed on their sign that The Creamery would be open until midnight on Memorial Day. "Can you get away then?" Equal parts fear and impatience amped his pulse. She might order him off the place afterwards and not give him another chance—wouldn't Victor love to enforce that? But for their relationship to grow past the initial stages of attraction, he had to tell her the rest of the story about himself.

"Probably. As long as nothing bends or breaks between now and then."

"Let Victor handle it."

"Okay."

"It's a date then." And, hopefully, not their last.

"It's a date." She agreed softly. Then her eyes twinkled. "But first, I have a volleyball tournament to win. I hope you're not a sore loser."

Kellan shook his head. This woman who'd lived through so much pain could make him smile like no one else. "I don't intend to lose." The game or *her*. Not without a fight.

(28)

"*U*mph!" JoyAnne landed on her rump with a thud.

"You okay?" Kel ducked under the net as one of her teammates ran for the volleyball Kel had successfully slammed past JoyAnne's defense.

She'd jumped hard to block it, but her reach had been too short, and she'd body-slammed into Kel on the other side of the net before hitting the ground.

"I'm fine." She accepted his hand and stood, brushing the sand off the seat of her shorts.

"Sorry about that. I didn't mean to run you down." He hovered over her, concern etching his forehead. He wore his almost ever-present sunglasses, but his ball cap was turned backwards to keep the brim from blocking his view during the game.

He was cute. And she wasn't the only female that

had noticed. But thankfully, they had seemed content with just an appreciative glance before returning their attention to the game, to their spouse or boyfriend, or to a child needing their attention.

"All part of the game. Now get back on your side so we can finish beating you."

"Yeah, get over here, Davis. Your flirting's holding up the game." Victor grumbled.

"Sorry." Kel ducked backwards under the net, keeping an eye on her.

Was it her imagination or were his cheeks the slightest shade of pink at the chuckles from their teammates? JoyAnne's grin widened. "S'Okay." His discomfiture emboldened her and she dropped one eyelid in a slight wink to reassure him.

He stumbled and blinked, not reacting as the ball sailed over his head, headed deep into his side of the court.

"Get your head in the game." Victor slugged Kel's shoulder as another team member hit the ball back over to JoyAnne's side.

Hmm… So her wink had distracted him, had it? The game had been tight with neither side gaining more than a point over the other. But she might have just discovered an ace up her sleeve.

The players rotated around the court as the game continued at a furious pace, each side determined to win. JoyAnne returned to the front line as "Set point!" was called. Her team served the ball. She split her focus between it and Kel, heart racing. Her chance came within seconds. Victor set up the ball for Kel to slam it across the net, but Kel made the mistake of checking JoyAnne's position before attacking the ball.

She winked again and jumped to block it.

Kel slapped the ball.

Into the top of the net.

It bounced harmlessly to the ground on his side.

JoyAnne's team broke into cheers and high-fives as Victor's team groaned in defeat. After a few minutes of back slapping, fist bumps, and good-natured congratulations from the losing side, the players dispersed to take it easy after the hard-fought tussle.

JoyAnne turned from talking to one of the players and nearly slammed into Kel. She grinned up at him and stuck out her hand. "Good game, K. C."

He crossed his arms. "Mm hmm." He'd twisted his hat around correctly, and it was hard to read his expression beneath its shadow and the dark glasses.

JoyAnne reached up, hooked her finger over the top of the glasses, and tugged them down to see his eyes. "Are you being a sore loser?"

He blinked at her unexpected action then cocked his head, his lips twisting to one side. "You cheated."

JoyAnne raised her eyebrows. "How in the world did I do that?"

"You winked at me, and you know it." His eyes sparkled.

A gurgle of laughter broke free. "We don't play by the strictest volleyball rules so maybe they've changed since we last checked. Is winking not allowed now?"

Kel dropped his chin and tried not to smile. "You did it on purpose to fluster me and make me choke at the most inopportune moment. Victor is going to have my hide for losing the game."

"So my winking flusters you, huh?" JoyAnne's cheeks ached from grinning so big.

Chocolate-colored eyes narrowed but laughter danced in them. "Keep it up, Joy, and I won't be the only one flustered."

JoyAnne's heart skipped a beat. It would be prudent to back down before her teasing spiraled out of control. She stepped out of the sand pit and picked up her bottle of water. "Winking doesn't fluster me." The retort came out before she could stop it.

A hand touched her lower back and slid around the curve of her waist.

JoyAnne swallowed hard, glad she hadn't taken a drink. She'd have probably drowned herself.

"No. But I can think of something else that will." Kel tugged her closer.

She scuttled away from him, sputtering and trying to clear her throat. If she didn't put some space between them, she'd lose all sense of propriety and let him carry out the promise of retaliation warming his eyes. "I think—" She coughed. "I think I'd better go make sure everything's ready for the firework show."

Kel inched closer. "I think we've got plenty of fireworks right here, Joy."

Every inch of her skin prickled with awareness, and she put more distance between them. "Playing with fireworks is a good way to get burned."

"Afraid of a little heat?" His smug grin revealed his enjoyment of her sudden nervousness.

She nodded decisively. "Yes. And that's why I'm getting out of the kitchen while the getting's good. If you need something to do, go see if Victor needs a hand with setting up for tonight. I'm going to go... someplace else." JoyAnne spun on her heel and jogged toward the gator loaded down with spare lawn chairs.

She bounded onto the seat and turned the key, flinching when a hand landed on her arm.

"It was a good game, JoyAnne Daye." Kel grinned at her. "And I had fun."

Her heart rate settled a fraction. "I did, too, Kelvin Costner Davis. You're a good sport."

"Nope. Still wrong, Brat. I'm biding my time until there aren't so many witnesses, but I fully intend to collect for that wink." He dropped his own eyelid in a slow move before stepping away from the vehicle. "I'll see you tonight, JoyAnne."

Her foot smashed the accelerator and she nearly gave herself whiplash getting away from the man who made her heart race, her skin tingle, and her head spin. Tonight was a bad idea. A bad, bad, bad idea.

The man was an enigma and scared her to death. She knew next to nothing about his life outside the bounds of Wad-a-Wa. Inside those boundaries, she knew he was a gentleman and a hard worker. He'd saved her many hours of extra labor over the last week, pitching in and working longer and harder than some of her paid staff.

And he had a relationship with God. Besides praying while they waited for news of Uncle George at the hospital and asking the blessing over several of the meals they'd shared since, he'd carried a worn Bible with him to the brush arbor service the previous morning and seemed very familiar with using it—not having to hunt for any of the referenced verses.

Little as she knew about the rest of his life, she instinctively trusted him. The problem was herself. She feared her reaction to him. She feared falling in love again. And the changes that might entail. Therefore, spending any more time alone with the man was not a smart idea.

At all.

But she wasn't going anywhere dripping with sweat. Victor and the rest of the staff could handle the place for a few minutes. Sand clung to her sticky skin and any trace of makeup had melted under the sun hours ago. A shower and fresh clothes—maybe a cute sundress—would make this evening's closing festivities much more enjoyable.

She'd hate to mess up Kel's fancy car with the rank smell of sweat or leave sand all over its leather interior.

Thought you said it was a bad idea.

JoyAnne bumped over a rough spot in the road and whizzed up the lane to the house. "I changed my mind. It is a woman's prerogative after all."

(29)

*S*tage fright. The worst case he'd had in years. That's what was wrong with him.

Kellan licked dry lips with an equally parched tongue. Thankfully, JoyAnne didn't seem to be aware of his nervousness as she sat beside him on a worn quilt at the edge of the assembled crowd. Then again, she had no idea what he intended to confess to her as soon as they weren't surrounded by sunburnt vacationers and sugar-high children, or surreptitiously watched by members of her family.

Lord, forgive me keeping my identity secret longer than I should have, and help her to forgive me for not telling her sooner.

Why had he thought it so important to remain incognito this long? The roiling in his gut warned him that decision had the potential to blow up in his face with the same spectacular and painful effects as holding an active Roman candle by the wrong end.

An explosion of light over the lake lit up JoyAnne's upturned face and drew appreciative murmurs from those gathered on the slope between the beach-access parking lot and the lake's edge. Tense as his insides were, he couldn't help but smile in response to her delight at the colorful sight. The woman had bowled him over from the first moment they'd met face to face and he hadn't stopped tumbling yet.

He shifted his legs out of the path of a group of youngsters playing tag through the obstacle course of lawn chairs and blankets scattered across the slope and draped his arm around Joy's shoulders. Like him, she'd obviously showered after their spirited game, and a light floral scent teased his nose and enticed him closer.

He felt a shiver run over her and he hugged her a little tighter. "Chilly?" The breeze coming off the lake was cool but it felt good to him after a day spent in the hot sun. And it was a great excuse to keep his arm around her.

She shook her head, keeping her face turned toward the pyrotechnic show.

"I don't think I told you how nice you look this evening." A slight understatement. The sleeveless, knee-length, fitted dress of blue and white striped fabric was probably meant to be simple and cool, but the sight of JoyAnne in it had robbed him of breath. The woman looked good in her everyday work clothes and ponytail. In a dress with her hair pulled softly away from her face and waving down her back, she blew him away. And made him want to punch every fellow whose gaze had followed her a little too long when she'd walked across the grassy lawn of the fireworks viewing area to find him.

"Thank you."

He leaned his head towards hers to hear her quiet words through the noise. "You smell good, too." Going off alone with her in the dark would be too much temptation if the whole purpose of the jaunt wasn't to answer the riddle of his initials. That conversation would effectively kill any romance. And he wanted her in his car where she couldn't get up and leave until he'd told her the whole story.

"So do you."

The low response accompanied by a brief, warm glance that held an endearing trace of shyness made Kellan's chest swell. But dread spiraled through the warm pressure. *Lord, help us get past this next hurdle.* He'd built it with his own hands but there was no way he could remove it safely without divine help.

Kellan held JoyAnne against his side as the explosive show reached its finale and lit up the sky in a storm of colored flashes and rolling thunder. After tonight, it might be a while before she'd let him this close again. He planned to take advantage of every second.

Applause and whistles approved the impressive Memorial Day tribute as people stood and began to gather their belongings. JoyAnne hopped to her feet leaving Kellan's arms cold and empty, but she immediately stuck out her palm and tugged him to his feet.

He held onto her hand. "How quickly can you get away, and what can I do to make it faster? My car's up in the parking lot and we can leave from here if you don't have to take your UTV back."

The glow from the parking lot lights touched her face allowing him to see the nervousness in her quick grin. "No. Dorothy can drive it back, but I have to give her the key and want to make sure everyone returns to their vehicles safely. We've never had any serious problems, but we've had a few incidents that might have gone sideways if we hadn't been keeping an eye on things."

"Then what can I do to help?" He squeezed her fingers.

She licked her lips and tugged her hand free. Leaning down, she pulled a flashlight out of the small tote bag she'd dropped onto the quilt earlier. "Uh... why don't you direct the golf cart drivers back to the gravel service lane so they're not competing with the bigger automobiles for room on the blacktop drive?"

"I think I can handle that." He winked and brushed the back of her hand with his fingers as he took the light.

"O...okay. Sounds good. I... I'll meet you by the parking lot in a... a few minutes then."

"Deal." Kellan grinned at his flustered lady before spinning on his heel and jogging toward the golf carts. The sooner this crowd dispersed, the sooner he could start clearing that hurdle between his and JoyAnne's future.

"Those of you with golf carts... remember to turn on your headlights and take the gravel service drive back to the main campground." Kellan raised his voice to be heard over the chatter of people making their way through the corner of the parking lot sectioned off for the low speed vehicles. "Now drive carefully and have a good evening." He flipped on his flashlight to direct drivers to the correct exit.

"Bobby? Where are you?" A woman hollered from across the parking lot, twisting her head back and forth.

"Here I am. I'm coming." The high-pitched voice sounded near Kellan and he jerked around to find the source.

A small boy darted from the shadows of a parked SUV and dashed toward his mother. Right into the path of a campground guest's private ATV speeding toward the service drive entrance.

"Stop!" Kellan's feet flew into action as he shouted at the little boy and the driver who was paying more attention to his glowing smart phone than his surroundings. "Stop!"

The little boy skidded to a halt, glancing at Kellan in confusion. Kellan sprinted faster. The driver still hadn't looked up from his phone to see the child directly in line with his vehicle.

Kellan dove for the boy, wrapping him in his arms to protect him from the inevitable fall as he carried him out of the line of the small-but-powerful vehicle.

Fire ignited in Kellan's leg and knocked him rolling. He tightened his arms and curled around the boy. His head slammed into something, restarting the pyrotechnic show behind his eyelids as the tumbling world finally squealed to a stop.

Only… the squealing didn't stop.

Squinting through the blinding pain, Kellan peered down at the blurry child. "Are you… alright?"

"That was fun. Can we do it again?" The boy bounced against Kellan's chest, giggling happily.

He chuckled through a groan. "Sorry. Only one per customer." The keening sound grew louder in his ears. He closed his eyes, trying to block it out.

"Bobby, Bobby, Bobby!"

The boy wiggled free, and Kellan melted against the warm pavement as too many head-piercing voices swirled around him.

"You, call 9-1-1!" Hands touched him, running along his neck, back. His legs.

A guttural sound scraped through Kellan's throat as the fire in his leg blazed into an inferno.

"Easy. Help's on the way. Just lay still, Buddy."

Not moving sounded like a really good plan.

"Kel!"

The frantic cry tugged at Kellan's heavy lids. "Joy?"

"I'm here, Kel." Gentle fingers touched his cheek. "Open your eyes and stay with us, okay?"

He squinted at the blurry forms leaning over him. "Joy, I need to... need to talk to you..."

"Yes, keep talking to me, Kel, until the ambulance gets here." Her voice sounded funny. Thick. And cracked.

"Are you crying?" The tall security lights behind her head put her face in the shadows.

"No." She sniffed. "My eyes are just taking a quick shower."

His eyes drifted shut with the effort of grinning. "That's terrible."

"I know. Sorry." She sniffed.

"Joy," he took a breath and the world spun again. "Don't worry. I'll be... okay. Just banged up..."

(30)

"*K*el!" JoyAnne patted his cheek, but his eyes remained closed and he didn't move. "Don't go to sleep. Stay with me."

When he still didn't respond, her eyes flew upward to scan the expression of the older gentleman kneeling on the other side of Kel's body, checking the pulse in his wrist.

No! Don't think body *like he's already gone*! *He's not! Lord, why do you keep asking me to go through this?*

"How far out is that ambulance?" The man looked up at Victor who hovered over them, phone to his ear.

"About ten minutes. How's he doing?"

"He's unconscious. His leg is scraped up and might be broken, and he sustained a pretty solid blow to the

214

head when he landed." He laid his fingers on Kel's neck. "His pulse is steady—which is a good sign—but I'll be happy when those EMTs show up. Somebody hand me a blanket. We need to keep him warm in case he goes into shock."

Victor relayed the information to the 9-1-1 operator.

JoyAnne clung to Kel's hand, the older gentleman's calmness numbing some of her initial panic. All the campground employees knew basic first aid skills and CPR, but she was thankful for this stranger and his quickness to the scene. Because right know she would be hard-pressed to remember how to apply a Band-Aid. "How did this happen?"

Several voices began to speak at once but Victor quickly hushed them as George appeared with a blanket.

The older gentleman helped spread the thick fabric over Kellan. "A little boy ran out in front of an inattentive driver. This young man's quick action got the boy out of harm's way, but he didn't get himself completely clear of it and took the blow to his right leg."

JoyAnne tried not to think about the bloody handkerchief that had covered Kellan's shin before the blanket had hidden it from view. He'd been wearing cargo shorts, leaving his lower legs bare and without a shred of protection from the blow. "Will he be alright?" Her voice shook.

The gray-haired senior reached across and patted her shoulder reassuringly. "I'm not a doctor, but I saw a lot of boys hurt back in 'Nam and picked up some first aid. This fella needs a bit of patching up, but I think he's going to be fine."

She managed a tight nod but didn't feel any better. It was awful to have to watch a loved one suffer when all you could do was sit and wait for help.

Loved one?

She ignored the question. *Lord, haven't I already had more than my share of pain and waiting for bad news?*

"I think I hear them." Victor lowered his phone to listen.

JoyAnne strained her ears and finally heard the faint wail through the clear evening air as the people gathered around them grew silent.

Victor and George went into action. "Step back, everyone. We need to clear this area so the ambulance can get through."

The last minutes of waiting dragged by in an agonizing blur of sounds as she focused on Kel's face—too pale in the glow of the tall parking lot lamps—a wordless prayer wringing from her heart.

"Excuse me, Ma'am. I need you to move aside." A stocky woman gently pushed JoyAnne out of the way to kneel at Kel's side, the reflective letters on her navy t-shirt announcing her profession as EMT.

Victor wrapped an arm around JoyAnne, and they silently watched the emergency personnel assets Kel's injuries while questioning the man who'd rendered first aid. Then they clamped a cervical collar around Kel's neck, strapped him to a long backboard, lifted him onto a gurney, and rolled him into the open doors of the flashing ambulance.

She jerked out of her daze when the doors slapped shut. "Wait. I want to go with him."

Victor held her back as the boxy vehicle pulled away. "I'll drive you there. We'll be right behind them."

"Judge Barrett? What happened here?"

JoyAnne blinked at the county deputy standing in front of them.

She felt Victor shrug. "I don't know. I didn't see it."

"I did, Officer." The calm veteran spoke up. "I can tell you what you need to know and who you need to talk to."

George stepped forward. "Victor, you take JoyAnne to the hospital. We'll finish up here with the deputy and then meet you there."

"Okay. Come on, Joy. My truck's on the other side of the lot." He pointed and JoyAnne took off at a run for the silver automobile.

They caught up with the flashing emergency vehicle on the county highway, and Victor lowered his speed and tucked in behind it. Silence filled the cab of the truck.

"He'll be okay, Joy."

She gritted her teeth. "Why does this keep happening, Vic?"

Victor's hands tightened around the steering wheel. "I don't know. I guess because we live in a broken world. And until Jesus returns to fix it, we can't escape pain."

"But I don't want to go through this again." It had nearly destroyed her before. She couldn't handle it again.

"JoyAnne breathe! That's not Micah up there." Victor's voice rapped through the dark cab.

She took a shallow breath. "I know who it is, Vic. But I lo… like him and he's hurt. Really hurt."

Vic glanced at her sharply before returning his eyes to the road. "Micah was as close to a brother as I'll ever have, but he's gone, Joy. And he's not coming back. It's okay to love someone else." He spoke slowly, deliberately. But his voice rasped a little. "And K. C.'s not dying. He'll be fine."

"But what if he's not? Life doesn't always have a happy ending."

"Stop it, JoyAnne!" Victor snapped on the overhead dome light.

She blinked in the unexpected brightness. "I'm sorry. I'm sorry. I know I'm panicking." She curled her fingers tighter into her palms, desperately trying to hang onto her sanity. *Jesus, help me! I should be praying for Kel and the EMTs working on him, but all I can think about is losing someone else I care for.*

Victor began praying out loud.

JoyAnne latched onto the words that lessened her swelling panic. *Father God, help me. I don't want to do this again. I'm not supposed to lose anybody else until George and Dorothy are old and gray.*

Let go.

The simple command whispered through her soul and arrested the fear. She stared out the windshield at the lights of the hospital. Let go of what?

Everything. I'll catch you.

She shook her head and piled out of the truck as Victor slammed it into park and raced toward the ER entrance. The last few years had taught her to dig in her heels and hold on to what she had left. She couldn't let go. If she did, she risked losing it all. And then she'd shatter. Into a million irreparable pieces.

JoyAnne skidded up to the Emergency Room desk. "The ambulance just brought in a man who was injured out at the campground..."

"Just a minute..." The nurse checked her computer screen. "K. C. Davis?"

"Yes. How is he?"

"I'll have someone come talk to you as soon as they can. Until then, you can fill out some paperwork for me." She slapped a clipboard onto the countertop.

JoyAnne took it, grateful for something to do. Until she scanned the stack of blank forms. "I... I don't know the answer to most of these." In fact, she really only knew his name. And not his full one at that. Why had she let her heart fall for a man she barely knew? "Since it happened on our property, our insurance will pay for it, but if I had his wallet, I might be able to fill in the rest of the blanks." For the hospital as well as herself.

The nurse tapped a few more keys and frowned at the monitor. "He apparently doesn't have anything with him. Just a car key."

"Why wouldn't he have his wallet with him? We were supposed to go..." Her voice trailed away as she caught the nurse's curious gaze on her.

Victor touched JoyAnne's shoulder. "Was his Mercedes in that parking lot?"

She nodded. "He said it was."

"Then his wallet might be still in his car. I leave mine in the glove compartment sometimes when I don't want to sit on it. I'll call Dad and have him look for it."

"But they don't have a car key and if Kel did leave it in his car, it's probably locked."

Victor turned and smiled at the nurse after a

surreptitious check of her name tag. "Good Evening, Melissa. I'm Judge Barrett. Co-owner of Wad-A-Wa Campground where Mr. Davis was injured. Do you think you could have someone get us that car key so we can get your forms filled out with as much information as we can?"

The nurse blinked and an enchanted smile cracked her weary-looking face. "Of course, Judge Barrett. It may take a few minutes but I'll see what I can do."

"Thank you, Melissa. I appreciate it." Victor's smile widened.

JoyAnne rolled her eyes and picked up the pen and clipboard. "I'll be over there." She pointed to a waiting room chair. Not that the nurse was paying any attention to her.

Five minutes dragged by as she read through the pages, growing acutely more aware of how little she knew about the man who'd stolen her heart in just a few weeks' time.

"I've got his key. You want me to go find his wallet or sit here with you?"

She looked up at Victor. "I'm okay now. I'd rather you be working on solving this problem."

Victor nodded. "Be back ASAP."

"Be careful, Vic. No more accidents."

He leaned down and gave her a hug. "I will. And you stop worrying."

Easier said than accomplished. She leaned her head against the wall behind her chair after he left and tried not to think as people came and went past her.

When that didn't work, she people-watched, counted the squares on the industrial carpet, carefully printed Kel's initials and last name at the top of the forms, watched nurses and other hospital staff come and go—and hold whispered conferences with each other behind the front desk.

JoyAnne convulsively tapped the pen against her thigh when she intercepted more strange glances from the nurses who huddled around the receptionist, whispering. Was something worse with Kel? Or were they simply aggravated at the delay in getting their precious forms filled out?

She turned her attention to the large wall clock and focused on counting the ticks of the second hand. She'd lost count and started over five different times before Victor rushed back through the sliding doors, George and Dorothy on his heels. A sigh released some of the buildup of pressure in her chest. She stood to greet them. Tensed.

Victor wasn't walking. He was stomping. And the glint in his eye and hard set to his jaw tightened her stomach.

"What's wrong?" She really, *really* couldn't take any more bad news.

He jerked to a halt in front of her, flipped opened a black leather wallet, extracted a card. Thrust it at her.

She read the name of a health insurance company at the top and shook her head. "We're going to use our insurance since he was working for us when the accident happened."

Vic's jaw tightened. "Read it."

She frowned and studied him a second before lowering her eyes to the card. It took two tries for the words to make sense.

Breath whooshed from her and the card fell from her nerveless fingers.

The whispers and stares from the nurses suddenly made sense.

(31)

"*H*ow are you feeling this morning, Mr. Davis?"

The doctor's penlight raked across Kellan's eyes and he squinted against the pain. "Like I've been run over. It's impossible to sleep around this place."

The doctor chuckled and stuck the torture device into the chest pocket of his white coat. "Sorry about that. But you have a mild concussion, and waking you up every couple of hours to ask random questions is all part of the fun."

"Remind me to not have another concussion." Kellan grimaced, his skull still protesting the bright light.

"I'll add it to your discharge orders." The doctor grinned and jotted a note before asking several questions similar to the ones the night nurse had bothered him with multiple times. Apparently, Kellan answered them satisfactorily and the doctor nodded before checking the bandages on Kellan's leg. "I want to see you in my office in a few days—the nurse can set up the appointment for you. By then the lacerations on your shin should be healed enough to transition you to a hard cast. But until then, absolutely no weight on that leg. It's braced, but stay off it."

"How long do I have to wear a cast after that?" If he'd been told last night, he couldn't remember. In fact, he couldn't remember much of anything after launching himself toward the little boy. George and Dorothy might have come into his room, but he could've dreamed it, too. He didn't remember seeing JoyAnne, though.

"We'll see how fast a healer you are, but typically six to eight weeks. You're lucky. The fracture wasn't near your knee or ankle, so it didn't require surgery."

The pain throbbing through his head and radiating up his leg didn't feel lucky. But according to the nurse, he'd kept the boy from being hurt so he didn't regret it.

"I'll get the discharge paperwork started and as soon as the nurse comes in to help you dress and go over your restrictions and care of your injuries, you can go home." He tucked his pen in his pocket and headed toward the door.

Home. The idea sounded wonderful. Especially if it included people like George and Dorothy. Even Victor. But most importantly… JoyAnne. "Thanks, Doctor."

"You're welcome." He opened the door and looked back at Kellan. "Feel up for some company while you're waiting for your nurse to return?"

Kellan started to nod then thought better of it.

"Yes."

"You can go on in." The doctor disappeared from view, and Joy entered the room.

The same emotion shot through Kellan's chest, immediately improving his headache. He pushed himself higher against the pillows the nurse had propped behind him earlier and let his eyes absorb the woman standing just inside the small room. She looked like she'd had a rough night, too.

Remorse for being the cause of it dampened the spurt of happiness. "I can't remember much from last night. Was anyone else hurt?"

She shook her head and walked a step closer, face tight. "How are you feeling?"

"Better now that you're here." He smiled at her, hoping to reassure her. Ease the strain around her mouth.

It didn't work. Her chin lifted and she crossed her arms over her ribs as if finding the air conditioned room too chilly. "So... K. C. Davis. Maybe your initials don't stand for an awful combination of names after all. Like Kentucky *Chicken*." A muscle along her cheek twitched.

Kellan froze. His brain was foggy from the goose egg on it and the pain medication, but he was beginning to catch on to the fact JoyAnne was mad.

"Or maybe you were just experimenting with the local yokel to see how big a fool you could make her." She finally approached his bed. "I'm sure you had a great big laugh at how well you succeeded." She lifted her hand and flung the object she carried onto his chest. "Kellan Campbell."

The name slapped him across the face. He closed

his eyes. "Joy... I—"

"You lied to me! About what you did. Who you are. Was it all a lie? No! Don't even try to explain. You've had more than enough time for that." She whirled and flew from the room, leaving behind a hint of perfume and a wave of remorse.

Kellan groaned as he clutched at the wallet she'd hurled at him. He'd been an idiot to think he could keep his identity a secret. An idiot for not telling her earlier. An idiot for ignoring his nagging conscience.

Victor burst through the door that had barely stopped moving from JoyAnne's hasty exit.

He groaned again. "Go ahead and kill me. Maybe I'll feel better."

Victor stomped to the end of the bed, glaring. "Don't tempt me, Mr. *Davis*. If you weren't already in a hospital bed, it would be extremely difficult to resist putting you in one. I'd like to wring your neck for lying to JoyAnne and putting her through more pain."

"Victor. That's enough. Leave the poor man alone." George entered the room, Dorothy right behind him.

Another wave of guilt submerged Kellan. "I'm sorry. It was never my intention to lie to all of you or hurt any of you. I handled this all wrong."

Victor's frown deepened. "You can say that again."

George looked stern but curious. "Why didn't you tell us your real name sooner, Son? Did you not think you could trust us to guard your privacy?"

"No!" Kellan winced at the volume of his voice and lowered it. "I used to go by K. C. in school, and it's easier to have a restful vacation if I'm not recognized. Not trusting you had nothing to do with why I didn't tell you—at least, not after the first few days. It was just… it was nice to be plain old K. C. Davis again for a change. Not Kellan Campbell of KWESTT."

"Except you *are* Kellan Campbell of KWESTT." Victor snapped. "One of Joy's favorite groups—*why* I don't know—and you've done exactly what I told you not to. Hurt her."

Kellan gripped his throbbing temples between his fingers. "That wasn't my intention. And I planned to tell her last night after the fireworks display. Only—"

"Too little, too late. I knew something was off with you from the first, but she wouldn't listen to me, and I backed off." Victor's hands curled into fists.

"That's enough." Dorothy took Victor's arm and turned him toward the door. "Victor. You take JoyAnne home and get the spare bedroom ready."

Victor stared at his mother. "What for?"

"Because I asked you to and because Kellan's coming home with us."

"What?" Victor and Kellan blurted the same question.

"No, Mom."

"I didn't ask your opinion, Vic. Do what I said." The small woman shoved her protesting son through the door and pulled it shut. "Now. When are they releasing you, Mr. Davis?" She returned to the edge of Kellan's bed.

He shook his head. "That's not necessary. I'll get a motel room until I can fly back to California." It wasn't home but it would have to do. His chances of having anything like that in the foreseeable future had died a quick death due to his secrecy. He'd never stood a chance, really.

Dorothy crossed her arms and pinned Kellan with a stern look. "You can't drive and I highly doubt the doctor will give you permission to fly across the country before you have a real cast on. You're coming home with us. Where you belong."

"As much as I would love to, I don't belong there." The admission knifed through his heart. "I won't make it any harder on JoyAnne than I already have."

George slipped an arm around Dorothy's shoulder. "I do think you should have told us who you were a lot sooner, but I think I can understand why you didn't. And I think our house is the best place for you *and* JoyAnne right now. She's been hiding from the risk of being hurt again long enough. You brought out something in her we haven't seen since Micah died. As much as she wants to shove you away right now, she's not going to get that chance. She needs to face up to the possibilities of what could be between you."

Kellan's cheeks warmed. "I don't deserve another chance."

"None of us deserve second chances," Dorothy patted his shoulder, "but God gives them anyway. So. You're coming home with us and no more arguments."

Kellan held her gaze and then looked at George. "Only if you'll forgive me for not being completely up front with you. It was wrong of me and I'm sorry." *So very sorry.*

"Done." George stuck out his hand and gripped Kellan's.

Dorothy leaned over and kissed Kellan's cheek. "You're forgiven, Kel."

Kellan's eyes burned, but a sliver of hope lightened the gloom that had settled over his insides with

JoyAnne's exit.

Dorothy straightened and smiled at him. A full, unreserved smile. "I'll go find a nurse. It's time to take you home."

Home. It was what the doctor had ordered. But it wouldn't be home until Joy had forgiven him. And given him a second chance.

(32)

"*H*ow long do you plan to avoid Kellan?"

JoyAnne scrubbed a dry cloth over the bathroom mirror, polishing away the last traces of the imposter's stay in the cabin. George and Dorothy had packed up the man's things and moved them to their house along with his car the day after he'd been injured. But she'd marked the cabin as unavailable in the computer and ignored cleaning it until today. She could've had one of the staff handle it, but for some silly reason, she'd needed to do the job herself.

Her nose burned from the cleaning supplies she'd used, but at least she couldn't smell the man's lingering cologne. Now if she could only scour him from her thoughts as easily. "How long do you plan on letting him hang around?"

George's lean face wrinkled in disappointed disapproval. "This unforgiving attitude of yours is wrong, Joy, and quite frankly doesn't suit you."

She slapped the rag into her supply carrier. "He lied to *all* of us about who he was. How can you forget that and invite him into your home like a long-lost relative?"

"I'm not forgetting it. I'm forgiving it. And if we're keeping score, we owe the man for all his help after I ended up in the hospital. But we're *not* keeping score. Dorothy and I genuinely like Kellan. You did, too, before you learned what he did for a living. You still would if you'd put aside your snit and stop using it to avoid your feelings for him."

JoyAnne stiffened but held her tongue. George had never spoken to her so sharply before. For him to do so now meant he felt very strongly about the matter, and she owed him the curtesy of paying attention. Even if it stung. But she needed a second to construct a civil reply.

She picked up her container of cleaning supplies and walked out of the cabin to put it in the back of the utility vehicle. George followed her. She turned to face him, and suddenly the patient, tender warmth in his light brown eyes dampened her ire.

Air whooshed out of her lungs. "Why does life have to be so hard, Uncle George?"

The tall man pulled her into a tight hug. "Because we live in a fallen, broken world, my dear girl, but it teaches us to lean on our Heavenly Father if we'll let it." He pushed her away to look her in the eye. "Easy roads don't make strong Christians."

JoyAnne folded her arms. "If that's true, I should

be as strong as Superman. But I'm not. I'm a weak coward who never wants to face another storm or bump in the road." She grimaced and shrugged. "Unrealistic, I know. But I can't help but hope."

George's fingers tightened on her upper arms. "Quit worrying about what tomorrow or next week or next month or next year might hold and start trusting a God who won't let anything touch you that hasn't already passed through His loving fingers. And quit trying to be strong in your own strength. The Apostle Paul said God's grace is sufficient for us, and His strength is made perfect in weakness. Lean on Him, Honey."

He held her gaze until JoyAnne nodded slowly, reluctantly. "I hear you, Uncle George. I'm just struggling to put it into practice." She inhaled and blew out a sharp breath. "But I'll work on it."

He pulled her into another embrace. "Good girl. And I like it when you call me Uncle. You can keep that up as long as you like."

Joy blinked back a spurt of tears. "I've thought of you that way for a long time, but I'm always afraid it will remind you too painfully of Micah."

"Never." George held her a long moment before releasing her and digging out a blue paisley handkerchief from his back pocket to blow his nose. "You ready for a morning break? It's a hot day, and I heard you leave the house before sunrise. Dorothy was mixin' a big pitcher of strawberry lemonade when I left, and I'd guess it's about ready to pour into a tall frosty glass." He winked. "Besides, we got a member of your favorite music group staying with us."

JoyAnne looked away to hide the panic that

spurted through her. "Sure." She took another deep breath and forced a smile. It felt more like a grimace. "I guess now's as good a time as any to face him."

"That's the spirit." He hopped into the front of the utility vehicle. "I'll drive."

"Great." She ground the word out, climbed in, and braced herself for the ride. And the upcoming confrontation.

She'd managed to evade it for a day and a half by staying with Victor—who'd been more than happy to let her crash on his leather couch when she'd learned Kellan Campbell would be moving into George and Dorothy's spare bedroom. Right below her cozy little apartment in the attic. And she'd planned to keep avoiding the man until he left. She should have known it was a fool's dream.

All too soon, she trailed George into the kitchen as Dorothy poured pink-tinted lemonade with slices of strawberries floating in it into two tall glasses.

"Good." Dorothy handed both glasses to JoyAnne. "Kellan's on the deck. Would you take his drink to him?" She grabbed George's arm and headed out of the kitchen.

George followed her.

JoyAnne frowned at their backs. "Where are you going?"

"I need George's help with a project in my room before he takes Kellan to his doctor's appointment later."

"But—" They disappeared down the hallway and a door closed off the rest of her protest.

"Dorothy? Did you need any—? Oh."

JoyAnne whirled, sloshing icy pink liquid onto her

hands. She ignored it easily for the more disturbing sight of K. C.—no—Kellan Campbell leaning on a pair of crutches outside the patio screen door off the dining room.

Silence stretched between them as she searched for something to say.

Kellan watched her, his expression unreadable.

JoyAnne cleared her throat. "How... how's your head?"

"Better."

"And your leg?"

"Painful. But the pain reliever helps."

"That's good."

Silence returned but this time he broke it. "Where did Dorothy go?"

"Um... She said she needed George to help her with something."

"Oh." His eyes dropped to the drinks in her hand. "One of those for me?"

"Oh, yes. Here." She set down one glass and walked to the screen door to slide it open to hand his drink to him, belatedly realizing he couldn't carry it anywhere because of his crutches. "Oh." Great. She sounded like a broken record. "Sorry."

He carefully maneuvered backwards on his crutches, his cargo shorts showing off a black splint that encased his leg over thick bandages. "Can you stay for a few minutes or do you have to get back to work?"

"No." She picked up her glass. "I mean... Yes, I can join you." She stepped onto the deck and elbowed the screen door closed.

"Great." A tentative smile tilted his lips and he made his way to a couple of padded Adirondack chairs that sat in the shade of the large pin oak.

After he sat and laid his crutches aside, she handed him a glass and perched on the edge of the second chair, sipping nervously at her own lemonade.

"I've been wanting to talk to you. To ask your forgiveness for not telling you who I was from the very first. And explain why I didn't."

JoyAnne swallowed too fast and had to clear her throat. "You don't owe me an explanation."

"I do. Besides, I like talking to you. I've missed it the last few days." His voice was quiet. Sincere. And she could hear the warm tones she loved listening to when he sang through her radio speakers.

Her cheeks heated and she slapped a hand over her eyes. How had she not recognized him? She'd had *Kellan Campbell* mowing grass, picking up fallen tree debris. Emptying trash cans!

"What's wrong?" Kellan's voice sharpened.

The anger she'd felt for days at being made a fool of disappeared in a flood of embarrassment that made her insides writhe. "You're Kellan *Campbell.* How did I not recognize you?" She moaned.

"Short hair and no beard helped, as well as having laryngitis when I first arrived. By the time my voice returned, you'd already accepted me as plain old K. C. Davis—my old school nickname by the way—and didn't look any further."

JoyAnne lowered her hand and peered over her fingers. "But still... Oh, good grief!" She slammed her hands back over her eyes.

"What now?"

"I *sang* in front of you!"

His soft laugh made her lower her hands. "You'll

never know how much I enjoyed that. After I got over the near heart-attack of thinking you'd discovered who I was, that is. You have a terrific singing voice."

"Which you will never hear again." How in the world could she have been so completely blind?

The smile drained from his face. "I hope that's not so. I really hope not, JoyAnne." He twisted the untouched drink in his hands. "Can you ever forgive me for not telling you sooner?"

JoyAnne dropped her gaze. The remorse on his face tugged at her heart, but following that unwise organ had gotten her into trouble before.

(33)

*T*he agonizing silence dragged until Kellan couldn't stand it any longer. He started to speak, to *beg* Joy's forgiveness, but the words snagged on his tongue.

She twisted the sweating glass in her hands. Around and around and around. Her eyes fastened to the swirling pink liquid, her eyebrows scrunched together.

Kellan slugged a mouthful of the sweet drink to moisten his throat. He'd screwed up big time. Major league big time.

She sighed and straightened, looking toward him but not quite at him. "I forgive you."

A "but" not only hung in the air, it also hung in JoyAnne's wary hazel eyes. She might say she forgave him, but he'd clearly lost any trust he'd won.

Regret knifed deeper. "I don't deserve it, but thank you."

She took a sip of her lemonade then sat it aside. "I guess I can understand why you would want to keep your identity a secret, but why did you pick here—of all places—to vacation?"

The stilted question felt like a tentative truce and Kellan accepted it gratefully. At least she hadn't bolted. "I wanted somewhere off the beaten track to relax and regroup. A place where people wouldn't be quick to..." He swallowed the last of the sentence.

"Wouldn't be so quick to recognize you? You found the right place for that." Self-derision dripped from the words, her gaze fastened to the grass separating their chairs.

"Ouch." Kellan winced. "But yes. That's exactly what I wanted. But don't beat yourself up. I didn't recognize you at first either."

JoyAnne's head jerked up. "Huh?"

A sliver of humor threaded through him and tugged up one corner of his mouth. "It wasn't until I saw you in your Friday R.E.D. that the fog of self-absorption started to clear, and I recognized something familiar about you." He paused for a second to appreciate the pink creeping up her cheeks. "But it wasn't until you sang in the truck and talked about the concert that I realized where I'd seen *you* before."

Her eyes widened and her mouth dropped before she covered her flaming face with both hands. "*Please* tell me you didn't see..."

Kellan couldn't stop his grin at her muffled moan. "You were the highlight of my night. But I didn't put two and two together until the answer stared me in the face."

She groaned. "You must have thought me such a klutz!"

"Actually, I saw you long before you nearly tumbled out of the balcony."

Her hands slid down her cheeks until she could peer over her fingertips again. "What?"

He nodded. "I was signing autographs at the merch table when you blew into the theater lobby like an old-fashioned movie star."

JoyAnne squeezed her eyes shut, and Kellan could tell her nose wrinkled even though her hands still covered the lower half of her face. "Oh, this just keeps getting better."

Kellan chuckled at her sarcasm. "You definitely caught my attention."

Her hands finally dropped from her face and she huffed out a breath as her arms crossed protectively around her. "I am so embarrassed."

"Why?"

"'Cause I feel like some kind of crazy-fan-stalker right now."

Her absurd answer made Kellan laugh. "You forget. I'm the one who followed you here. Not the other way around."

She wrinkled her pink nose again. "But you said you didn't know who I... Okay. I get it. That was a dumb statement. I'm changing the subject now. Sorta. I really did enjoy the concert that night." JoyAnne picked up her glass and took a drink.

"It was the first concert I'd enjoyed in a while, too."

Her forehead creased. "Why?"

"For the same reason I escaped to the back woods of Missouri." Kellan took a breath and tried to think of a way to explain without sounding like a spoiled diva.

His own forehead crinkled. Maybe that had been his problem. He'd unwittingly become a diva. If so, hopefully a few days of sweaty, manual labor sprucing up the campgrounds for the holiday weekend had knocked it out of him.

"What reason?"

The question recalled him to their conversation. The fact JoyAnne was still talking to him gave him hope that they might have a future past this apology. "It sounds selfish and whiny when I put it into words, but I was worn out. It's been about three years since I've had more than a week's vacation between appearances, practices, recording studios, interviews, tours... The cities we visited and the crowds we performed for were all blurring together. My agent and the group's management team were butting heads over who was going to relinquish some creative control, and singing had stopped being fun and had become work." He winced at how whiny his reasons sounded but continued with his explanation. "Until I saw you. And then I had someone to think about other than my own measly problems."

"I can see how worrying about a crazy fan throwing themselves out of the balcony would make anybody temporarily forget their problems." JoyAnne rolled her eyes.

Kellan grinned. "What were you trying to do anyway?"

She ducked her head and shook it. "Thought it would be less hassle if I climbed over the back of my seat instead of the knees and feet of a whole row of people. And it was. Until I stubbed my toe and nearly face-planted. I didn't think anybody but my friends and a few others seated beside us had noticed, though."

"Oh, I noticed. I flubbed the end of a song because you made me catch my breath." She'd been affecting his breathing ever since, too.

A tiny glimmer of a sheepish grin appeared in her eyes. "Sorry 'bout that."

"Mmm hmm. After meeting you in person, I'm beginning to wonder if you didn't do it on purpose to trip *me* up."

A faint twinkle made the green flecks in her eyes glow, and she slowly, deliberately shrugged her shoulders. Fake innocence in every line. "I don't know what you're talking about."

Her small, tight laugh mingled with his and some of the tension melted from Kellan's shoulders as she finally relaxed enough to slide deeper into the chair.

"So…" JoyAnne studied him, her eyes narrowing slightly. "Is that why I never caught you sitting beside your campfire here, strumming your guitar and crooning a ballad? You were worried about being recognized and bothered, I mean?"

Warmth touched Kellan's cheeks. "No. Not really. I didn't want to play, actually." He cleared his throat. "Until the last week or so, I had only touched my guitar when I absolutely needed to for the show. I wanted a break from all things music business. Even my guitar."

"Oh." JoyAnne faltered. "I'm sorry. I always thought it sounded like you loved what you did. I thought I heard that emotion come through your voice." A hint of a blush returned.

The warmth of it settled in Kellan's heart. She'd given him one of the best compliments he'd ever received. "Thank you. I did. But as I mentioned earlier, it had become more about business and less about loving what I do. Being here has made that love return. And I've started writing again."

"I'm glad. You already know that KWESTT is my favorite group. But one of my favorite songs is 'You Hold My Hand.' I think you wrote that one didn't you?"

Kellan nodded cautiously, warned by the wobble in her voice.

She was silent for several seconds before taking a deep breath. "I know what it's like, in a way, to lose the music. After Micah died, it felt like music died, too." JoyAnne twisted in her chair to face the lake. "It was a long time before I wanted to listen to any. It hurt too much—even sad songs sounded too happy. But one day, I heard KWESTT for the first time over the speakers of a store I was in. The radio station was playing one of those bouncy, funny Celtic ballads you all do so well, and the lyrics made me laugh. I hadn't laughed in close to two years. I ordered the CD with that song on it that afternoon."

The words socked Kellen in the chest. First she gave him the sincerest compliment he'd ever had, then she humbled him and effectively robbed him of speech.

"When it arrived in the mail, I popped it into my player and listened to it three times straight through. 'You Hold My Hand' made me cry. But it was a good cry." She hastened to add. Then she looked toward the lake. "'You hold my hand through the storms. When I fall you help me stand. You hold my hand.' Those lyrics… You might have written them about someone else but they reminded me of my Heavenly Father, and I put the song on repeat. It reminded me that God hadn't left me to struggle through my grief alone." She caught her breath then slowly turned to face him again, her eyes glistening. "Some people might think what you do is just entertainment, but it's more than that. You bring joy and encouragement to many people. Sometimes when no one else can reach them."

Hot emotion stung the corners of Kellan's eyes. His music had done that?

Even though he sung mainly secular songs?

He *had* written "Hold My Hand" as a tribute to how God had walked with him through the loss of his family. But then he'd rewritten it with vaguer terminology so that KWESTT could sing it without offending those who didn't believe in God. And he'd felt a pang of guilt the first few times he'd sung the weaker version on stage. But in spite of that, it had helped JoyAnne. The one person in the world he now wanted to help—to love—more than anyone else.

"So I hope you don't decide to give up writing songs or playing your guitar. You never know when your words might help someone through a rough time."

Kellan leaned his head against the back of his Adirondack chair and closed his eyes. Otherwise he'd jump out of it and haul JoyAnne into his arms and kiss her.

And probably send her running back to Victor's place. "I won't stop. In fact, I've rediscovered the inspiration hours on a tractor seat can bring."

"You're writing a song?"

He opened his eyes and smiled at the excitement on

her face. "Yes. More than one." Lyrics had come fast and furious the last few evenings in spite of his injury and his agony over JoyAnne's reaction to who he was. Or maybe because of it, since it had driven him to his knees before his Heavenly Father. And if his current record label wouldn't let him record a solo album of his decidedly-more outspoken Christian songs, he'd accept the offer Patricia had found for him because it was time to be more upfront about his faith.

Kellan sat bolt upright in his lounge chair, ignoring the pain the movement flared through his leg.

Patricia! He'd forgotten all about the deadline his agent had given him. His cellphone had even less reception up here at the Barrett's cabin, so she'd had no way to get ahold of him since the accident. His barracuda agent had to be gnashing her teeth at his silence.

(34)

*K*ellan Campbell.

Principal performer with a world-famous group.

Staying in George and Dorothy's house.

Sleeping one floor below her attic apartment!

The realization had yet to completely sink through her thick skull, but it definitely managed to distract her from what she should be doing.

JoyAnne shook her head and tried again to concentrate on the spreadsheet open on the computer screen in front of her. Working at the furthest edges of their property the last two days in an effort to avoid Kellan had put her behind schedule in the bookwork department. But no matter how hard she tried to focus this afternoon on numbers, and spreadsheets, and supply orders, her mind insisted on replaying this morning's conversation with Kellan.

With his identity finally exposed, she'd expected him to be different somehow. But he wasn't. She'd been talking to Kellan Campbell of KWESTT, but he was still K. C. Davis. The man she'd found it so easy to talk with, joke with, work with the last couple of weeks.

The quietly-sophisticated Mercedes-Benz made sense now, though.

Her mouth slanted in a crooked grin. So did the brand new, top-of-the-line outdoor gear he'd arrived with. Contrary to her initial impression of him, he really *had* known how to use it all. She might not be the kind of crazy fan who followed the members of KWESTT on every available social media site, but she'd read the magazine articles that mentioned the members of the group's love for the more extreme versions of outdoor activities. Rock climbing, white water rafting, sky diving, backpacking into remote areas to camp.

Cheeks heating, JoyAnne remembered the condescending way she'd taken over securing his tent the day he'd arrived.

If she'd known who he was from the beginning…

You'd what? Asked for his autograph? Avoided him?

"I'd've treated him like any other camp guest." As soon as she said it aloud she knew it wasn't true. She'd liked the man from the moment she'd walked onto his campsite. And now she was suffering from a full-blown case of fan-girl crush. She'd never quite cared for the scruffy look Kellan Campbell had sported on all their album covers, but she'd started to see past that while watching him perform in St. Louis. Now that he was a clean-cut…? *Pshew!*

Her pulse kicked up several notches. She slapped the desk with her hands, shoved her chair back, jumped to her feet, and stomped to the office window. "Get a grip, JoyAnne Daye. He'll be gone as soon as the doctor hands him his walking papers. Which might happen today."

And therein lies the rub.

He would leave.

She would stay.

That thought had fueled her restless dreams before pushing her out of her bed this morning before sunrise and out of the house—skipping her normal habit of reading from Micah's Bible—to escape the nagging realization.

It had dogged her steps all day, however.

"Is it true?"

"How could you not tell us, JoyAnne?"

JoyAnne spun around. "Alyce. Jordyn. What are you doing here?"

Victor's younger sisters hurried forward to hug JoyAnne then stepped back and studied her, crossing their arms over their stylish tops. They weren't twins, but they were close enough in age and mannerisms that they were sometimes mistaken for them.

Alyce spoke first. "Mom didn't want us to come up until we were completely over whatever crud our *benevolent* offspring brought home and shared with us, but now that we're cough and sniffle free, we came to see for ourselves that Dad is well and behaving. And to check on our suspiciously-silent cousin. The one who conveniently forgot to mention the fact *she's been hobnobbing with Kellan Campbell!*" Her accusation ended on a small shriek.

"And you didn't think to share that bit of news with your best friends in your emails?" Jordyn crossed her arms and donned a wounded look.

"Who told you?"

"We had to hear it from Mom. Because *you* didn't tell us."

JoyAnne rolled her eyes. "I didn't say anything because our guests deserve their privacy." It had taken all her persuasive powers to convince Tayleigh to not immediately post the news to all her *friends* on the internet once the college girl had discovered the identity of their guest. Tayleigh had been more than slightly excited to learn a celebrity had been hiding in their midst all this time—she'd even re-dyed the streak in her hair to match KWESTT's latest album colors. After that, Joy hadn't had the energy to explain the situation to anyone else.

Especially not her sharp-eyed cousins.

"So it's true? Kellan Campbell really is here?" Alyce, mother of two middle schoolers and one kindergartner, squealed like a teenage girl at a boy band concert.

"Are any of the other ones here?" Jordyn peered around as if expecting KWESTT to pop out of a file cabinet drawer and perform an impromptu, private concert.

"Yes, Kellan Campbell is really here. By himself. Incognito. So he can have a restful vacation." Seeing these grown women's reactions and vocalizing Kellan's reasoning for keeping his name a secret made it impossible to retain any resentment at him for not revealing his identity to her sooner. "And I didn't tell you because I didn't know who he was until after he got injured. Saving a little boy from being run over." Okay. Now she sounded as infatuated as Alyce and Jordyn.

"Girl! You have to spill all the juicy details! How in the world could you not instantly recognize Kellan Campbell? You listen to KWESTT all the time! You're like one of their biggest fans." Jordyn propped a hip on the edge of the cluttered desk.

"Yeah! Spill it, Joy!" Alyce pushed JoyAnne into the desk chair, plopped onto the other corner of the desk and crossed her arms.

JoyAnne shrugged at her two interrogators. "There's nothing to tell. I didn't recognize him because he'd cut his hair and shaved and looks different than when we saw him in concert. And it's not like he goes around singing all day. He's just a nice, quiet guy on vacation."

Nearly identical, exasperated looks speared her. "*Have* you heard him sing?"

"Of course I've heard him sing."

Jordyn's eyes widened then slowly narrowed at the matter of fact reply. "I don't mean at the concert or on a CD. I mean here! Has he sung to you here?" Her smile turned sappy. "That would be so romantic."

JoyAnne shook her head, hoping the heat building in her cheeks wasn't noticeable under her deepening tan. The man hadn't needed to serenade her to be romantic. He'd kissed her for goodness sake!

She cleared the sudden rasp from her throat. "That would kind of ruin the whole 'incognito' thing, don't ya think?"

Alyce squinted at her with a speculative twinkle in her eyes. "You *like* him, don't you?"

A muffled squeal outside the office saved JoyAnne

from having to answer the question and distracted Alyce and Jordyn's all-too-discerning scrutiny. Footsteps scampered down the short hallway to the small corner office.

Tayleigh skidded into view, eyes dancing, face flushed, splayed hands beating the air. "He's here! He's here! *Kellan Campbell* is standing at *my desk*!"

Her hissed proclamation launched Alyce and Jordyn from their chairs with involuntary shrieks.

"Shh! He'll hear you!" JoyAnne waved her hands in an attempt to quiet the three giddy females. They should all know better. Alyce was married with three children, Jordyn had two small girls and ran a successful home-based graphic-design business, and while Tayleigh might still be a college student, she was a brilliant one with a higher IQ than her current tizzy would lead one to believe. "What does he need?"

"He wants to see you, of course." Tayleigh sighed.

"Ooooh!" Alyce and Jordyn directed excited grins at JoyAnne.

"Good grief! He's just a guest." Her words did nothing to extinguish the gleam in her friends' expressions. "You three stay here. I'll see what he needs and be back in a minute." She pushed past the orange-and-magenta haired college girl standing just inside the office. The effect was rather startling, but Tayleigh's younger brother was probably relieved at the color change since she no longer sported his ball team's colors.

"Oh no you don't. We're coming with you." Three eager women hustled after her.

(35)

Kellan leaned against the tall front desk, facing the hallway to the back rooms. A smile appeared in his eyes then grew to his mouth when JoyAnne entered the store. "George dropped me off from driving me to my doctor's appointment and said I might find you here. I got my cast." He gestured to the hard blue cast encasing his foot and ankle and extending up past his knee. Then his gaze shifted over her shoulder, and he tucked both crutches under one arm as he straightened to his full height. His smile cooled slightly. "Good afternoon, ladies."

The breathless replies from her normally level-headed friends set fire to JoyAnne's cheeks. "May I introduce some of my friends?"

Kellan's eyes glinted with amusement. "I'd love to

meet your friends."

She barely resisted the urge to roll her eyes again at Alyce and Jordyn's noisy sighs. "You know Tayleigh of course."

"Yep." Kellan grinned at the awe-struck college student. "She's the first friendly face I saw when I arrived at Wad-A-Wa."

"He just autographed my copy of their newest CD." Tayleigh gushed, snatching up a plastic case and waving the orange-and-magenta hued album back and forth.

"Since when do you..." JoyAnne bit off the rest of the question when she caught sight of Tayleigh's desperate glare.

Okay. So KWESTT and their eclectic musical stylings had gained a new fan. Apparently, Kellan had completely won over the wild-haired, die-hard country-music-only fanatic.

"And these are my best friends, Alyce Clark and Jordyn Smith. George and Dorothy's daughters." Joy motioned to each woman in turn.

"You were with JoyAnne at the concert, weren't you?" Kellan leaned forward and shook their hands.

"Y... yes. How did you know?" Jordyn's eyes rounded in surprise.

Kellan grinned. "I remember seeing you with JoyAnne."

The sisters blinked, mouths hanging open. Alyce recovered first. "You *saw* us?"

Kellan nodded, sending a quick teasing glance at JoyAnne. "Yep. Sure did."

"Wow!" Jordyn stared at him. "I can't believe you picked us out of that crowd and remembered us. We were all the way in the balcony."

Kellan's grin developed a worrisome quirk that JoyAnne rushed to derail. "Was there something you needed to see me about, Kel—I mean Mr. Dav— Campbell?"

He eyed her for a moment then shook his head. "It's nothing that can't wait. You have company, so I'll head on to the house."

"No! Uh..." Alyce cleared her throat. "We were waiting on Dad to return and stopped in to say hi to JoyAnne. Now we'd better get back to the house to see him. Before we have to head home. To St. Louis." Joy had never heard the no-nonsense mother of three rambunctious youngsters so rattled. "You stay. Talk to JoyAnne as *long* as you like." She jostled her sister with her elbow. "Right, Jordyn?"

Jordyn nodded, looking a little dazed. "Right."

"Maybe we'll see you again. Before we leave." Alyce grabbed Jordyn and dragged her toward the door.

Jordyn dug in her heels. "Wait." She frantically dug in her purse. "Before we go, would it be too much to ask..." Her voice trailed off when she caught sight of Joy's are-you-kidding-me stare.

"I'd be delighted to." Kellan reached over the desk and plucked a pen out of the chipped Wad-A-Wa mug by the computer keyboard then graciously flourished his name across the crumpled fast food receipts Alyce and Jordyn produced from their voluminous purses.

JoyAnne didn't know whether to be embarrassed or jealous. *She* didn't even have the man's autograph. And she'd rescued him from a lightning storm!

"Thank you so much! It was so nice to meet you!" Jordyn gushed all over the man as Alyce tugged her—

too slowly in JoyAnne's opinion—to the exit.

"Yes. It was *really* nice to meet you. Maybe we'll get to see you again. Before you leave." Alyce repeated herself as she waved and backed through the campstore entrance, pulling Jordyn with her.

"I'll look forward to it, Ladies. Good bye." Kellan smiled and watched them go before looking at JoyAnne. "They're nice."

She crossed her arms and glared through the front plate glass window at the two women who hopped into a red minivan, giggling like a couple of lunatics. "I am so sorry about that. I have no idea who those two women are. They're usually so… *sane!*"

"Don't worry about it. I'm used to it." As he laughed, his eyes slid to something over her shoulder.

Oh yeah. They still had a very avid audience of one in the room. Tayleigh.

"Was there something you needed to see me about?" She asked the inane question again.

"George loaned me his key to the utility vehicle." He held up the key and wiggled it. "Said you were probably ready to escape the toils of paperwork and would be ready to do a drive-through of all the sites and make sure everything was shipshape before calling it a day. And since I've been bored out of my skull with nothing to do lately, here I am to bug you."

"But your leg. You shouldn't be driving."

"That's why I need a chauffeur." He wiggled an eyebrow and gave her a smile that would charm a squirrel out of its winter supply of acorns. "Was George right? *Are* you ready to head outside for some fresh air?"

To hang out with Kellan Campbell after her

friends' mortifying behavior? No. To escape Tayleigh's big ears and eyes? Absolutely. "Yes."

She held the door for him, and he swung through it easily before taking the steps two at a time.

"Careful! You'll end up breaking your other leg if you don't slow down."

He grinned at her, tossed the crutches behind the front seat, and climbed into the green vehicle. "Let's go, Driver. And by the way, my name's Kellan, or Kel, or K. C. to you. Whichever one you prefer as long as it's not Mr. Campbell or Mr. Davis."

She slid onto the seat behind the steering wheel, her cheeks heating again. "I'm sorry my friends embarrassed you."

"They didn't embarrass me." Kellan glanced over as she pulled out of the parking lot. "Looks like they embarrassed you, though."

"How in the world do you put up with that all the time?"

He chuckled. "It doesn't happen *all* the time, but we've had some success so it's part of the job. I won't lie. It can get old by the end of a long tour when I'm burned out, but most of the time it's fun. Especially after I've had a break from it."

"Thank you for being gracious about it."

"No problem. I could get a little offended that *you* haven't asked for my autograph, though. A fellow might get the impression you didn't like him."

Her jaw dropped. "I— I thought it'd be rude."

"Or maybe you aren't as big a fan as your family claims you are. After all, you didn't even recognize me."

"Because you looked nothing like you did on

stage!"

"It's just a haircut and shave, Joy."

She glanced at him then back at the road. Was he really offended or just pulling her leg? She went with the second option. "To tell the truth, I never cared for the long-haired, scruffy look. On you or anyone. And while I liked listening to you, I didn't watch you all that much. On TV specials or internet videos, I mean."

Kellan twisted toward her, draping his left arm over the back of the seat. She saw a crease appear between his brows.

Oops. She'd picked the wrong option. She hurried to rectify the mistake, pressing down on the accelerator as if she could outrun the foot she'd stuck in her mouth. "But you really are handsome. More so than I ever suspected. The shorter hair totally changed the shape of your face, and with the beard gone, I can actually see your jaw line. I don't know why whoever's in charge of your group didn't demand you clean up a long time ago. You'd sell as many albums based on your looks as on your voice." JoyAnne hauled in a breath. Then realized what she'd revealed.

Kellan's eyes danced and the corners of his lips turned up. "So you like my looks, huh?"

She opened her mouth but couldn't get any words out for the shoe leather wedged between her teeth.

He leaned over and brushed a kiss against her cheek. "For the record, I like the way you look, too. And have from the first moment I saw you. Both times. At the theater and then at my campsite the day I arrived."

JoyAnne's jaw swung so low she should have been able to pull her foot out of her mouth. But all she could do was yank her gaze away when Kellan winked at her. She was supposed to be holding him at arm's length. Because he would eventually leave and would carry away a chunk of her heart.

(36)

"*W*here are *they* going?" JoyAnne slowed to let George's truck pull out of their long driveway, Dorothy grinning and waving as George tooted the horn.

A red minivan followed the pickup. Alyce rolled down the window. "Have fun, you two. Good bye." She winked and sped after her parent's truck after Jordyn leaned across her to wave and shout a farewell.

Joy stared after them. "I thought they were going to spend the afternoon here, visiting."

Kellan swallowed a nervous grin. It was nice to have an ally in the camp. More than one from the look of it. "George told me he was taking Dorothy on a date night and not to look for them until around ten. Maybe he invited Alyce and Jordyn to go with them for supper."

"Oh." JoyAnne took her foot off the brake.

Kellan touched her arm, stopping her from driving forward. "Unless you have something in particular you wanted to do, why don't we head up to the house?" He gestured up the blacktop drive to their right.

She grimaced. "Guess I have been driving around rather aimlessly. Tired of my company already?"

"On the contrary. I have permission to kidnap you for the rest of the afternoon—or evening since it's almost five now." The knot behind his breastbone tightened. Their budding relationship was on shaky ground, and he desperately wanted to move it to more solid footing before his life intruded into this hideaway any more than it already had.

JoyAnne grew very still before a tiny smile quirked one side of her mouth. "Permission to kidnap me? Is that even legal?"

"Not sure. I'm unfamiliar with Missouri laws on the subject. You can check with Victor later, though. I'm sure he'll know." Kellan shrugged.

"I might just do that." She didn't look at him again but pressed the accelerator to the floor and zoomed toward the log home as she licked her lips and tucked a blowing strand of hair behind an ear.

Kellan dragged his eyes away from the lovely profile beside him in order to rein in the desire that had shot through his veins at her unconscious action.

When she parked inside the garage and cut the engine, he twisted toward her, his emotions under firm control. "So here's the plan, should you choose to accept. With George and Dorothy gone, I figured you'd want to stay within radio range of your staff rather than taking off for town. And since this annoying thing limits what I can do," he tapped the cast on his leg, "I had to get creative."

"Okay…" Wary curiosity darkened her eyes.

"Do you like old movies? Like forties, and fifties old movies?" Who'd've guessed that simply asking a girl to hang out with him for an afternoon would parch his mouth worse than a dentist's cotton wadding? The social media tabloids who speculated on his love-life—or lack thereof—would never believe it of him.

"I love 'em."

"Me, too." A sliver of relief slid through him. He hadn't thought about her movie preference until just now. If she'd said no, he'd have had to execute some fancy footwork in order to come up with another plan. "There's a Cary Grant evening marathon starting on the classic movie channel in about fifteen minutes. Would you care to join me for it? With Coke floats, popcorn and M&Ms, of course."

Humor flashed across JoyAnne's face, but she dodged the question. "I didn't know kidnappers asked their victim's opinion."

"You'll have to cut me some slack. I don't have a lot of experience with this whole kidnapping gig." Kellan gave her his most pleading expression.

A delightful giggle trickled out. "It doesn't sound like a kidnapping. It sounds more like a…" She broke off, her gaze flicking away.

"A date?" He waited until she glanced toward him again, her fingers gripping the edge of the seat. "Yes. That's exactly what I'm hoping it is."

Their eyes met. Held.

"Are you sure this is a good idea?" Indecision warred with another emotion in JoyAnne's gaze.

Something Kellan hoped was anticipation. "Absolutely sure." The decision to pursue a relationship with her was the easiest one he'd ever made.

Joy dropped her gaze and licked her lips again. "Then I guess you have yourself a date, Kellan Campbell. Davis."

"Good!" His cheeks ached with the force of his pleasure. "After you." He waved her out of the vehicle as he reached for his crutches and lurched upright. "Time's a-wasting."

He followed her into the house, enjoying the view but nearly slammed into her when she halted abruptly just inside the kitchen. "What's wrong?"

She pointed to the large bowl of fluffy white popcorn sitting on the cabinet beside two smaller, empty bowls, and a dish of colored chocolate candies. "Umm… why is popcorn sitting there?"

Kellan hobbled around her so he could see her face. "Because we're going to watch a movie."

She looked at the fragrant snack then to him, eyes narrowing. "I think I've been set up."

Kellan grinned. "I might have had a bit of help. Being a gimp has some perks." He opened the freezer and his grin deepened. They'd chilled two glasses for ice cream floats.

JoyAnne watched in silence as he extracted them.

"Would you like your float now or later?"

She squeezed her eyes shut and groaned. "Did they all know about this…?"

"Date? Yep. Dorothy told me you sometimes like popcorn suppers—with M&Ms, of course—and coke floats. But there're also sub sandwiches in the refrigerator if you want actual food."

A tiny smile broke the grimace. "You do realize I'm never going to hear the end of this from Jordyn and Alyce. I've half a mind to give them your number when they call me tomorrow to grill me for details."

"Go ahead. I'm sure they'll be great sources of information about you." He wiggled his eyebrows. "Speaking of which…" He strode to the pad of paper by the telephone and scribbled his cell phone number across it. After ripping off the paper, he handed it to her. "I'd prefer you didn't give it to too many people, but now at least *you* have it."

She colored prettily and shook her head, tucking the slip into her pocket. "Uh uh. I've changed my mind. Them plus you…" She shuddered playfully. "Bad idea. If you want to know something you ask me."

"Deal!" He grabbed the offer before she had time to realize what she'd said and retracted it. "Now. Float?" He held up the glass and wiggled it.

"Water. I'll save the float for later. And let me get it. You should get off your feet."

Kellan protested but let JoyAnne bully him to the sofa in front of the large television while she carried in the drinks and snacks. It felt really good to have her fuss over him. She helped prop his casted, aching leg on a padded footstool, making sure a side table was in the right place to easily reach his drink and bowl of popcorn.

Kellan settled into the comfortable couch and accepted the remote control, enjoying the attention.

Until JoyAnne plopped onto the far end of the extra-long couch. Well out of reach of his arm. Not quite what he had in mind when envisioning sitting in front of the TV with her.

"I don't think I'm contagious."

"What?" JoyAnne nibbled on a handful of popped corn, eyes on the opening credits of the black and white Cary Grant and Katherine Hepburn film.

"I'm not contagious. You could sit closer."

She choked and started coughing.

Kellan leaned over and tugged her arm until she slid close enough to pat her back like his mother used to do when he got choked as a little boy.

When she finally cleared her throat and caught her breath, she collapsed against the back of the couch and gave him a look that held equal parts accusation, shyness, and humor. "You did that on purpose."

Kellan stretched his arm over her shoulders. "I didn't mean to make you choke, but I can't say as I mind the results. Now let's watch the movie." He turned the volume up a notch, laid the remote aside and grabbed his bowl, leaving his other arm where it was.

After a while, she relaxed and leaned a fraction closer as they laughed at the comical trials of Cary and Katherine.

Kellan closed his eyes and inhaled. This. This was what he'd been searching for. Enoch would approve. Roots weren't just a place. They were people. Like George and Dorothy. And one person in particular. JoyAnne. She grounded him. Made him feel that he'd come home.

He wanted her to be his family. He wanted George and Dorothy to be his family. He'd even claim that big lug Victor.

He turned his head slightly to study JoyAnne. She'd experienced so much heartache, but she hadn't let it make her bitter. She might work too hard, but she worked to make others happy. To relax and have a good time with their family. With her family. She was good with people and would be a perfect fit with his tour family. He couldn't wait to introduce them to her.

Pink stained her cheeks again and she shot him a look out of the corner of her eye. "You're not even watching the movie."

She was far more interesting than a movie he'd seen several times before. "You said if I wanted to know something I could ask?" He reached for the remote and lowered the volume a few notches.

JoyAnne snagged one of the throw pillows and hauled it onto her lap, playing with the fringe. But she didn't pull away from the arm he'd kept around her shoulders through the film. "I might have said something like that."

Kellan rubbed his fingers over the curve of her shoulder, feeling the tension that had drawn it up. "You told me your parents were gone and about your husband, but I don't know anything else about how you grew up or where. And I'm curious."

"I could say almost the same thing about you." She twisted toward him, pulling her legs onto the sofa and crossing them Indian style, hugging the pillow, and leaning her shoulder into the couch cushions.

He liked being able to see her eyes but missed the physical contact so he laid his hand on her bent knee. "You first."

(37)

*J*oyAnne took a deep breath. Let it out. "I'm not *from* anywhere in particular. I was the daughter of a military chaplain. So I've lived a lot of places. Bounced around a lot of military bases. Seen a lot of the world. Picked up a smattering of survival words in several languages."

Kellan grinned. If anyone could handle his travel schedule while KWESTT was on tour, it would be a woman who grew up with the pressures of military life. At least *he* didn't have to move lock-stock-and-barrel at the whim of the government. "We have that in common. Although I've seen my share of it since I graduated high school and sounds like you saw it before."

She nodded. "Yep. I'm a military brat who learned early never to throw away a good packing box. It made me really close to my folks, though. They were the one constant. Until another automobile lost control on black ice and plowed into them."

Kellan gripped her knee. "I'm sorry. I didn't mean to bring up a sad topic."

"That's okay. I'll always miss them, but the pain's not so sharp anymore. And it's time to start remembering the good memories again."

"Tell me one."

She thought for a moment and then her smile reappeared. "My dad was a chaplain, but he looked more like the hardest, toughest sergeant you can imagine. Anyway, we had an agreement that whenever a boy asked me out, I would let Dad meet him first. In my senior year, a cute boy at my newest school asked me out. When I got home and told Dad a young man was coming over to ask his permission to take me to a movie, Dad got the wickedest gleam in his eye. To my utter mortification, when the boy arrived, Dad was sitting on the front porch, cleaning his .45 pistol." Joy's grin grew. "The kid had guts, though. He actually climbed the porch steps, stuck out his hand, and introduced himself."

Kellan wasn't quite sure how he felt about this tale, but he couldn't take his eyes off Joy's animated face.

"I was watching from behind the curtain in the living room and thought this cute guy would decide the new girl wasn't worth the effort and hightail it out of there and never speak to me again. Especially when after several awful, awkward minutes of silence my dad asked, 'If you died right now, do you know where you'd spend eternity?'"

Kellan's eyes widened. "He didn't. Seriously?" If

he'd confronted that situation as a skinny, acne-tormented teenager, he'd have given up dating for the rest of high school.

Joy chuckled. "Yep. The boy backed up a couple of steps, but in the squeakiest voice I ever heard from him said. 'I'd go straight to heaven, Sir. But if you don't mind, I'd rather not go today. I was hoping to take your daughter to a movie first.' He swallowed hard enough for me to hear on the other side of the screen then said, 'If I don't have her back by the time you want, you can shoot me then. Okay?'" Joy laughed. "My dad stood up and said, 'Young man, it's a deal. Just let me know where you want your body sent.' Then he laughed, shook the boy's hand, and said he was glad to know him.

"He and Micah—two of the best men I've been privileged to know—were best of friends before we even became engaged."

She looked down at the pillow fringe she was knotting. "I hadn't thought of that story in a long time. And I'm sure you didn't come here to hear me talk about my dead husband."

Kellan stilled her hands. "I came here to talk about whatever you want to talk about. And don't ever be scared to talk about Micah to me. He's an important part of your past. Part of what made you who you are today."

JoyAnne swallowed hard. "Thank you. But it's your turn now. Tell me some more about you."

So Kellan did. He talked about his mom—her love of music. His grandparents. Growing up on a farm. And in between, JoyAnne shared more about herself. Cary Grant marathon forgotten, they talked, and laughed, and fixed themselves coke floats with chocolate syrup, and talked some more.

Kellan's straw slurped when he tried to suck out the last of the creamy mixture from the bottom of his glass, and JoyAnne giggled.

"Are you laughing at me, Joy?" He purposely slurped the straw again.

Her eyes danced merrily. "Yes, and I warn you. If you don't stop making that noise, I'm going to come down with an awful case of giggles. Because I've had entirely too much chocolate and caffeine."

"Go ahead. It won't bother me." He slurped the straw and grinned as she tried to fight back the giggles. "But I think I should mention... you have a little chocolate syrup right there." He pointed to the side of her mouth and set aside his empty glass.

"Why didn't you say something?" She quickly rubbed her mouth but missed the spot.

"I just did." He leaned forward, tugging her toward him at the same time. "Here. Let me."

She froze as he gently rubbed his thumb over the brown smudge then stuck it in his mouth. "Mmm. Sweet." His voice rasped, and the air between them crackled into a million sparks. "Hold on. I don't think I got it all..."

Kellan angled his head, heart racing as she met him halfway. When her lips touched his, the sparks dancing around them exploded in his chest. She was new worlds to be explored and the safety of home all at the same time. His hands cradled her cheeks, fingers sliding into the tendrils of hair curling around her ears.

He forced himself to hold her lightly. To go slow, giving her time to back away. But when her hand crept around his neck, he groaned and pulled her into his chest, deepening the kiss. She tasted of ice cream and chocolate, popcorn and soda, and one hundred percent JoyAnne.

He pulled away slowly, feathering kisses across the top of her lip, the tip of her nose, her forehead.

Her eyelids fluttered open and she blinked at him like a sleepy owl.

"Are you okay?"

She nodded. "Uh huh."

He leaned his forehead against hers. "So the kiss was okay?" It would be only natural for her to compare him to the husband she'd loved for so many years, but it would sting, too.

"Uh huh. More than okay."

He grinned. "You keep looking at me like that, and I'm gonna kiss you again."

"Okay." Her soft lips curved up.

Kellan dropped another kiss on them but held his desires in check. "I want you to know that I'll never try to erase Micah's memory or try to take his place, but I would be extremely honored, if I could be the next man you loved. And if your dad were here, I'd ask his permission, too."

Her smile faded and her eyes grew large.

"Because I love you."

Her mouth dropped open and tears turned her hazel eyes into sparkling topazes.

Kellan's boldness abandoned him as he watched her struggle for a reply. He placed a finger over her lips, removed it for another quick kiss, and replaced it. "No. Don't say anything yet. I know we've only known each other a few weeks, and you need more time to get to know me. Sort out your feelings." He was rattling. But he had to stop her from maybe saying no. "I won't press you for an answer. I just wanted you to know how I felt."

JoyAnne blinked and a tear escaped down her cheek. "Thank you." She cupped his jaw in one hand. "God's blessed me with good men in my life, and you're one of them."

When she kissed him, the sparks danced through the air again and right into Kellan's veins. He gently but firmly pushed JoyAnne away and caught his breath. "You'd better call it a night and head up to your little apartment."

She frowned and glanced at the wall clock. "Why? George and Dorothy won't be home for another half hour or so."

"I know. That's the trouble. If your father were here and could read my mind, he'd be getting out his .45 again."

JoyAnne ducked her head, another blush kissing her cheeks the way he wanted to. "Oh."

"Yes. Oh. Now scram. Before I'm anymore tempted to do something we'll both regret and keep you right here with me."

She stood, her eyes darting everywhere but to his. "I'll just straighten up real quick…"

Kellan grabbed her hand. "No. I'll clean up. Good night, Joy. And sweet dreams."

She looked at him then. "I think they will be sweet. Good night, Kel." She winked in spite of her rosy cheeks and blew him a kiss before scampering out of the living room.

"Brat."

Her laugh put a huge smile on his face, and he laid his head against the couch, listening to her run up the staircase to her room and shut the door.

"Lord. Thank you. She's perfect. Let her love me, please. I would love to travel the world with her by my side or know she's waiting at home for me with little ones of our own—if you see fit."

He got to his feet to clear away the remains of their snacking, dreaming of the possibilities for their future until he heard George and Dorothy pull into the garage.

Yep. Life was good and getting better.

(38)

*L*ife had just careened around a ninety-degree turn into uncertainty.

JoyAnne kicked off her tangled sheets and flopped over to stare at her ceiling through the predawn shadows. She'd grown up with the drop-everything-and-change-your-plans-at-the-last-minute uncertainty of military life. Lived it again as a Marine's wife. Barely survived the worst kind of uncertainty waiting to learn whether her husband was dead or alive.

When she'd finally crawled out of the ruins of her old life, she'd built her new life around the comfort of knowing what each day would bring. Established it on the stability of controlling her environment and the security of knowing she had a home with George and

Dorothy for the rest of her life if she wanted it.

But suddenly a handsome, charming man had stormed the gates of her sanctuary, laid siege to her scarred heart, and made her wonder if maybe she'd been too quick to lock it away after Micah's death.

When she was with Kellan, the answer swung toward yes. Especially when he kissed her.

JoyAnne yanked her flattened pillow from beneath her head and hugged it to her chest, reliving last evening's kisses. Oh, they'd been absolutely exquisite!

Kellan Campbell had kissed her. More than once. And she'd kissed him back. Even initiated one of them. And felt every corner of her battered heart come back to life as he'd held her. Caressed her. Shared stories of his life. Listened to her reminisce about her parents and late husband without flinching. Said he *loved* her.

JoyAnne squeezed her eyes shut and cradled the words to her heart. He loved her. He hinted at life with her.

And that's when the fear had stormed from its barracks to reinforce the walls around her heart. Falling in love with Micah had been easy. The decision to marry him had been easy.

A relationship with Kellan Campbell Davis—there was nothing easy about that. Exciting, maybe. But she'd lived through too much for falling in love to ever be easy again.

Kellan might think he wanted a life with her. But did he have any clue what that looked like? She had no desire to leave here. And there was no way he was going to give up his career. He was too good at what he did. Too well-known. She wouldn't even consider asking him to give it up.

But how long would he be happy with a long-distance relationship? With having to travel to a backwoods corner of Missouri every time they wanted to see each other? He'd tire of it in a year if not sooner.

She'd survived the deaths of her parents and Micah, but they hadn't had a choice in leaving her. She didn't know if she'd survive the death of a relationship with Kel. Because he'd leave of his own free will. And it would crush her.

"I can't handle losing someone I love again, Lord. I can't! I wish you'd never allowed Kellan to come here." JoyAnne gulped in air. She didn't wish that. But she should. "What am I going to do?"

The dark ceiling offered no answers so she rolled over, flipped on the bedside lamp, and squinted in the light of a bulb that seemed dim at the end of the day but too bright at five in the morning. She grabbed the brown leather Bible that lay beside the lamp and scooted against the headboard, rubbing her fingers over the worn, scarred cover.

Micah's Bible. The book had given her much comfort over the last few years, not only from the words contained within, but from the fact that Micah had held and treasured this book above all others.

She flipped through the pages, looking for answers, stopping when it fell open to a section containing several highlighted passages. Her eyes landed on one of them.

Fear though not; for I am with thee: be not dismayed; for I am thy God: I will strengthen thee; yea, I will help thee: yea, I will uphold thee with the right hand of my righteousness.

A tear trickled down her cheek. Isaiah 41:10.

274

Micah had inked the verse inside his helmet, had engraved it on his memory. Had quoted it every time she'd uttered her fears for his safety when talking to him while he was deployed. Micah had believed that verse. Lived and worked and fought standing on the truth and comfort of that verse. And if she knew her courageous husband like she thought she did, he'd probably died with those promises on his lips.

"But what good did it do him, God? He still died! My parents still died!" The explosive bitterness rocked her back against the headboard.

She'd dealt with those feelings years ago. Hadn't she?

"I'm sorry, Heavenly Father. Forgive me. I didn't realize the hurt and anger were still so deep." She read the highlighted words again.

Fear though not: for I am with thee:

I was with him, JoyAnne. Every single second. Every step of the way I asked him to walk. And now he's with me. Safe. Happy. And at rest.

The assurance that whispered across her heart made her catch her breath and hug the Bible to her chest, tears raining down her cheeks. "I know they're with you, but I miss them. I miss the innocence of not knowing what it's like to have your world fall apart. Please help me. I don't want to be fearful, but I am. I don't want to have to experience that kind of pain again."

She laid the Bible aside and got up to wipe her face, deciding to go ahead and get ready for the day when she reached her bathroom. She needed to keep Kellan at arm's length. If this was a summer fling that would end the moment he returned to his normal, everyday life, she wanted to know it before these feelings for him had a chance to get a stronger foothold in her heart.

JoyAnne flung on her regular workday attire, but took a little more care with her hair than usual and even added a touch of concealer under her eyes and brushed on a thin coat of mascara. She didn't have to look like she'd had a sleepless night even if she had.

She slipped down the stairs to the kitchen in her sock feet, carrying her shoes in her hand, careful to avoid the squeaks so that the rest of the household could catch a few more winks. With a little luck, she'd be out of the house before anyone else stirred.

"Morning, Joy."

The quiet greeting startled her. "Oh. Good morning. You're up early. It's not even six yet."

Kellan smiled and gestured with his mug of steaming coffee. "Couldn't sleep. How 'bout you? Did you sleep well?" The twinkle in his eye hinted he was remembering her parting statement last night about sweet dreams, too.

"Fine. Just wanted to get an early start on the day. It's Friday and always busy, you know." The way he looked leaning against the counter, eyes still a little sleepy, hair not quite combed down... It was killing her resolution to keep him at arm's length.

"Really? I thought it was, but since you aren't wearing red I wondered if I'd gotten my days mixed up."

She blinked and looked down at the blue camp shirt she'd paired with her khaki shorts and the blue canvas shoes she still held. Then she looked at the calendar beside the refrigerator. It *was* Friday. The first

Friday since Micah's second deployment that she hadn't worn red. Hadn't Remembered Everyone Deployed. Hadn't pulled on her pair of combat boots to remember to pray for the troops and their families with every step she took.

The realization hit her, but it didn't hit as hard as she expected it to. And that scared her.

"Hey. You alright?"

She looked up to find Kellan directly in front of her. "I can't believe I forgot."

He pulled her into a hug, resting his chin on her head. "It's okay. You can always go change. No harm done. The day's just getting started."

JoyAnne wrapped her arms around his waist, dodging his crutches to accept the mix of excitement and comfort his touch offered. "No. It's fine. It won't hurt to miss one Friday." It's not like she'd ever forget to pray for the men and women in uniform. But it did feel like betrayal to her husband's memory. Especially since it was turmoil over another man that had made her forget.

"Oh, wait a minute. I can't believe I forgot." Kellan abruptly released her and spun on his crutches. "I'll be right back. Wait here."

The speed with which he disappeared proved how well he was adapting to the crutches. And reminded her that his injury wouldn't necessarily keep him at Wad-A-Wa until the cast came off. But either way, he'd soon be gone, too.

She yanked open the refrigerator door and retrieved the quart of orange juice for something to do with her trembling hands. She was going to get hurt, but she couldn't seem to stop herself from tumbling headlong after the man.

"Here. I saw these at the store yesterday when George and I picked up the ingredients for our snacks last night, and I immediately thought of you." Kellan swung back into the room and over to her, holding out two stretchy rubber bracelets.

They were red.

"I got two. One for you and one for me. So I could remember, too. See." He propped himself on his crutches and turned the bracelets so she could read the black lettering. "'R. E. D. Remember Everyone Deployed.' Now you can wear red today and not have to go change." His smile faded when he looked back up at her. "Not a good idea, huh?"

She shook her head, fighting back the sudden spurt of tears. "No. I mean yes. It's perfect." She tugged one of the bracelets from him and worked it onto her wrist. "It's one of the nicest things anyone's ever done for me."

Kellan shrugged. "It's only a cheap piece of plastic."

JoyAnn couldn't resist any longer. Her arm's-length plan had already flown out the window. She hugged him. Hard. "It's a lot more than that to me. It means you were thinking of me. And know how much R. E. D. means to me."

"I'm always thinking about you. And if cheap jewelry gets this kind of reaction, make room for lots more." He kissed her temple, returning her hug with equal fervor.

JoyAnne's giggle sounded watery. "Thanks. I think."

Kellan nudged her back far enough to drop a sweet,

too-short kiss on her mouth. "You're welcome."

A door latch clicked down the hallway, and they stepped away from each other.

"So." Kellan cleared his throat. "What's on the agenda for today?" He picked up his mug and took a drink.

"I'm heading for the camp office to tackle some more of the paperwork I didn't get done yesterday—because *someone* who will remain nameless distracted me—and to start the coffee makers." JoyAnne dug in the cabinet and pulled out four of Dorothy's homemade chocolate-nut-granola bars. She needed to get her mind on her work, and a quick, on-the-go breakfast would help her accomplish that quicker.

"Great. I'll go with you and help."

She handed him two of the bars. "No. You stay here and put your foot up." She needed space to do some more thinking. When the effects of that kiss wore off.

"Nope. Put me to work. I can count inventory or make coffee or watch the desk for you, but I'm going with you. If I'm going to be in your life, I want to know all about it."

Her breath left in a whoosh and she was thankful she hadn't bit into her breakfast bar yet. She'd have choked to death. "O... okay. That sounds... okay."

"Good. Let's go. I bet I can even drive the utility cart with my left foot." He grabbed the key off the rack and winked at her. "Besides. I'll wager the office will be quiet for a while yet, right?"

She nodded. Trying desperately to get her mental feet under her, she followed him into the garage, carrying her cup of orange juice and granola bars.

"Great. Then prepare to have some kisses stolen. Unless of course you want to give me some free ones." He fired up the small vehicle and shot her a blinding grin. "Come on. Hop in. Daylight's a wasting, Miss Daye."

Completely at the mercy of the handsome, cheerful rogue, JoyAnne slid onto the seat to be immediately tugged into Kellan's side and tucked under his arm. If she shut off her brain and let her heart do the thinking, this was where she wanted to be. For the rest of her life. Right next to the man who made her heart brave again. Made it sing again.

She looked up at Kellan when the utility vehicle stayed stationary. "Something wrong?"

Kellan searched her face, his grin returning. "Nope. Not a thing. Just checking to see if you were with me."

"Well quit checking. I'm here. And daylight's a-wastin'!"

"Yes, Ma'am." He stole another kiss. "Yes, Ma'am!"

He backed around George's truck and out of the garage, handling the driving with his left foot well enough to keep her from insisting she take over.

She snuggled under Kel's arm and let the morning breeze blow a few loose tendrils of hair out of her face and the worry and uncertainty out of her mind. Not having control of a situation might not be so bad after all.

An irrepressible smile bloomed across her face. Especially when Kellan Campbell was the situation.

(39)

"*I*s this place ever quiet?" Kellan sank into one of the extra chairs behind the front desk and propped his casted leg on an overturned metal crate.

"Probably. In the winter. But I'm not around then." Tayleigh laughed and closed out of the reservation screen on her computer that she'd just filled in with information from the most recent phone call. "You can ask JoyAnne to find out for sure."

"What do you mean?"

Tayleigh shrugged. "Oh, just that she's the only one around then. Mr. and Mrs. Barrett take their vacation during the off season—to someplace warm. But JoyAnne stays here to keep an eye on the place."

"They don't shut down the campground for the winter?"

"Yep. They do."

"But JoyAnne doesn't head 'someplace warm' for a while, too?"

"Not that I've ever heard. I think she's here year round. Yes, Ma'am, I'm coming." Tayleigh darted out from behind the desk toward the campstore shopper who'd waved to her for help.

Kellan tucked that bit of information away to examine later and picked up the ringing phone to take a message. Barely nine o'clock and it had rung off the hook since before the campstore's official opening time of seven a.m. He had entered the darkened building with JoyAnne shortly before six-thirty, looking forward to the quiet privacy of the building in the early morning hours to do exactly what he'd promised her. Steal some more kisses. And to spend some more time talking and getting to know each other on a deeper level.

None of that had happened. Almost the instant JoyAnne had flipped on the overhead light, the interruptions had started. First there'd been an emergency with a stuck water valve in the women's shower house, followed by an RVer who wanted to check out early. The day had avalanched from there. Kellan had started the coffee makers, but that's all he'd been able to help JoyAnne with before being forced to stand back and watch or ride along as she effortlessly handled each task thrown at her.

When Tayleigh had arrived, JoyAnne left the front desk in the college student's capable hands and headed out the back door—Kellan limping after her, feeling like a lonely puppy. She gave her high-school-age summer work crew their orders for the day before a problem with the delivery of bagged ice for the campstore freezers had sent her jogging around the building.

This morning had *not* turned out the way he'd envisioned it. While he admired JoyAnne's confident ability to do her job and apparent enjoyment of it, he'd gotten the feeling she might be using her busy-ness to keep him at a safe distance. If he hadn't been hobbled by a cast and pair of crutches, he might have been able to at least keep up with her as she bounced from interruption to interruption.

The bell over the front door jingled and Kellan felt the object of his attention enter the room even before he saw her. Did she feel the same electric connection between them that he did?

"Young man, has anyone ever told you that you look like that singer from... oh, what's that group's name?"

Kellan jerked his gaze away from JoyAnne and eyed the silver-haired lady dumping a pile of shirts and postcards onto the counter. "Uh..."

"You mean KWESTT and Kellan Campbell?" Tayleigh rounded the corner of the front counter, a huge grin on her face.

"Yes. That's the one." The lady snapped her fingers and returned to studying Kellan. "Doesn't he kind of remind you of him? Without the long hair, of course."

Tayleigh turned to eye him, too, propping her hands on her hips and cocking her head. "You know? Now that you mention it... The resemblance is rather uncanny." She swallowed as if trying to contain a laugh. "Has anyone ever mentioned that to you, Mr. *Davis?*"

Kellan smiled tightly. "I believe I've heard something like that before." At least three times already this morning. And maybe the reason why JoyAnne had started to withdraw. Why she looked less than amused now.

Tayleigh's eyes twinkled impishly as she turned to ring up the woman's purchases, handing them to Kellan to bag up for her.

"There you go, Ma'am. And thank you for staying with us at Wad-A-Wa." Tayleigh set the two large plastic bags on the desk, but the woman was digging in her purse again.

"Young man, would you mind if I took a picture with you? My friends will never believe I met a handsomer version of Kellan Campbell." She held up her small camera with a pleading smile.

The backhanded compliment caught Kellan off guard before tickling his sense of humor. He lowered his leg to the floor and pushed to his feet. "Sure. JoyAnne there can take the picture." He hobbled around the desk on one crutch and put his arm around the shoulders of the stout little lady. "Make it a good one, Joy. I've never been told I'm better looking than Kellan Campbell."

JoyAnne ignored his wink, accepted the camera with a stiff smile and snapped the picture.

When the door swung closed behind the older woman, Tayleigh let out a long laugh. "That's the *funniest* thing I've seen this year. Just wait till she figures out you really *are* Kellan Campbell." She laughed again. "She'll *flip!*"

JoyAnne came around the desk, smiling slightly at Tayleigh's amusement, but the shadow had returned to her eyes.

Kellen sighed silently and sat down again. He'd begun to think they were getting past his deception, but it looked like he still had a lot of damage to repair.

The bells over the door jangled before Kellan could think of anything to say to repair the situation, and JoyAnne seemed relieved to turn and greet the latest arrival along with a grinning Tayleigh.

The two women and the tall front desk blocked his view, but an unexpected, strong whiff of perfume stiffened him an instant before a familiar voice removed any hope of salvaging the rest of the day.

"Well, isn't this place just... darling. But what exactly is it? A resort of some kind?"

Kellan had the strongest urge to pull one of the large Wad-A-Wa plastic shopping bags hanging beside him over his head in an attempt to be invisible. A childish impulse, but there all the same when it hit him how abruptly and completely his vacation was over.

"Umm... Welcome to Wad-A-Wa *Campground*. How may we help you?" JoyAnne sounded gracious despite her suddenly bolt upright and tight posture.

She hadn't missed the condescension Patricia hadn't deigned to hide. Kellan ordered himself to stand up and stop his agent from being any more of a jerk, but he couldn't take his eyes off the train wreck of his chaotic everyday life and the idyllic peace of the last few weeks with JoyAnne and the Barretts.

"An Indian name. How quaint. I thought they only used those out west. Shouldn't you have something more appropriate to this area like Hillbilly Acres or something?" Patricia uttered a shrill laugh as if she'd told a great joke.

"I'm sorry? Were you interested in booking a night, or are you lost? I'll be glad to give you directions on how to get out of here." Tayleigh's arms were crossed, her spine as stiff as JoyAnne's, and Kellan silently cheered at the blatantly false concern in her voice.

"Honey, I'm never lost. And I wouldn't stay out here if you paid me. Last night's *motel* room was enough of a nightmare." A snarl licked through Patricia's laugh. "I'm here to speak with my client. I believe *he's* been staying here—although I can only guess why. We'll discuss later how much you want for the pictures I'm sure you've taken of him, but they are *not* to be used for any kind of promotional material for this place. Now, point me to where Mr. Campbell is staying, and I'll let you return to… whatever it was that you were doing when I came in."

Kellan jerked out of his shock and to his feet. "Sheath your claws, Pat. These are my friends."

Two abruptly *unfriendly* females spun toward him, and Kellan regretted, for the first time in his life, being six foot tall. Because it prevented him from crawling under the desk.

Tayleigh looked disgusted—at him or Patricia he couldn't tell.

There was no expression on JoyAnne's face. The shadow in her eyes had deepened to pitch black—locking him out in the cold.

"Kellan! What in the world are you doing back there? I cannot believe you dragged me all the way out here into the boonies to find you." Patricia's ever-present, impossibly thin high heels clattered around the side of the desk, but Kellan lurched to his feet, grabbed his crutches and swung out of Joy and Tayleigh's work space. It was the least he could do to keep his rude agent from invading what personal space they had left.

"How did you find me, Patricia?"

"Your face is splattered all over the tabloids, Kellan!" She swiped a finger across the screen of her phone and flashed him a quick view of a small picture of him leaving the hospital. "Somebody at the hospital where you were treated snapped a couple of pictures and they're going viral! People speculating about what happened, where you are, and why you've suddenly cut off your gorgeous hair and shaved. The press is hounding me for what really happened—and of course I have no idea because you *won't answer your phone!* And the record deal I made is in danger of falling off the table because, again, you won't answer your phone! I told you taking off into the wild unknown for months on end was a bad idea. What were you thinking staying in a back-of-beyond place like this? It was almost a given you'd wind up injured. And what did happen, *if* you don't mind your agent asking?"

"I'll explain later, Pat. Why don't you head back to wherever you're staying and I'll meet you there." After he'd had a chance to talk with JoyAnne. It was time to deal with the rest of his life, but not before he made sure Joy knew what was growing between them wasn't over. Not by a long shot.

"Oh, no you don't." His agent grabbed his arm, ignoring the nickname she hated. "I'm not letting you out of my sight. I'll help you get whatever you want to take with you packed and then we need to hit the road. We have a flight out of St. Louis in four hours and a meeting with music execs in Nashville in the morning.

We are *not* missing that meeting. I've already moved it twice while trying to find you!"

"Patricia, you should have asked me—"

"And you should have taken my calls and called me back when you said you would." She cut him off. "If you want to leave your stuff behind, I'm sure your *friends*," she flicked her fingers at JoyAnne and Tayleigh in a dismissive gesture, "can pack it up and have it shipped to our Nashville address, but the clock is ticking, Kel."

"Whatever you want to leave behind, we'd be happy to mail to you, Mr. Campbell. Along with the bill for your stay. Thank you for staying at Wad-A-Wa. It's been… interesting." JoyAnne's voice was colder than the inside of the bagged-ice freezers as she stomped away from the desk, disappeared down the hall, and slammed her office door.

The reverberations hit Kellan square in the chest. He needed a chance to talk with her—promise her they'd figure out how to incorporate his life with hers. It might take a little bit of adjusting on both their parts, but they could do it.

He turned to follow her.

Patricia grabbed his arm. "Since that's taken care of, we need to go."

Kellan's jaw tightened, but then he nodded. Maybe he should give JoyAnne a chance to calm down first. "I need to run up to the Barrett's house first and pick up my phone—"

"Which you don't use." Patricia sniped at him.

"And a couple of other things and say good-bye. Then we can go. But first…" He snatched a pen and pad of paper off the desk and scribbled down two telephone numbers then shoved the paper at Tayleigh. "Give these to JoyAnne. Tell her she can call me anytime. She has my cell number, but these are two other numbers where she can reach me. Tell her I'll call her as soon as I can. We need to talk."

Tayleigh accepted it warily, eyeing Patricia with barely veiled hostility. "Okay."

Kellan gripped her hand. "It was nice to meet you, Tayleigh. Take care of her until I can."

"It was nice to meet you, too. I think." She sighed and cocked her head toward Patricia. "You better go before your *handler* there blows a fuse or something."

"I'll be back, Tayleigh. You can tell Joy that."

"Sure you will. Good-bye, Mr. Davis."

Kellan clamped his jaw at her skepticism. He *would* be back. As soon as he tended to this meeting with the music execs and got his career straightened out he would return. And he'd be calling JoyAnne every day until that happened. Because he wasn't leaving her behind. She was as much a part of his life now as his music. More, actually. She was the woman who'd given him back the music.

(40)

She was an idiot. A one hundred percent, undiluted idiot.

JoyAnne slapped the surface of the water below the dock with her feet, relishing the sting against her bare soles and wishing it would take away the sting of foolishness of falling for a guy she knew would leave. Then maybe she could ignore the larger ache of missing the same guy who'd been gone less than a week.

She twisted the red rubber bracelet around her wrist. It silently accused her of idiocy every time she saw it, but she hadn't been able to make herself take it off since Kellan had given it to her.

After his sleek and gorgeous agent's insults had so rudely but effectively contrasted the stark difference between Joy's life and home and Kellan's, JoyAnne had spent the rest of the day trying to escape thinking about any of it. But memories of Kellan permeated nearly every inch of the campground and she'd finally given up and returned to the spot he'd first kissed her to wallow in the pain of once again losing someone she loved.

She wrapped her arms over her stomach and leaned over to stare into the murky water. *Why* hadn't she kept her distance? She'd known she would get hurt. And she'd been right.

Feet thudded onto the dock behind her and she straightened but didn't turn. The footsteps were familiar, and when gray trouser-clad legs came to a halt beside her, she wasn't surprised.

Victor squatted on his heels and glanced her way before looking out over the lake. "You gonna come eat supper, Squirt?"

JoyAnne shook her head. "Not hungry."

Vic exhaled roughly. "It's a good thing that guy left before I arrived. I'd have been hard pressed not to slug him."

"Why would you want to slug him?" She tried for a careless chuckle but only managed a choking sound.

"Because he hurt you. Something I expressly forbid him from doing."

It was a good thing they weren't fishing. Victor's low, rumbling growl would've scared the fish away. "He didn't hurt me. I hurt myself. He was a guest and guests leave. Even if they're *not* famous singers. I somehow managed to forget that fact. I'll get over it." In fifty years or so.

"This is me you're talking to, Squirt. You fell for him."

She shook her head. "It was just a fling. You know—the kind people have on vacation and then leave behind." Her throat closed.

"Maybe for him," Victor growled again. "But you don't do flings." He studied her for several long seconds before sighing. "You fell in love with him, didn't you?"

She swallowed hard then lifted her chin. "Like I said. I'll get over it." Her eyes burned with the lie.

"Ahh... Squirt." Victor sat on the weathered boards, disregarding his good suit pants, and wrapped a thick arm around her shoulder, pulling her close. "I'm sorry."

She rested her head against his shoulder. "You tried to warn me."

"You want me to make out an arrest warrant for him so we can haul him back here?"

"Is that even legal?"

"Hey. I'm a judge. If you want his sorry carcass hauled back here, I can figure out a way to get it done. And if he spends a night or two in the county jail, I'd consider it payback for lying to you."

JoyAnne half-heartedly elbowed him in the ribs. "No, I don't want you throwing him in jail. He's a nice guy and he doesn't deserve your anger." But it was nice to have somebody who cared enough to be mad on her behalf. Another reason she never wanted to leave this place.

Victor's hand tightened on her other shoulder. "From the amount of times Mom says he's called wanting to talk to you this week, I have to admit that it might not have been a simple fling for him, either."

She looked away.

"If he's serious about you, his leaving won't change that. The man doesn't have to live on the place to have a relationship with you, you know."

"When he gets back to his real life, he'll forget about me." A tear escaped before she could blink it away.

"Much as I hate to admit it, I don't think he's that kind of man, Squirt. He might be an entertainer, but unless there's something I haven't been able to uncover, he's not a playboy."

She caught her breath and twisted out of Victor's grip to stare at him. "Did you have him investigated?"

Her cousin-in-law didn't look one bit ashamed. "Yep. And he's exactly what he appears to be. A hard-working musician whose group happens to have some fame so people make up things about him and speculate about him in the tabloids and online. But he doesn't play around with women."

That made her feel better but only slightly. "I can't believe you did that."

"I think you should give you and him a chance, Joy."

"How am I supposed to do that, Vic? I'm here and he's... all over the world."

"Ever heard of a thing called a long-distance relationship?"

"Yeah. I have. But nothing good about 'em." JoyAnne snapped. Vic was supposed to be in her corner. Not Kellan's.

Victor eyed her, his expression somber. "You made it work with Micah."

The words knifed through her. "And look how well that worked out! He's gone! And I'm alone!"

Pain slashed across Vic's face and JoyAnne had to turn away from it. She hadn't intended to hurt Victor, but once again, her own pain had spurted out and splashed on those closest to her. "Vic... I'm sorry. I didn't mean it that way."

A muscle flexed along his cheek and he didn't look at her. "I know."

"JoyAnne?" Dorothy called from the back porch.

Joy grabbed the interruption and shot to her feet. Anything was better than continuing this conversation. She jogged barefoot across the grass. "What is it?"

The woman raised the cordless phone JoyAnne hadn't noticed until too late. "Kellan's on the phone for you."

She stopped cold and shook her head. She wanted this conversation even less than the one she'd just had with Vic. "I'm not ready to talk yet."

Dorothy frowned and shoved the phone at her. "Then you tell him that. I'm not making any more excuses for you."

JoyAnne took the phone to keep it from hitting the deck and watched as Dorothy and Victor disappeared inside the house, leaving her alone. The traitors.

Reluctantly, she raised the phone to her ear. "Hello?"

"From the sound of that conversation, I take it you're still mad at me?" Kellan's solemn voice was as clear as if he were standing right in front of her. Except he was about five hundred miles away.

"I'm not mad. We both knew you'd have to leave eventually." JoyAnne tried to put a smile in her voice. "But it was fun—"

"Don't you dare say it was fun while it lasted."

Kellan interrupted her. "As if what happened between us is over."

"You don't have to let me down easy, Kellan. I understand you have a whole life I'm not part of. And from what your agent said, you've spent far too much time away from it."

"I could cheerfully strangle Patricia right now. The 'deal' she pulled me away for is nowhere near as final as she led me to believe, and I still had several more weeks of vacation time coming to me. Which I fully intended to spend getting to know you and your family better. I never planned to leave so abruptly and with so much unsettled between us."

JoyAnne sank into a deck chair. "It's probably for the best."

Silence filled her ear for a long moment. "The best for whom, Joy?" Kellan's voice was tight.

"For both of us."

"You're wrong. There is something very special between us and it doesn't end just because I had to leave on business. I'll be back. And until then, we can call and video chat with each other every day."

"Kellan…" She wanted to believe him, but she knew what long distance did to a couple who were united in marriage. What would it do to two people who didn't have that bond? "I don't think it will work. You're there, and I'm here."

A growl of frustration came over the line. "You are not allowed to give up on us, JoyAnne. You hear me? If you can wrangle rookie campers who have no idea how to set up a tent or drive an RV and ensure they all have such a safe, fun experience at your campground that they want to return, you can handle figuring out how to make *us* work. Okay?"

His tenacity sparked a flicker of hope inside her. "Maybe."

"JoyAnne. I think you've forgotten something I said to you."

"What?" She probably had. The man had her so confused she didn't know whether she was coming or going.

"I said I love you. I meant it when I first said it, and I mean it more now." His voice dropped, low and husky.

"I haven't forgotten." She whispered. They were three words she'd treasure. Even if she didn't believe they'd last.

"Then don't give up on us. Okay?"

JoyAnne sucked in a huge breath. Closed her eyes. Curled her free hand into a fist. "Okay."

"Okay." Kellan sounded relieved. "I really, really hate to cut this short, but I have a couple more business calls to make before I can call it a night, but I'll call you tomorrow on your lunch break."

"Okay. I hope your calls go well."

"Thanks, Honey. Remember I love you, and we'll figure this out."

"Okay." She was stuck on that word. "Goodnight, Kel."

"Night, Joy."

She punched the power button and dropped the phone to her lap. It would be wonderful if he were right. And maybe he was. But they'd only been apart a few days. She'd give it a chance like he wanted, but she'd also steel her heart against the inevitable distance that would grow between them as the separation lengthened. He'd soon discover that a long-distance girlfriend was a lot of effort with little reward.

Hauling herself to her feet, she went inside and returned the phone to its base.

"I kept a plate of food warm for you." Dorothy turned from her place at the sink.

The sounds coming from the family room indicated Victor and George were watching a ballgame.

JoyAnne was grateful. Dorothy's questioning eyes were more than enough to face right now. "No, thank you. I'm not hungry." If her stomach churned any more, the remaining contents of her meager lunch would come up.

"That boy was not happy about having to leave so soon. But he was very sweet to George and I. Thanked us over and over for our hospitality and promised to return as soon as he could. I believed him. I think you can, too."

"Can we talk about this later? I just want to go to bed. I'm exhausted." JoyAnne rubbed her eyes. Believing he would return wasn't the problem. It was the fact that if he did, he'd only have to leave again. Delaying the inevitable—that one day he'd be gone for good.

Dorothy's face softened with something that looked uncomfortably close to pity. "I'll talk or not talk about it whenever you want, Sweetheart. As long as you promise me one thing."

"What?"

"That you'll talk to the Lord about this before you go to bed. And ask Him what *He* wants you to do about this. Don't depend on your own wisdom here. God may have something entirely different for you than what you envision if you'll give Him a chance to work."

JoyAnne nodded and gave the same weak answer Kellan had accepted. "Okay." She exited the room before Dorothy could elicit more of a promise than that. It was the only one she could make right now. She'd had too many years of living a life that was more than just half empty from the loss of her parents and husband. It had been shattered, destroying the naïve optimism she'd once possessed.

(41)

"*G*ood job, Guys! That's our best rehearsal so far! I can't wait to see what our fans think of this show!" KWESTT's director beamed and clapped her hands. "I believe this tour is going to be our greatest one yet!"

"Thanks, Coach!" Trev mimicked the woman's enthusiasm with a smirk.

"Despite Trevor's horsing around." Sandra continued as if she hadn't been interrupted. "Now. You have two days to rest up, pack your bags, and get ready to hit the road." She clapped her hands again. "This is going to be fun! And Kellan…"

"Yeah?" He was glad *she* thought rehearsal went well because his enthusiasm and attention span had been nearly non-existent. She was probably about to peel a strip off his hide for that, too.

"I think I speak for all of us when I say we're *very* happy you're staying with KWESTT."

Several of the crew stopped dismantling sound equipment to express their agreement with a smattering of applause, and Enoch slapped Kellan on the back. "Same here, Man."

"Thanks. I didn't want to leave anyway, so I'm glad everything's straightened out." He managed a halfway-genuine smile.

"Aww! Admit it. You couldn't leave because you'd miss my sparkling personality too much." Trevor slugged Kellan on the shoulder. The story of Trev's near drowning on their whitewater rafting trip had been recounted several times by Ty and Sawyer, but the incident hadn't dampened the adrenaline junkie's bold personality that Kellan could tell.

"Actually, I think you were the reason he considered abandoning us in the first place." Westin shoulder-bumped Trev aside and grinned at Kellan. "Glad you didn't let him run you off, Kel. I'd've missed you."

Kellan chuckled at Trevor's scowl at Westin. "Thanks. But before the rest of you get too maudlin on me, there never was any real danger of me quitting the team. That was an idea Patricia cooked up all on her own. End of story."

"Good thing you've got a new agent then." Ty smiled and grabbed his backpack, but quiet earnestness enforced the statement. "C'mon, Trev. Let's find food."

The magic words quickly dispersed Kellan's band mates, and he grabbed his own messenger bag and headed for the door, pulling out his phone to check for any messages that might have come in during their rehearsal session.

There were five missed calls, but all were business related and could be returned tomorrow. His shoulders drooped, and he stuffed the phone into his back pocket.

"You wannna talk about it?" Enoch caught the door Kellan had slapped open and caught up to him on his slog across the parking lot to his car.

"Not really."

"She hasn't called you, huh?"

Kellan unlocked the passenger door, tossed in his bag, smacked both hands against the car frame, then pushed off in frustration. "No. My professional life is in the best place it's ever been, but my personal life is in complete shambles. I'm almost sorry I ever took that vacation."

Enoch leaned against the side of the car trunk and crossed his arms. "You don't mean that."

Kellan frowned, sighed heavily, and slammed the passenger door. "No... I don't know." He scrubbed his face. "Professionally it was a good thing because it forced things to come to a head with Patricia and opened my eyes to what she was doing."

The woman had been sabotaging his career with KWESTT in an attempt to get more money and prestige for herself in a new record deal for Kellan. The directors of KWESTT had been receiving a greatly inflated version of Kellan's requests, and he'd been given a fabricated report of the creative freedom they were willing to allow him. In truth, they were more than happy to let Kellan cut a solo project and eager to talk about adding a few of his original songs to the new show.

When Kellan had realized what was going on after

the first few weeks back in Nashville, he'd confronted Patricia about it. The woman was responsible for getting him the job with KWESTT in the first place and he'd owed her a chance to explain. But she'd been blatantly unrepentant and grew angry when Kellan flatly refused to leave KWESTT for a new record label. So they'd parted company—if not amicably, at least without the threat of a breach of contract lawsuit on either side.

"I can't say that I'll miss that woman, but how exactly did you get out of your contract with her without winding up in court?"

"The judge I met in Missouri knew a good lawyer in Branson who specializes in the entertainment industry. After one meeting with him, Patricia surrendered. He also introduced me to my new agent who seems to be working out very well. Personality wise, he's more laid back than Patricia, but according to his other clients, he's a bulldog when it comes to working for his clients' best interest. Emphasis on his *clients'* interests. Not his."

"I'm glad to hear it. I assume this judge is the brother or whatever of the woman you fell in love with? JoyAnne?"

The sound of her name made Kellan clench his fists. "Technically he's a cousin-in-law—if there is such a term—but he's more like a brother in every other aspect."

"So her family will talk to you, but not the woman herself?"

Kellan leaned against the car beside his friend and crossed his arms. It was the first day of fall and thanks to a storm front, it actually seemed like it. The cooler air felt good on his heated skin and was a relief after a long, hot summer of legal wrangling, writing, arranging, rehearsal sessions, and missing a woman who wouldn't return his calls. "That pretty much sums it up."

"Maybe you should fly out to see her before we leave."

"Tried that. I've been back twice since I left and each time I'm there, I see more of her family than her. She acts like I'm barely a friend—much less the woman I fell in love with. It's almost like going to see her made the distance between us worse. At least before that second visit she would talk to me on the phone. Now I don't even get that." And it was killing him. He'd only made it through today's session by pretending she was in the front row of the theater seats and that he was singing to her.

"At least her family seems to be on your side."

"For whatever good that does." Kellan took a deep breath and fought back the urge to kick something. "I think she's never gotten over the loss of her parents and husband and it's become a barrier she can't or won't get over. A barrier I can't seem to get around."

Enoch stood beside Kellan in silence for several minutes. "So are you giving up?"

Kellan rubbed his face. "I don't know. Maybe she'd be happier if I did." He wanted her to be happy. And if it came at the cost of his dream of a life and home with her... Well, he'd give it up. Even if it killed him in the process.

"Or maybe she needs someone willing to keep fighting to scale the castle walls and tear down the fears that hold her prisoner. You haven't experienced what you told me she's lived through, and those kind of wounds take time to overcome. But from what I've heard, she's worth fighting for."

Kellan could see JoyAnne as clearly as if she stood on the blacktop parking lot in front of him. Her loyalty to the family she now claimed as her own. Her hard-working dedication to her job—her love of that job. Her quirky sense of humor. The inner beauty that shone even brighter than her outer beauty. "Yeah. She is. But not seeing her or being able to talk to her might kill me before she gives in."

"No, it won't. You're tough. You might have to prove it to yourself as well as to JoyAnne, but you are. And if it makes you feel any better, my family is praying for you as much as I am. The girls pray for their Uncle Kel and his 'girlfriend' every night."

Kellan nearly lost his shredding composure. He looked up at the darkening sky and cleared his throat. "Thanks, Enoch. Tell them I'll drop by to see them tomorrow afternoon. I need my bear hugs before we load up the busses again."

"Will do. See you tomorrow, Bro." Enoch gripped Kellan's shoulder before pushing off the car and heading toward his own. "Oh." He turned around and grinned. "It may sound trite, but remember what they say about faint hearts and fair ladies."

Kellan huffed a laugh and shook his head. "I just hope that old adage about *absence* and hearts is true."

Enoch laughed and climbed behind the wheel of his car. "Guess you're about to find out."

Kellan waved the man off and slid behind the wheel of his latest rental. He was looking forward to the show's fresh arrangements and new songs, and he'd give each show all the energy he had. He owed it to his fans. He owed it to himself. He owed it to JoyAnne. Because he prayed she cared about him enough to follow the tour through the media coverage and fan videos of concerts. Because he'd be singing for her.

And when he wasn't on stage, he'd be working on storming her fears. She had told him a long-distance relationship wasn't fair to either one of them since she didn't plan on ever leaving her little corner of Missouri, and then she'd tried to convince him they should only be friends. But he wanted more than that. Much more.

She might think a long-distance relationship during his touring schedule would never last, but she was about to find out that a long-distance siege would. She'd met her match in the stubborn department. He was going to prove she could trust his love for her.

And he had a distinct advantage. Her family was on *his* side. Even big old Victor—after a serious bawling out for hurting his cousin.

JoyAnne had no idea what she was up against.

Kellan cranked the key, fired the engine to life, and sped out of the theater parking lot. He had a siege to plan.

(42)

"*O*h, Jooooyyy." Dorothy sing-songed from the echoey campstore. Empty racks had been moved out to allow the floor to be cleaned, stripped, and waxed "Delivery for you."

JoyAnne rested her forehead against the shelf she was refilling with sorted and inventoried leftover summer stock. It had started at the end of September—just when she thought she was making headway on convincing Kellan to forget about her.

First it had been the mail. Cards, postcards, letters. Every couple of days. All addressed to her. All from Kellan. Then small packages started interspersing the letters.

She'd grown to alternately dread and anticipate the mailman's arrival. The packages had contained everything from her favorite candy bar to a poster of KWESTT autographed by all the members. From a beautiful foot-tall stuffed plush horse that looked like Ladybug, to a delicate necklace with a filigreed heart locket with a tiny red ruby in the center and *Kel loves Joy* inscribed on the inside.

That one was tucked away out of sight in a drawer, but it still found its way into her hand too often for her peace of mind. Just like the newsy notes and sweet cards he sent her, keeping her informed about what was going on in his life—she couldn't help cheering silently when she read that he had a different agent now. A man.

Mail from Kellan had lasted until the week of Thanksgiving—which had been dismal no matter how hard she'd tried to fake otherwise. And then for ten days... nothing. The anticipation, dread, and wondering if he'd finally given up had robbed her of sleep and appetite.

Then last week the deliveries had started. Fresh flowers with a tiny card that simply said he was thinking about her followed by her favorite type of pizza three days later delivered hot, right at meal time. That one hadn't surprised George and Dorothy—the spies.

Already this week, a fancy-schmancy smart phone with all the bells and whistles, already set up and programmed, had been hand delivered by a courier. A courier! She hadn't known they had those in this part of Missouri. And she didn't even have to pay for a phone plan as a note in the box explained that it was already taken care of.

She'd turned it on and played with it out of sheer

307

curiosity and boredom but had quickly powered it off when it started ringing and Kellan's picture appeared on the screen. It hadn't been a professional photograph, either. It had been a selfie. And his grinning face had made her miss him even more. And lured her into turning the phone on to look at the picture more often than she'd admit.

"This has got to stop." She muttered into a pile of t-shirts.

"Why? I think it's the most romantic thing I've ever seen. It would be nice if you'd at least give the poor man a little hope." Dorothy's dreamy sigh turned into a scold as she set the tissue-wrapped vase of flowers onto the storeroom work table. "Come on and see what he sent this time."

"I don't even want to guess what he's spending to have fresh flowers delivered all the way out here from town. He's going to go bankrupt." JoyAnne tried not to hurry to the table, but she reached it too soon and couldn't stop herself from tearing back the protective paper to see the tall arrangement.

"Oh, Joy. They're gorgeous!" Dorothy clasped her hands and sighed.

They were. Thirty pale purple, white, and pink tulips filled a tall, etched crystal vase.

She pulled the card from the tiny envelope tucked in the greenery.

I miss you.

Love, Kel.

P.S. These tulips reminded me how much I enjoy kissing you.

A smiley face punctuated the sentence.

Cheeks burning, JoyAnne jammed the note into her

pocket to keep Dorothy from reading it. "How did he know?"

"Know what, Dear?"

"That tulips are my favorite flower?" JoyAnne bit her lip, trying to be aggravated enough at her family of snitches to keep from crying.

Dorothy plopped her hands on her hips. "I didn't tell him, but I would've if he'd asked."

JoyAnne blinked at the heat in her aunt's normally gentle voice.

"Because he brought the first smile to your face I've seen in months! When are you going to stop this foolishness? He's in love with you, and you're in love with him. Yes, you are." She frowned at JoyAnne's head shake. "Who are you trying to convince that a relationship won't work? You or him? He obviously doesn't believe it, and all you've accomplished is to make him miserable and yourself ill. You've lost weight and you walk around like the shadow you became after Micah died. But Kellan's not dead!"

"He's miserable?" JoyAnne whispered. He didn't look miserable from the clips and videos she'd seen of their current tour. He looked entirely too good and too sincere singing love songs to audiences of strangers.

"Yes, he is. And you'd know that if you'd ever answer one of his phone calls, Young Lady."

"What's all the shoutin' about?" George entered the storeroom and glanced between them.

Dorothy huffed and grabbed her coat off a hook on the wall. "I'm trying to talk a little sense into your niece, but it's like talking to a brick wall. Maybe you'll have better success." She stormed out the back door, letting the gust of raw December air slam it behind her.

"Shoo wee! What put the bee in her bonnet?" George stared after his departed wife.

JoyAnne pulled out a chair and sank into it. "I did. I guess I've been a royal pain in the neck. I didn't mean to be. I just…" Her voice trailed away and she shrugged as she pulled on the rubbery red bracelet around her wrist.

George eyed the tulips before perching on the edge of the table beside them. "What are you so scared of, Honey?"

A tear slid down Joy's cheek. "Of leaving here. Of losing you guys." The deeper truth bubbled to the surface and whispered past her lips. "Of losing him."

"Seems to me, if you stay here, you will lose him."

"But this is my refuge. My safe place. It's the only permanent home I've ever had."

George patted her hands that were fisted on the table. "True refuge can only be found in your Heavenly Father. No earthly place can ever completely fill that need." Compassion filled his brown eyes. "Let me ask you something. Is this place really safe for you anymore? Or has it become a prison? Keeping you from all God wants to give you?"

Tears poured down JoyAnne's face, and she stood to bury herself in the older man's gentle embrace. "I don't know anymore."

"I think you do know. But you need to let go. Let God be your security, and *let go*."

"But if I leave, what'll you do about all the work around here?" She sniffed, grabbing at excuses like lifelines.

George laughed. "What work? It's winter time. The campground is closed. You've been creating work where there is none. If you're here next season, your job will be, too—if you still want it. If not, we'll get someone else to fill it. I might remind you that we ran a successful campground long before you came around, Honey."

"I know. I'm sorry. I'm just so scared." Tears flowed hard, and she dug in her pocket for a tissue for her runny nose.

"Oh, Honey." George hugged her harder. "Do you love him?"

JoyAnne nodded her head against his soft sweatshirt. She did. So much it hurt.

"Have you prayed about what to do?"

She sucked in a snotty, convulsive breath. "Not really. I think I kinda told God what I thought I needed."

George chuckled. "We're all guilty of that from time to time. But maybe it's time to change tactics, huh?"

"Yeah. I'm sure you all would appreciate that." She moaned glumly.

George pushed her back and lowered his head to look at her. "Quit worrying about us and get your relationship with Him," he pointed upward, "right. And then, for your sake as well as his, go tell Kellan you love him!"

JoyAnne wiped her face with both hands and scrubbed them on her inventory-grimy jeans. "I guess I'd better." She picked up the waxy green tissue paper and carefully wrapped it around the beautiful blossoms.

"Well don't sound so excited about it. I'd hate to see you hurt yourself in your haste." George teased and handed over her coat.

She shrugged into it. "I think I've held on to what felt secure and safe for so long that my hands have gone numb. It's hard to open them."

"I know. But you know what I've learned?" He flipped off the lights and opened the back door.

JoyAnne cradled her tulips carefully to her chest. "What?"

"Home really is where the heart is. So ask yourself. Where is your heart?"

(43)

*W*here was her heart?

George's question echoed through her head over and over as JoyAnne sat in her room that evening and stroked a velvety-smooth petal of the delicate tulips. She'd popped a KWESTT CD into her player and listened to Kellan singing for the first time since he'd pulled away from the campground with his snotty former agent. And she'd cried into her pillow until she'd thought there were no tears left. But more had come when she'd slid off the rumpled comforter and knelt beside her bed to confess her fears and stubbornness to the Lord.

"Father, forgive me for not trusting you. Help me to let go of my fear of losing everything again. Help me to rest in you. To hide my heart in you so that no matter where I am, I'll be home because you're with me."

She opened Micah's Bible to Isaiah forty-one and ran her finger over the highlighted verses. "Fear thou not. For God is with me." She paraphrased. Then she read the rest of verse ten to herself before backing up and reading the familiar, comforting verses at the end of chapter forty.

Laying the Bible on her lap, she wiped her aching eyes on her sleeve. "Okay, Lord. I'm letting go of this place and my right to a safe future. Show me what *you* want me to do."

It had been a long, hard struggle, but peace finally entered her heart with the surrender.

JoyAnne stared at the darkened window that in the daytime showcased a view of the lake she loved. She was okay with leaving it behind now, because life without Kellan was much more painful.

An idea sent her flying off the bed to her computer. She wiggled the mouse and quickly found the web page she was looking for. She'd bookmarked every site that mentioned KWESTT and Kellan Campbell and checked them several times a day now. If anyone saw her recent browsing history, they would accuse her of internet stalking.

She went to the list of upcoming tour dates and found the next one. In two days. Their big Christmas show and their last appearance until after the New Year. She clicked through to buy a ticket before slowly sinking into her desk chair.

Sold out. Of course it was. Probably had been for weeks.

She propped her elbow on the edge of the desk, plopped her cheek on her fist, and stared at the computer screen. Now what?

"Knock, knock? Can I come in?" Victor called through her door.

"Sure." Joy twisted around to watch the big man enter her room.

"How ya' doin', Squirt? Dad and Mom said you…" He frowned and crossed the room to lean over and stare at her face. "You look terrible."

"Thanks for the ego boost, Vic. Just what I needed." She rubbed her puffy, sore eyes. A soul-cleansing cry wasn't exactly easy on the face.

"You don't need an ego boost. You need a kick in the pants for worrying all of us. But I think you need a hug first." He grabbed her hands, pulled her to her feet and into a hug. "You okay?"

JoyAnne accepted the hug. One of the best things about this family was their hugs. "I am now. I'm sorry for making your life miserable, too, lately."

"You're forgiven, Squirt." He released her and grinned slowly. "Does this mean you're finally gonna put Kellan out of our—I mean *his* misery?"

She shrugged, nervousness replacing the earlier peace. "I'm gonna try. If he even wants to talk to me after all this time."

Vic rubbed his hands together. "Good. So what's the plan?"

"You've certainly changed *your* tune about him."

"What can I say? You were right. He's a nice guy. Now quit stalling and tell me what you're going to do."

She gestured toward her computer. "I was going to go to their last Christmas show, but I'm too late. They're sold out."

"So? What's the problem?"

315

"Uh… I won't be able to get in to try and see him without a ticket?"

"Go anyway." He winked.

"And do what exactly? Stake out his bus and try to get through security to ambush him? They'll haul me off to jail before I ever see him." Victor could be extremely exasperating at times. Exactly how a brother should act. And she loved him for it. After she got past the urge to smack him.

"Give your name at the ticket counter and see what happens." A sneaky grin flashed across his face.

JoyAnne's heart did a funny little kick. "Why would I do that if they're sold out?"

"Maybe because there's been a ticket waiting for you at every one of their shows since he left."

She struggled to suck in enough air to speak. "What…?"

"Kellan told me to tell you whenever I thought you were ready to hear it. He wanted you to be able to get in whenever you decided to go see him."

JoyAnne covered her mouth and blinked rapidly. She was *through* crying for the night. She'd never get her eyes open in the morning if she didn't stop weeping. "He really believed I would come?"

Victor managed to decipher her raspy, choked whisper and nodded. "I also might have told him not to give up on you just yet."

"We all did." George and Dorothy stepped into her room. They'd obviously been eavesdropping.

She found herself wrapped in a three-way hug and sniffed and laughed through the tears that were starting to annoy her. "I see how it is. You want to get rid of me."

"No. We want you to be happy and where God wants you to be. If that's here or there or both, we'll always be in your corner, cheering you on. You're part of our family, and you couldn't get rid of us if you tried." Dorothy kissed Joy's cheek. "So where are you headed?"

"I guess I'm flying to California. If I can get a flight this late. It's too far to drive." Panic gripped her. Why hadn't she thought about a plane ticket earlier? If there was anything left at this late notice, it'd likely clean out her savings. But it'd be worth it.

"Then maybe I should give you your Christmas gift early." Victor pulled an envelope out of the inside of his jacket. "One round-trip ticket good for anywhere in the U. S. at any time, although I'd better get on the phone and make sure we can get you a seat tomorrow." He grinned, obviously pleased with his little surprise.

JoyAnne cleared her thick throat. "How'd you know I'd need it?"

"After years of serving on the bench, my instincts are razor sharp." Victor struck a pompous pose.

She took the ticket he handed her and swallowed hard. "If you don't stop making me cry, I'm going to whack you and your razor-sharp instincts."

"No violence, please. We need to pack." Dorothy dragged a suitcase from beneath JoyAnne's bed and opened the door to her walk-in closet.

The reality of what she was about to do hit JoyAnne full force. "Lord, give me courage."

Victor touched her shoulder. "Want me to go with you for moral support?"

She nearly nodded her head then shook it at the last second. "No. I have to do this myself. If I crash and burn, you can scrape me off the pavement. But I'd love to have you all drive me to the airport."

"We'd be offended if you didn't." George wrapped an arm around her and steered her toward the large closet where Dorothy stood frowning at JoyAnne's clothing selection. "Now you'd better get started packing while Vic and I call the airlines and before Dorothy decides you need to fit in a shopping trip first. I know that look of hers."

JoyAnne found a watery smile. "In case I haven't mentioned it lately. I love you guys. With *almost* all my heart."

"I bet I can guess who has the rest of it." Victor grumbled, grinning. "We've been bumped down the list by a musician with a pretty face."

She smacked him on the arm.

"Victor, don't you have something you need to be doing?" Dorothy squinted at her son.

"Yes, Ma'am. I'm going." Victor saluted and hurried out.

"George?"

"Yes, Dear. I have other things to do, too. I'm leaving."

"Joy? What do you think of this dress for the show?"

She hugged her twinkly-eyed aunt. "I think it's perfect. But first things first." JoyAnne grabbed Micah's Bible off the bed, carefully laid it in the small trunk of keepsakes sitting on her closet floor, and gently closed the lid with a slow caress. Then she pulled her own Bible off her bookshelf and stuck it in the outer pocket of the suitcase. It was past time to put the past behind her and walk into the future. "Now I'm ready to pack."

(44)

"*G*reat job, tonight, Boys! You sounded fantastic. Kel, your new song is one of the hits of the show and you nearly had *me* in tears tonight."

"Thanks, Sandy." He'd been singing it for JoyAnne. His hope fluctuated on a daily basis between barely there to fully expecting to see her face in the crowd. Tonight, he could almost feel her in the audience, but no matter how often he'd looked, she'd never appeared.

Had Victor not been able to tell her yet that there was always a front row seat waiting for her if she wanted it?

It was three days till Christmas and starting tomorrow they had a two week break. All he wanted for Christmas was to fly to Missouri and see his Joy.

Actually, he wanted a lot more than to see her, but she wasn't ready yet. So he'd grit his teeth and stay away and do the next best thing. Send her the nicest Christmas gift he could find—something he was having trouble accomplishing. Especially when he only wanted to send himself.

Sandra continued congratulating each singer and the other musicians on different aspects of the successful Christmas-themed show.

"Trev, Ty, you *nailed* your number tonight." Sandra gave the twins a huge smile.

Trev high-fived his brother then stuck his thumbs under the lapel of his tux. "Thanks. I was in my best voice tonight."

"Where's it been the rest of the tour?" Tyrone spoke up with a straight face.

Laughter broke out at Trev's startled blink. Even Kellan couldn't help laughing at the self-satisfied smile worn by the twin who was normally content to stay in the shadow of his more boisterous brother.

Sandra clapped her hands to regain their attention. "I'm proud of *all* of you for the power-house performance you gave. Now go get out of those tuxes so wardrobe can pack them. I'm catching a flight home in two hours to see my grandbabies, and I'll see you in Chicago in two weeks for our January fifth show. I hope you all have a wonderful Christmas and are able to get some rest so we can hit the New Year running. Trev and Ty. Do *not* go break a leg on the ski slopes or something."

"Yes, Mother." Trev bent and hugged her, and the short post-concert meeting broke up.

They all bid the energetic tour director goodbye

and headed to their dressing rooms to change before helping the stage crew finish packing up and loading all the gear it took to produce a KWESTT show.

Kellan was tugging a favorite, worn red t-shirt over his head when someone knocked on the closet-sized dressing room. He settled the hem over the waistband of his jeans and opened the door. "Yes?"

"I'm sorry to bother you, Mr. Campbell." The tall, skinny theater security guard shifted uncomfortably.

"It's not a problem. What can I do for you?" He snatched a black permanent marker out of a side pocket of his duffel bag. He always tried to keep a few within reach to sign autographs.

The young man grimaced. "We've got a bit of a situation, Sir."

Kellan frowned. "What kind of 'situation?'"

He sighed and tugged at the utility belt that held a thick ring of keys and a radio. "Somehow one of your fans made it around back where your busses are parked and refuses to leave until she gets a chance to meet you."

Kellan shook his head. "Tell her I'm sorry, but the meet-and-greet was before the show. I'm unavailable for pictures or autographs now."

"We tried that, Sir. Even some of your crew tried to get her to leave by offering her a signed KWESTT t-shirt. But she politely declines and continues to sit on the edge of the loading dock. I kind of hate to have to bodily remove her."

A crazy fan appeared from time to time, and the young man who looked more like a starving college student than a security guard had evidently met his match. "If she's in the way, I guess you'll have to call the police."

"I suppose I might have to, but she's not really in the way. And…" He hesitated.

"And what?"

"She sort of looks like she's been crying. And even though she's really persistent, she's been polite about the whole thing. Maybe she's sick and this is her last chance to meet you or something. She *does* look a little skinny."

"Did she tell you that?"

The security guard shook his head. "She hasn't said anything except she's not leaving until she sees you. Sir, you'd make my job a lot easier if you could spare just a couple of minutes to see her.

Kellan nodded reluctantly. This kid might actually *be* a student working his way through school. Law school. He'd certainly plead his case effectively enough. "All right. I'll do it for you." It wasn't like he had any place to be except a hotel room before driving to his condo tomorrow morning.

The young man grinned with relief. "Thank you! I'll show you where she is." He turned on his heel and headed deeper into the bowels of the big theater building.

Kellan grabbed his duffel bag and hurried to catch up. They quickly reached the loading docks where the crew rolled cases of equipment into the semi-trailer that hauled it from show to show.

The security guard halted and pointed to a figure sitting on the far edge of the two-bay elevated concrete loading dock. She sat in the shadows, well out of the way of everyone, her back to the controlled chaos. "She's over there."

"Thanks." Kellan made his way around those working to quickly load up their stuff, smiling at a couple of the guys who glanced toward the woman and shook their heads in silent sympathy for him.

Fifteen feet away from the motionless figure, Kellan froze. They'd opened both bay doors on the loading dock, but they hadn't turned on the lights over this one, and his eyes were playing tricks on him. He'd wished for her to appear so many times he was now seeing things.

But she couldn't be here. He'd left instructions that if a JoyAnne Daye picked up her ticket he was to be told immediately. And the seat she would've been given had remained empty the whole show.

His heavy duffel bag slid out of his lax grip and thumped to the floor.

The woman stiffened and slowly looked over her shoulder.

Kellan couldn't breathe. Couldn't move. It *was* her.

Unless it was another dream that would leave him hating the alarm clock when it pulled him away from it.

"Umm… Hi." A tentative smile graced her beautiful face. She twisted toward him a little more but didn't stand up.

She wasn't wearing the red dress he'd seen her in the first time, and he kind of missed it, but she looked pretty good in purple, too.

Who was he kidding? She looked wonderful! His eyes roamed over her seated form, absorbing every inch that he could see. She was even prettier than he remembered. He'd lost count of how many times he'd kicked himself for not snapping some pictures of her when he'd had the chance.

"I know you weren't expecting me, but..." She lifted her shoulders then dropped them, her smile slipping.

Kellan pried his dry mouth apart. "What... what are you doing here?" *Why* was she here? That's what he should've asked. But the stark question took all the breath he had available.

He saw her throat work. She pulled her legs up from over the edge of the loading dock, tucked them under the skirt of her long-sleeved sweater dress, crossed her arms, and lifted her chin with a determined smile. "I came to talk to you. But if you don't want to see me, then I'll sit out here, get pneumonia, and die. And then what will you do with the body?"

His eyes snagged on the faded red plastic that encircled JoyAnne's wrist and peeped from beneath her sleeve, matching the one on his wrist. This woman had managed to catch him off guard since the first moment he'd laid eyes on her. Spoken to her. And he loved it. Even when it took him a second to catch up.

His ability to breathe, move, and think returned, and he took a couple of slow steps toward her, fighting to keep his growing hope in check. "It's San Diego. It's not that cold."

"It is if you sit here long enough."

"Then I suppose I'll have to talk to you because dealing with bodies requires more paperwork than I want to mess with tonight."

"You will?" Her voice squeaked.

"Yep. And flattering as it is to have people fall at my feet, it is rather awkward. It'll also be a lot more comfortable if we find some place more private." He'd heard the snickers behind him at her dead-body remark.

She looked at her lap and back up at him. "I might need some help getting up."

"I think I can handle that." He stretched out his hands and took both of hers. The electricity that zinged through their hands made him want to release her so he could experience it again. But he didn't let go, instead he let his gaze wander slowly over her as he tugged her upright. "Did your legs go to sleep waiting on me?"

She shook her head, eyes darting away. "No. They're... they're too shaky to stand on."

Kellan tugged her closer, rubbing his thumbs over the backs of her hands. "Why are they shaky?" His voice dropped to match hers.

She met his eyes again. "'Cause I'm scared to death." Her face scrunched with the whispered admission.

He grinned and lowered his head. "That's okay. I'm feeling braver by the minute."

"I'm glad one of us is." She muttered and glanced around at their very interested audience. All work on breaking down and loading up had stopped. Enoch, Sawyer, Westin, Trev, and Ty were standing well within earshot, grinning like a bunch of idiots.

"Ignore them." Kellan shifted to block their view of his girl and noticed something. He released one of her hands and slowly reached up to the locket resting in the modest vee of her dress's neckline. He scooped it up, letting his knuckles brush her skin. "You got it. I wondered." And the fact that she was wearing it tonight, here, could only mean one thing. Right?

She shivered then nodded. "Yes. I got a lot of very thoughtful, lovely things. You shouldn't have wasted your money like that."

He grinned and lowered the locket to its smooth resting place and trailed his hand to her shoulder, down her arm, and to her hand. "It wasn't a waste. Not when it brought you here. I simply took a page out of the Greek history books and sent you a Trojan horse."

A grin quivered at the corner of her mouth. "A Trojan horse, huh? I though it looked more like Ladybug."

"Pure coincidence." He studied her face. It did look like she might have been crying earlier. There was a small black smudge below her left eye, and her eyes looked a little red. She also looked like she might have lost some weight. She was too skinny like the security guard had mentioned.

Fear stuck a pin through his hope. "Did you come because something is wrong back home?"

Her eyes widened and she shook her head.

"Then why have you been crying?"

Chagrin creased her face and she pulled her hands out of his to rub beneath her eyes. "I must look a fright."

He recaptured them. "No. You don't. But what's wrong?"

"Me."

He frowned, not understanding the blunt answer.

"I've been doing a lot of crying lately after some pretty painful soul searching and putting some things in the past where they belong. But that's not what made me cry tonight."

He waited.

"I saw the concert." She blinked rapidly.

"You were here? Where? You weren't in the seat I told them to save for you."

"No. I stayed in the back and made them promise not to mention that I was here."

"Why?"

"I wanted to watch you without you knowing I was here. And work up my courage." She bit her bottom lip, and the tears welled in her pretty green eyes. "And then you played your guitar and sang that song." Her voice disappeared.

"What song?" He knew exactly what song. He'd written it for her, but he wanted to hear her say it.

"Joy's Song." She swallowed, blinked hard, and cleared her throat. "The program showed that you wrote it. Did you... did you write it for me?"

She wasn't close enough. Kellan released her hands and settled his hands on her hips, nearly sighing in relief at being able to hold her again. "Every word."

She closed her eyes and a tear slid down her cheek.

He pulled her in another inch. Almost there. Another couple of inches and she'd be where she belonged. In his arms.

> *One day, Joy touched my life.*
> *Made it worth living.*
> *And tho' Joy went away,*
> *Life's still worth living.*
> *'Cause she'll return one day,*
> *And Joy'll be my wife.*

Kellan quietly sang the final chorus of the song he'd written in a moment of hopeful despair in the weeks following his last visit to Missouri.

Enoch had found the lyrics several days later and set it to a haunting melody. Then he'd given it to Sandy, telling her it needed to be added to the show and that Kellan should sing it. She'd agreed, and Kellan hadn't argued when they'd added it to the play list. He'd hoped Joy would one day be in the audience to hear it. Hear his heart.

Thank you, Lord!

JoyAnne ran her fingers under her eyes. "It was so beautiful. But you made me cry. Again."

"Is that a bad thing?" Kellan sort of liked her spiky, wet lashes.

"Yes. I'm tired of crying. It's becoming an annoyingly regular occurrence." Her sparkling eyes ruined her attempt at a frown.

"So tell me, Miss Watering Pot, why *did* you come here tonight? Was it just to see KWESTT and obtain an autograph or was there something else?" *Please! Let it be something else.*

"I came to... Oh, shoot. There go my knees again."

"Don't worry. I've got you." Kellan pulled her closer, but she pushed away.

"No. I've got to do this right. Hold on." She turned and picked up a purse he hadn't noticed beside the jacket she'd been sitting on, dug through it, and pulled out a familiar-looking phone. "I came to tell you I learned how to text. On the new phone you gave me."

"You... learned how to... text."

"I'll show you. Wait." She swiped twice at the screen on her phone then starting tapping it slowly. When she finished, she looked up at him.

The phone in his pocket buzzed, making him jump. He yanked it out and saw Joy's name on the screen with a message notification. He glanced up at her.

"Go ahead. Read it." Her knuckles were nearly white from clenching her phone.

Kellan swiped the screen without taking his eyes

off her then lifted the device so he could see it. A variation of the words he'd had inscribed on the inside of the locket she wore jumped out at him. He read them twice.

Joy loves Kel!

She'd even added a fat red heart emoticon.

Kellan closed his eyes. *Thank you, thank you, thank you, Lord!*

He jammed the phone in his back pocket and strode toward her. He plucked the phone out of her fingers, slid it into his other pocket, and hauled her into his arms. "Do you mean that?"

She buried her face in his shoulder. "Yes. I love you. With all my heart. And I want to be wherever you are. I'm sorry it took me so long to realize that."

"Hearing those words makes it all worth it, Sweetheart. Completely worth it. I love you, too." He slid his right hand up to cradle the side of her face. "I love you so much."

Lowering his head, he did what he'd been aching to do for months. He kissed her. With every ounce of pent up longing in his heart. Ignoring the wolf whistles, cheers, and applause from behind him.

(45)

"*H*ey, Kel! Come up for air and introduce us to your girl."

The laughter-filled shout jerked JoyAnne out of a kiss that had been worth every fearful mile to get here. Her cheeks burned as she buried her face in Kellan's shoulder to hide for a second while trying to catch her breath and gather her scattered composure.

"I will never apologize for kissing you," Kellan whispered, tightening his arms around her, "but I am sorry for the poor timing and location."

She looked up, reveling in the warmth in his eyes that banished the last traces of anxiety that he would reject her after pushing him away for so long. A small part of her wished she'd won the battle over her fears sooner, but maybe the victory tasted that much sweeter for being so hard-fought. "It's okay. I'd like to meet your friends. I just hope they don't think I'm some kind of crazy girlfriend."

A smile burst across Kellan's face. "Girlfriend. That title will do for now." He winked, sending the butterflies in Joy's stomach back into a frenzy.

He turned to face their grinning audience, tucking Joy securely under his arm against his side as he did so. "Guys, I'd like you to meet JoyAnne Daye. My girlfriend."

The band members and a couple of other people who'd been rolling big, black cases in and out of the theater while she'd waited grinned and came over to shake her hand, each with a quick, kind word as Kellan introduced them.

However, the guys Kel sang with hung back, eyeing her, and she began to think they did in fact believe her to be some kind of crazy, stalker girlfriend. But when the last crew member walked away to finish loading the long trailer, the brown-haired twins stepped in front of her.

The more animated twin crossed his arms and studied her with a skeptical expression, but she noticed with relief that his eyes were twinkling. "*Now* we know why Kellan disappeared without a trace this spring. I'd keep it a secret, too, if I found someone as pretty as you, 'cause nothing's safe around these guys." He jabbed a thumb at Westin and Sawyer who'd moved in behind him. "I'm Trevor Diamond, by the way," his grin was charming and infectious. "And this is my twin, Tyrone, but you can call us Trev and Ty."

Ty slanted a frown at his brother before giving JoyAnne an apologetic grimace. "It's nice to meet you.

Don't pay any attention to Trev, though. He likes to hear himself talk." He smiled, a bit of his brother's mischief appearing in it. "But you really are as pretty as Kel said you were."

"Thank you. It's nice to meet you both, too." JoyAnne ignored her hot cheeks and grinned at the twins. "I really enjoyed listening to you sing tonight. All of you." She shifted her gaze to include the rest of the guys in her statement.

"We all know you really only came to listen to Kel, there. But we'll forgive you. This time. I'm Sawyer Slade." The black-haired singer of the group elbowed Trevor out of the way, his dark eyes shining with good humor. "It's a pleasure to meet you, JoyAnne." He took the hand she offered and held it. "We've heard a lot about you—and discovered the knucklehead beside you obviously doesn't know how to use the camera on his phone because he has no pictures of you. I know. I checked." His grin grew at Kel's growled promise of retribution. "And much as I hate to agree with Trev on *anything*, he's right this one time. Kel *was* smart to keep your location a secret. If I'd seen you first, he'd have had a fight on his hands." He leaned down to press a kiss on the back of her hand, his short facial scruff rasping her skin. When he straightened, his eyes danced with merriment, and he released her hand to punch a glaring Kellan in the shoulder. "And he knows it."

JoyAnne giggled and placed her freed hand on Kellan's chest where he promptly covered it with his own, feeling a blush warm her throat. She'd been an idiot to ever think the black-haired man in front of her was the best looking of the six singers. "Thank you for the flattering words, Sawyer, but I happen to love this 'knucklehead' so you wouldn't have stood a chance."

Sawyer's blink and the shouts of laughter from the other guys proved she'd scored a point against the handsome flirt. He touched the brim of an imaginary hat and backed away, grinning. "Touché, Miss Daye. Touché."

"I'm Westin." The smallest in build of the six members of KWESTT didn't seem to smile as easily as the rest, but his expression was friendly as he nodded to her.

"It's nice to meet you, Westin Grant. I *love* listening to you play the piano."

A hint of a smile appeared about his rather solemn mouth. "Thank you, Ma'am."

"Call me, JoyAnne. Please."

The hint *almost* turned into the real thing. "Thank you, *JoyAnne*." Westin nodded once more then walked away to lend a hand pushing a large, heavy looking case onto the trailer.

The largest and darkest member of KWESTT stepped in front of Joy, his enormous smile contagious. "Miss JoyAnne. It is truly an honor and a pleasure to meet you. I've been praying for you all summer."

"You have?"

He nodded his shaved head. "Since Kel first mentioned you. Let her go for just a second, Kel. I'll give her back, but I want to hug this little gal." The big man tugged her away from Kellan and into a muscular but gentle hug. "Yes, Ma'am. It's so nice to meet you. I've been praying for this day for a long time. You've made my friend happier than I've ever seen him." He released her and smiled down at her.

She blinked back the sudden burn. The man's eyes

were as caring and warm as Uncle George's and Aunt Dorothy's. "Thank you, Enoch. For your prayers and your kindness."

Enoch's smile broadened on a bassy rumble of laughter. "Well, what do you know? The pretty lady knows my name." He shot a pleased grin at Kellan. "You've found yourself a smart lady. She already knows the most important member of the group."

JoyAnne laughed. "I know all your names. You're my favorite group. But if I had to pick a favorite member," she scrunched her face and nodded, "it would be Kellan." She directed the next words at him. "Hands down."

Kellan looked as pleased as punch, and he gave her another wink.

Enoch released his wonderful deep laugh again. "As well it should be. As well it should be. Now why don't you two scoot out of here and let us finish up without any more distractions—no matter how pretty they might be." He patted JoyAnne's shoulder. "I'm sure you have plenty to talk about and it's getting late."

Kellan scooped up her purse and jacket along with his duffel bag and grabbed her hand with his free one. "You don't have to tell me, twice. We're out of here. See you after the New Year."

He pulled her along in his wake, replying to shouted goodbyes without slowing his pace as he jogged down the concrete stairs at the side of the loading dock and past the semi and tour busses.

"Hey, not so fast. Some of us are wearing heels." JoyAnne protested, tugging his hand to slow him down.

"Sorry!" Kellan slowed—barely.

"Where are we going?"

"Someplace I can kiss you without a lot of nosy guys looking over my shoulder." He grinned at her in the glow from a tall security light. "Any objections?"

She shook her head, a thrill shooting through her. "Nope. Just curious where that might be. If it's too far, I need to take off my heels. Especially if you're going to turn it into one of your long-distance runs."

Kellan laughed. "No long-distance needed. We're here." He dropped his duffel bag beside a sleek dark blue car in the corner of the small, fenced back lot, pulled out a key fob and pressed a button. When the doors clicked unlocked, he opened the passenger door for her, helped her in, threw her purse and his bag in the back seat then rounded the car and climbed in the driver's seat.

After locking the door, he twisted toward her with a grin. "Now. Where were we?"

JoyAnne leaned against her door and grinned, excited quivers raising goosebumps on her skin. "San Diego?"

"Very funny." His eyes sparkled in the dim light coming in through the windshield. "Come here, you."

She leaned into his arms and into a very slow, very long, breath-taking kiss.

When they parted, she twisted around and leaned against him as he wrapped his arms around her waist and held her. It was awkward to do with the console between them, but she couldn't think of anywhere else she'd rather be. She loved this man.

Kellan rested his chin on her shoulder. "By the way, how'd you get here?"

"Took a plane." Her smile felt muzzy. After a kiss like that one, she didn't need a plane. She could just float anywhere she wanted to go.

"No. I mean how did you get to the theater?" He squeezed her a little tighter.

"Oh." She giggled. She'd been doing that a lot lately. "I took a cab from the hotel where I left my bags."

"Good. We don't have to worry about another car then, and I can get a room at your hotel. What do you want to do while you're here and how long can you stay? I've got two weeks off, you know."

"I don't care what we do as long as I can hang out with you. That's why I came." And right now, she wouldn't worry about the future. That was in the Lord's hands. She'd followed his leading—and her family's urgings—to come spend time with Kellan and for now that was enough.

"Do you want to explore San Diego for Christmas?"

"If that's what you want to do. I bet I could show you some places around here you've never seen." She cocked her head to look up at him.

He leaned back. "You know San Diego?"

"Yep. My dad was stationed here for a couple of years. Military brat, remember?"

"My brat now." He kissed the corner of her mouth. "But I think I've got a better idea for Christmas." His smile grew.

"What?"

"How 'bout we go *home* for Christmas?"

"Home?" JoyAnne wrinkled her brow, trying to remember if he'd ever mentioned the place he considered home. She knew he had two places. One out here in California and one in Tennessee.

"To Missouri."

She blinked. "My home? I mean Uncle George and Aunt Dorothy's?" It would always be home to her, but she was trying not to hold on to it so hard anymore.

"Yep. I kind of fell in love with that place as I fell in love with you, and it feels more like home to me than anyplace in more years than I care to count. I also kind of like the thought of spending Christmas with your family there."

JoyAnne absolutely refused to let anymore tears dampen her day. "That... that sounds like a wonderful idea."

Kellan turned her toward him. "Then how 'bout in the morning, we take a road trip home? We'll have two days to talk with no interruptions, and arrive home on Christmas Eve, just like the old song. It'll be perfect."

Joy snuggled into his chest. "You're a big, ol' sentimental softy, aren't you?"

"Where you and your family are concerned?" He returned her hug. "Absolutely."

She lifted her head and smiled up at him, the love she felt for him warming every inch of her being. "Then let's go home, Kel."

"Home." He sighed and rested his forehead against hers. "I love the sound of that. Almost as much as I love you."

EPILOGUE

*T*he steam from the frothy hot chocolate swirled under JoyAnne's nose, tempting her to brave another careful sip of the steaming-hot, marshmallowy brew as she watched fat snowflakes that had started falling sometime during the night drift past the front porch and pile on the ground.

She smiled and licked the sweet froth off her lips. They were having a white Christmas. And she was home. But no longer did the roots she'd sunk into this place strangle her future. Her wings had healed and she was relearning to fly. New places and adventures tempted her to stretch those wings—no longer terrifying her with uncertainty.

Thank you, Lord, for not giving up on me. For loving me enough to give me a place to heal and then pushing me out of my carefully constructed prison. I'm ready for whatever you have next for me, and I'll trust you to catch me when I fall.

"There you are." Arms slipped around her waist and tugged her into a warm chest. "You're going to freeze out here without a coat."

JoyAnne shivered and pressed into Kellan. "I didn't realize I was cold until just now. I was too busy enjoying the fact that we're having a white Christmas." She nodded at the ground that had collected enough snowflakes overnight to turn white and soft looking. They had at least two inches already, and the weatherman predicted another couple of more. It was perfect.

"Have I mentioned that your family does the best old fashioned Christmas I've ever experienced?" Kellan accepted the tall mug she handed back to him and took a sip of the liquid cocoa.

"I think you might have mentioned it once or twice yesterday evening." They'd arrived about noon on Christmas Eve, and Kellan had gotten to experience their tradition of reading the Christmas story before bed and opening one gift apiece. A new pair of pajamas for everyone to wear on Christmas morning. And this year, Aunt Dorothy had added in a thick, fleecy new robe in everyone's gaily wrapped package.

JoyAnne had the sneaking suspicion the woman had been planning on having Kellan with them for the holiday long before Joy'd called from California to warn her they were heading home.

Kellan handed her mug back. "You also make the best hot chocolate I've ever tasted."

"Thank you," she set her mug on the railing and

turned in his arms, "for the best road trip I've had in too long. Actually the *first* road trip I've had in too long." They'd talked, sung along to KWESTT songs on her mp3 player—much to Kellan's chagrin at first—eaten too many snacks, stopped to do some rushed Christmas shopping, and laughed the miles away.

"It was fun, wasn't it?" Kel dropped a kiss on her lips, then lingered there. "Mmm. You taste like chocolate and marshmallows." He raised his head a fraction. "And you're as soft as a kitten in your pink fleece. If George and Dorothy and Victor weren't waiting for us, I'd be tempted to sit out here and watch the snow while we cuddled on the porch."

JoyAnne's face warmed. She wouldn't mind doing that, but it was wiser—and safer right now—to stay around other people. She understood why Aunt Dorothy had added robes to the traditional gift. Everyone's new pajamas were thick and completely modest, but the soft, warm robes added another layer of modesty with the presence of one who wasn't a family member. Yet. She hoped.

"You're pretty cuddly yourself." She stroked the dark blue fleece of his new robe. "But we'd better go in before Vic comes to find us. He gets as antsy as a kid when he has to wait to open gifts."

"I heard that." Vic opened the front door, releasing a stream of warm air and reminding JoyAnne how cold it actually was. "If you two lovebirds would get in here, we could get started."

"See what I mean?" She grinned at Kellan and tugged him inside to the living room where a large tree graced one corner.

The gifts were passed out and opened slowly with

many smiles and much laughter. Each giver and recipient taking time to enjoy a thoughtful or funny gift before going on to the next one.

When the last present had been opened, they sat back and surveyed the remains of the wrapping paper in the floor. Kellan shifted on the loveseat beside her and cleared his throat in the comfortable silence that had settled over them.

"I don't think I'll ever be able to adequately explain how much being a part of your Christmas has meant to me. You've opened your hearts and home to me, and I can never thank you enough. There's only one thing more that would make this the best Christmas of my life." He stuck his hand in the pocket of his blue robe and slid off the loveseat to his knee.

Aunt Dorothy gasped and clapped a hand over her mouth, but JoyAnne didn't react. Because she'd stopped breathing.

Kellan picked her hand up off her lap and placed a red velvet box on her palm, a smile trembling on his lips. "There's one more gift that hasn't been opened yet."

JoyAnne blinked at him.

"Go ahead. Open it." He urged quietly. And maybe a little nervously.

JoyAnne desperately tried not to think about what the box might or might not be in case she was disappointed. Her hands shook as she opened the lid.

The overhead lights shot fire through the brilliant diamond perched proudly on top of a silver band. Joy's eyes shot to Kellan's, her breath freezing in her throat.

He gathered her hands—still holding the velvet box—in his. "JoyAnne Daye. From the first moment I saw you, I knew you were someone extra special, and the more I got to know you, the longer I wanted to know you. I spend a lot of time traveling back and forth, so we have some logistics to work out—but I want to spend the rest of my life with you." He took a deep breath. "Would you do me the greatest honor? Be my wife?"

JoyAnne closed her eyes. God was so good. He'd given her more family in Uncle George and Aunt Dorothy and Victor and given her the love of another good man.

Kellan's grip tightened on her hands. "You don't have to travel with me all the time if you don't want to. You could stay in my condo in California or in Tennessee, or we could get a different place if you don't like those. You could also stay here and work. I don't mind, although I would love to have you with me as often as possible. I also want to find some land around here for sale and build our own place to escape to between tours and recording sessions—maybe even build my own private recording studio. I know it's a big decision, but—"

She stopped his rapid, rambling speech with a hand over his mouth. "Would you like me to answer your original question now?"

He nodded behind her hand. "Pleath."

Her grin was shaky as she removed her hand and placed the red box in his hands. "My answer, Kellan Campbell Davis, is..." She gathered her breath and stuck out her left hand, palm down. "Yes. I would love to be your—"

He cut her off with a hard kiss.

The soft thud of something hitting the floor dimly

registered, but the happiness and excitement flooding through JoyAnne pushed it into the background.

Kellan released her long enough to pull her to her feet and into his arms. "Did you really say 'yes'?"

"Mm hmm." Her smile was huge as she cupped his face with her hands. If her eyes were anywhere near as starry and dazed looking as his, it was a wonder they could see anything.

A loudly-cleared throat interrupted another kiss. They pulled back from each other, flushed and breathless.

"I think you're forgetting an important part of your engagement." Victor poked a small red box between their noses and wiggled it, grinning. "You dropped something."

JoyAnne giggled at Kellan's reddening face as her family broke into amused chuckles.

He grinned good-naturedly as he extracted the ring, lifted her left hand, and slid it onto her finger. "I love you, JoyAnne."

She didn't spare but a glance at the sparkling ring. His face was so much more dear. "I love you, Kellan. And wherever you and God are, that's my home."

Once again, she was in his arms as her family moved in to circle them both in a big, warm group hug.

Home.

Kellan had wanted one but hadn't had one.

She'd had one but held on so tightly, God had had to teach her how to let go.

But in his wonderful wisdom and grace, he'd given them both the desires of their hearts.

Uncle George had been right. Home really was where the heart was.

ABOUT THE AUTHOR

Check out other great stories at
www.forgetmenotromances.com

An avid reader by age seven, Clari Dees loved to hang out at
the public library, and the local bookstore staff knew her by
name. Her favorite books ranged from Marguerite Henry's
horse stories, to Louis L'Amour's westerns and Grace
Livingston Hill's romances. Her fascination with books and
libraries continues, and Clari now works as a public librarian by
day and a writer by night. When she's not locating books for
an overdue term paper or tracing down a missing genealogy
link for patrons at the library, she can be found at her
computer plotting the lives and fortunes of hapless fictional
characters. You can visit Clari on her Facebook page at
www.facebook.com/ClariDees or drop her an email at
cdeesbooks@gmail.com

Made in the USA
Las Vegas, NV
28 March 2021

20331097R00203